KATHERINE CECIL

(1875-1911), was born at Woo... child of Paul Madden, a bank... Cork, and Catherine (Barry) ...

In 1901, when Katherine wa... the English novelist and dramatist, ~~Ernest~~ ... Thurston. Two years later her first novel, *The Circle*, was published. But it was the appearance of *John Chilcote, MP*, which made Katherine Cecil Thurston into a wealthy celebrity. Set against a political backdrop, it is a famous novel of impersonation and mistaken identity and, when serialised in *Harper's Bazar*, produced a stream of letters to the editor, imploring for advance information as to its conclusion. Published simultaneously in England and in America (where it appeared as *The Masquerader*) in 1904, the novel became a bestseller on both sides of the Atlantic. It was dramatised by her husband the next year and produced at the St. James' Theatre. Two cinematic versions — one of which was silent — were also made.

Her next novel, *The Gambler*, was serialised in *Harper's Weekly* and published in 1906, followed by *Mystics* (1907) and *The Fly on the Wheel* (1908). In 1910 Katherine Cecil Thurston obtained a divorce from her husband and in the same year she published her final novel *Max*, another, less successful, tale of impersonation.

She was a vivacious and humourous personality and, after the success of her second novel, was much in demand as a speaker at literary and other functions. Her flamboyant lifestyle drew the interest of the press and there was some surprise when her body was discovered at Moore's Hotel in Cork. Katherine Cecil Thurston died at the age of thirty six, during the month in which she was due to remarry. Said to have been in delicate health for some time, the cause of her death was recorded as suffocation as the result of an epileptic fit. Some of those who were acquainted with *The Fly on the Wheel* speculated as to the accuracy of that verdict.

VIRAGO
MODERN
CLASSIC

NUMBER
265

KATHERINE CECIL THURSTON

The Fly on the Wheel

WITH A NEW AFTERWORD BY
JANET MADDEN-SIMPSON

Published by VIRAGO PRESS LIMITED 1987
41 William IV Street, London WC2N 4DB

First published in Great Britain by William Blackwood 1908

Afterword Copyright © Janet Madden-Simpson 1987

British Library Cataloguing in Publication Data
Thurston, Katherine Cecil
The fly on the wheel. — (Virago modern classics).
I. Title
823'.912[F]   PR6039.H95
ISBN 0-86068-659-0

Printed in Finland
by Werner Söderström Oy

THE FLY ON THE WHEEL.

CHAPTER I.

IT was an April morning in the Irish town of Waterford; beyond the suburbs, the grass lay thick and green upon the country-side in the virgin freshness of the spring, and the chestnuts glinted with the delicate sheen of bursting leaves; but in the streets, the dust of March was whirling to the April breeze, powdering the narrow byways with a cloak of grey, eddying in a mad dance along the open spaces.

Portion of this dusty, characteristic, sparsely-populated town is dedicated to business—the business of the shops; a second and more important portion of it is given over to the quays, from whence a constant traffic is carried on with the hereditary enemy, England; while a third part, that holds itself aloof from commerce, is to be reckoned as half residential, half professional. It is to this third quarter that the eye of the story-seeker must turn on this April morning; for it is here, in Lady Lane,—a thoroughfare as long

and narrow as a Continental street, composed of
tall old houses with square-paned windows and
mysterious hall doors giving entry to vast and
rambling interiors, — that the story, comedy or
tragedy, is to find its stage; here, in the dining-
room of one of the flat-fronted houses, that the
student of human nature is to take his first glance
at Stephen Carey — hero, so far as middle-class
Irish life produces heroes, of the anticipated
romance.

A man's room, one would have said at half a
glance,—moreover, the room of a man self-made!
There was no art, no beauty suggested or displayed; but there was comfort of a solid kind in
the fire that burned ruddily in the grate, and
in the breakfast-table that stood awaiting occu-
pation.   A man's room, although a closed work-
basket stood on the sideboard, and the china on
the table indicated breakfast for two.

And this first impression would have proved
correct; for if the title of man be won by work, by
patience, by a spirit that holds firm in face of
great odds, then Carey's room was unquestionably
the property of a man; for he had carved his
own path to worldly success, hewing it from the
rough material by days of toil and nights of
thought.

Carey was a type,—a type of that middle class
which by right of strength has formed its huge
republic, and spread like a net over civilisation—
invincible, indispensable as the vast machines from
which it has sucked its power.   It is as parent of
this new republic that the nineteenth century will

go down to futurity; and it is from the core of
this new republic, virile in its ambition, tyrannical in its moral code, jealous of its hard-won
supremacy, that we have garnered such men as
Carey—the men of steel, drawn from the great
workshops, tempered, filed, polished to fit the ap-
pointed place; helping to move the mighty engine
of which they are the atoms, useless if cast out
from its mechanism.

There is no corner of the civilised world over
which the ubiquitous army of this republic has not
marched. Even in countries where advance is
slowest and change most subtle in its inroads—
even in Ireland, where the people still instinctively
bend the knee to the fetish of old name, and
the aristocrats, dwindling year by year, hug their
pride the closer for decay—this invasion of the
middle classes has become a fact raised above
denial. A century ago the rich Irish trader,
the manufacturer, even the lawyer or the doctor
—unless by chance he could produce a pedigree—
held little place in the social scheme; but to-day
his grand-daughters flaunt it with the best in the
world of sport and the vaster world of education.
True, the entry to these new pastures is through
a gate that still stands barely ajar and hangs
upon rusty hinges, but there is incentive in the
thought of a forced passage, and the constant
sight of a social Mecca stirs this section of a
naturally indolent community to unprecedented action. For this, the well-to-do shopkeeper gives
his son a profession; for this, the successful doctor
sends his boys to an English university; for this

the mother of a large family stints and saves to educate her daughters abroad.

It is not an exalted class: it is a class held together by material ambitions and common ideals; but it is a section of society strong in its own narrow purpose—an outpost in the great progress.

From this class Stephen Carey had come, as the new, strong grass shoots up between the cobble-stones of an ancient street. His story was that of many another Irishman—the story of a boyhood bred upon false conceptions, and a youth called upon before its time to grapple with realities. The eldest of seven brothers, he was the son of a builder, a man of dogged, taciturn nature who had risen from obscurity to a position of consideration. Forty years ago Barny Carey had been a well-known figure in Waterford commercial life, and there were few of the older business men who could not still recall his large, pale face, his shock of sandy hair, and his short, thick-set figure invariably clothed in an ill-fitting frock-coat. But despite the fact of a large acquaintance, not one among his fellow-townsmen could recall an intimacy with Barny: there had been something daunting in the man's reserve, something deterring in his proud, silent stubbornness that had precluded friendship; and not even the workmen by whose toil he had mounted the ladder of success, or the sons in whom the core of his heart centred, had known what it was to hold him in affection.

Yet it was these sons—these seven sons—on whom his whole inarticulate nature had bent and spent itself. There are always these chinks in the hard man's armour, and it is the business of fate to search them out with cunning shafts. For himself, Barny Carey had made no secret of the fact that he was a common man, the son of a mason, trained in his youth to the mason's trade; he had accepted it as a thing defined, and had made no move to alter or ignore it. But with his sons it was to be a different matter. His sons were to be gentlemen!

This was his dream — his dream as he had worked in his office, his dream as he had watched his buildings rising storey upon storey, monuments to his success. Stephen—Stephen, the first-born— was to be a lawyer; the law had always appealed to Barny as something impressive and formidable, and his soul yearned to see Stephen deal in justice as he himself had once dabbled in mortar and bricks; Joseph, the second son, was to be a priest, for God had been generous to him, and he must not grudge his offering to the church; Tom, the third, was to be an architect; Barny, his namesake, was to be a civil engineer; Maurice was to go into a bank, and Patrick to sea; while for Frank, the youngest, there was but one possible career,— being a seventh son, he must, in pursuance of time-honoured superstition, become a doctor. So he had lived in his schemes, uncomprehended and unloved, meting out education with a liberal hand; and in due time Stephen had been articled to a solicitor, Joseph had been sent to Maynooth, and Tom had gone to Dublin to study for his profession.

Then it had been, in the very weaving of the plot, that the threads had tangled. The tale of how a business, apparently impregnable, can be undermined by any one of the contingencies that arise in commerce is too long and too immaterial to the story in hand to be followed here. It must suffice that one bad year had followed another, that money had become scarcer, that Barny Carey had been forced to draw upon his reserves. At first his dogged nature had refused to see facts as they really were; then the gravity of the situation had forced itself home, and common-sense had whispered that it would be wiser to recall Tom and put new blood into the business; but the old narrow pride that had become as the breath of Barny's life had risen to scout the suggestion — and so had come the beginning of the end.

Money had been needed—and still more money: he might have borrowed, for his credit in Waterford was good, but here again the stubbornness had been tyrannical. He had never gone into debt, and he would not begin in his old age! So in pride and silence he had taken the infinitely more risky course,—he had departed from his previous scheme of safe investment, and had begun to speculate.

There is no need to describe the first plunge and the first failure; the second plunge, necessitated by the first, and in turn the second failure: it is depressing in its commonness. All that really concerns is that within two years Barny Carey died, broken by secret anxieties; and that

Stephen, just crossing the threshold of life, woke from the imaginary position of a rich man's heir to the reality of finding himself guardian to six brothers, only one of whom was self-supporting.

What Stephen did in that tremendous crisis, rather what he did in the long toilsome years, when the actual crisis was passed and the daily burden was still to be carried, is among the un-written records of heroism. In plain words, he worked as men only work in such circumstances, garnering the spoils saved from the wreck with a hand almost miserly in its rigid severity, stinting himself to the point of penury that his brothers might not turn back from their allotted paths; and in his own career struggling, struggling un-ceasingly, turning an impassive face to the slaps of fortune, grasping unquestioningly at every help-ing hand. Until now the story - seeker, looking into his room at Lady Lane, finds a man of thirty-eight—a citizen with a wife and three children—a solicitor with a growing practice — a matured controlled, successful Stephen Carey, possessing but one responsibility remaining from the past—Frank, the youngest brother, the seventh son, still studying medicine in Paris in fulfilment of Barny Carey's dream.

CHAPTER II.

THE hour of nine was proclaimed by a clock somewhere in the town; and a moment after, the announcement was made further patent by the cessation of a dozen mass bells that, for a quarter of an hour, had been chiming from north and south, east and west. In this newly made silence the door of the empty dining-room in Lady Lane opened slowly, to admit a servant carrying a tray of eatables for the prospective breakfast. She entered the room in a leisurely, easy fashion, moved forward to the table, and, still holding the tray, allowed her eyes to wander to the window and become riveted upon two errand-boys, who had deliberately set down their baskets to play a game of marbles in the narrow roadway. With the calm absorption of the born idler, she would have remained indefinitely rooted to the spot, regardless of the boiled eggs and bacon that were fast growing cold, but that the sound of steps in the hall outside brought her forcibly back to the realisation of duty. In obvious perturbation she twisted round, almost overbalancing the tray; then, with equal suddenness, she gave a little gasp of relief.

"Gracious, ma'am, I thought you were the master!" she explained. "I was just seein' how them boys of Clery's do be idlin' their time. 'Tis a fright, surely!"

The person addressed was Mrs Stephen Carey —Daisy Carey,—blue-eyed, fair-haired, girlish in face and figure, despite five years of domesticity and the three babies in the nursery upstairs. She was attractive, distinctly attractive as she stepped into the room; but it was a passive attractiveness—the sleek, uninspiring attractiveness of one whose days are full of small concerns, and who is obviously content to shape the future on the pattern of the past. Moving forward to the breakfast-table, she seated herself in her accustomed place, and picked up two envelopes that lay upon her plate.

"Are these all the letters, Julia?" she asked. "I thought I'd have got three."

"Them are all this mornin', ma'am,—except the master's. I took him up seven with his tea."

"Oh, well, put the things on the table! And, Julia——"

"What, ma'am?"

"See that nurse gets her breakfast soon, will you? Baby cried a lot last night, and she didn't get much sleep. She must want a cup of tea."

"All right, ma'am! She can come down now; I'll stop above with the children."

"Oh, will you? That would be awfully good of you! Thanks very much!"

"Not at all, ma'am! Why wouldn't I?" Julia set down the breakfast things, paused to straighten

her cap, which always drooped a little to one side
or the other, and departed, closing the door behind
her.

Left to herself, Daisy began to open her letters.
The action was not very enthusiastic, for she knew
by the envelopes exactly where they came from, and
could even have hazarded a very shrewd guess as to
what each contained. One was from her aunt, the
Reverend Mother of a convent in the County Clare;
the other was a bill from a local dressmaker. She
opened the former first, and, propping it against
the sugar-bowl, began to skim the thin sheets
covered with close writing, while she mechanically
poured herself out a cup of tea and took an egg
from the stand in the middle of the table. But
presently her attention wandered, and her gaze, as
Julia's had previously done, strayed to the window,
through which the shrill voices of the boys came
raised in dispute over their game. She sat for a
minute or two in idle, uninterested contemplation;
then, as in the servant's case, her truant wits
were recalled by the sound of a step, and, turning sharply round, she bent forward in a listening
attitude.

The steps drew nearer, and with the confirmation
of their sound she rose from her seat, moving so
hastily that the nun's letter fluttered down from
its upright position, and picking up a cover-dish
that stood upon the table, carried it across the room
and set it in the fender.

She was seated again, and apparently absorbed
in the dressmaker's bill, when the door opened and
her husband walked into the room.

There was nothing dramatic in Stephen Carey's entrance, nor was the man himself arresting by right of mere personal appearance. In figure he was tall beyond the average, but lean and a trifle ungainly; and his face—hard, strong, and clean-shaven—was too obviously the lawyer's face to lend itself to expression; his mouth alone of all the features gave promise of hidden emotions in its wide, thin-lipped flexibility, and for the rest, a well-shaped nose that broadened at the nostrils, a square jaw, and a crown of rough red hair made up a rather commonplace exterior. Yet, despite the lack of physical attractions, the man was a personality. You felt it instantly he came into a room, and, moreover, you felt that others felt it. He was one of those beings to whom it is given to claim consideration by a frown—service by a single word. As he came forward now, carrying a bundle of open letters in his hand, his wife knew without looking up that, for some unknown reason, his anger had been roused; and with a sense of uneasiness, her mind sped over the possible household incidents that might have annoyed him. The baby's crying last night! Julia's habitual lateness in the filling of his morning bath and the making of his morning tea!

This dread of having displeased him was subtly —most subtly—indicative of Carey's position in his own house; for though he rarely lost his temper, and still more rarely gave proof of its loss, the whole household—from Daisy herself to the little four-year-old Ted, just beginning to form conclusions as to those about him—each and all were imbued with the dislike of irritating him.

Five years ago, with the taking of this high-ceiled, many-roomed house, Carey had faced the problem of his marriage, — for in middle-class Ireland the choosing of a wife follows the making of a home by a natural sequence of events. It has been illustrated that he was by necessity a practical man ; he was also a man self-satisfying, and to a great extent self-centred ; and when it came to a question of marriage, it was scarcely to be expected that he would lose his heart or even his head — though neither was it to be expected that he would choose carelessly. His idea of a wife had the faint savour of Orientalism so frequently to be found in his country and his class. A wife, in his opinion, was useful—possibly attractive as well, but fundamentally useful ; a chattel, a being to be clothed and fed and housed to the best of man's ability, but beyond that hardly to be considered ; and he had looked round his little world much as the Eastern might have studied the slave-market.

Age and ugliness, even when compensated for by money, he had dismissed from his consideration with the contempt of his race for physical disability, and when at last his eye and his choice had fallen upon Daisy Norris, the daughter of one of the richest men in Waterford, it was not, as gossip had unanimously held, entirely an affair of ducats ; there had been pride in the matter, too, and a subconscious self-approbation—for Daisy had pretty blue eyes, pretty fair hair, and was barely turned twenty.

The fruit of that attitude was visible now on

this spring morning, as he seated himself at breakfast; for Daisy, without a word, poured out his
tea and pushed the cup across the table, then rose
again and carried the cover-dish back from the
fire.

"Will you have some bacon?" she asked in
a low, pretty, rather mincing voice. "I was keeping it hot for you!"

Carey looked up, as if seeing her for the first
time; and in the light from the window the
strong line of his jaw showed prominently.
"No!" he answered shortly; then his glance
fell again to the letters in his hand, and he
burst suddenly into speech. "I declare I'm sorry
the children aren't girls, if this is the return
boys make you!"

"Is that from Paris? Is it from Frank?"

"Yes! It is from Frank!" He answered her
question abruptly, in the deep masterful voice
from which he had never troubled to expel the
native intonation.

"And what is it about?"

He ignored the words, and, with abrupt irrelevance, rapped out a query of his own.

"How much did old Dan Costello leave his
daughter?"

Surprise — and behind the surprise, extreme
curiosity — gleamed in Daisy's eyes, but she
answered in the native roundabout way. "Why,
nothing, of course! What would an accountant
in a bank have to leave? Don't we all know
her aunt is supporting her?"

"And where is she now? The girl, I mean."

"Why here, in Waterford. She and the aunt came back from France on Monday. I know, because Mary saw them both at the ten o'clock mass yesterday."

Carey gave a short sarcastic laugh. "Oh!" he said. "Then I expect there isn't much we couldn't find out about Miss Isabel Costello! I suppose Mary could tell us the price of her gloves and the size of her shoes."

Daisy said nothing; for it was a fact, testified to by many a characteristic scene, that her unmarried sister Mary and Stephen were actively antagonistic. She felt no impulse to defend her absent relative; incidentally, because Mary Norris was so exceedingly capable of defending herself, but particularly because her curiosity was still aflame and prompting conciliatory action. For a while she remained silent, in the hope that Carey would unburden himself without prompting; then at last, as the hope faded, she delicately approached the subject.

"I wonder if Frank saw the Costellos at all, while Miss Costello was taking Isabel away from school! 'Twas funny, their all being in Paris at the same time!"

"Funny! I don't think I'd call it funny! Listen to this!" Carey caught up the letter that he had been brooding upon, and, without comment or explanation, began to read aloud:—

"DEAR STEPHEN,—I write this because it's only fair to tell you that, since you heard from me last, something very important has happened

to me. I am engaged to be married! I suppose
you know that old Miss Costello of Waterford
came over to Paris a fortnight ago to take
her niece home from a convent school. Well, I
came across her by the merest chance the first
day she was here; and—as she seemed rather out
of it with the language and one thing or another,
and as 'twas nice to see any familiar face—I
made myself civil. The end of it all is that
I've been going about with her and her niece for
the last ten days; and that Isabel and I have
fallen in love with each other, and have decided
to get married as soon as ever I can make a
way for myself. Of course I expect you will
be awfully upset when first you read this, and
will think me an awful fool; but don't answer
too soon, for I don't mean to spring it on you—
and I think you'll understand when you see Isabel.
Any way, as I say, take time to think it over!
And don't imagine I'm forgetting how much
I'm in your debt—and always will be.—Your
affectionate brother,

"FRANK.

"*P.S.*—Give my love to Daisy and the boys.
I hope she will be nice to Isabel; it's dull for her
living with Miss Costello.

"*P.P.S.*—Of course all this is strictly private.

"F. J. C."

Carey read the letter to the end without comment; then he rolled it into a ball and flung it
across the room into the fire.

"In love!" he ejaculated with biting contempt. "In love!"

Daisy's eyes had remained wide open in the effort to grasp, whole and entire, this astounding news; now her pretty mouth opened as well.

"What are you going to do?"

Carey glanced at her. "Do? Break the whole thing off, like you'd lop a dead branch from a tree!" He drew his cup towards him, swallowed some of his tea, and, with absent-minded annoyance, helped himself to some of the bacon he previously refused.

"Do you think it's for this I'm making a doctor of him?" he demanded after a moment, not especially of his wife, but of the world in general. "Do you think it's for this that I've saved him from sweating in some Waterford office—perhaps even standing behind a counter?"

He was very angry when he alluded thus openly to the monetary straits from which he had emerged; and outbursts of passion had not been frequent enough in the five years of m. rriage to eliminate the slight, fastidious shudder with which Daisy met the revelations. She drew herself up now with a faintly affected movement, indicative of her own superior refinement.

Carey caught the action. "Oh, it's all very well for you!" he said, "but I can tell you, people like Frank, who are dependent on others for their bread and butter, had best see which side the butter is put on at. A man with a position to make has nothing to do with love. Love! Rot!"

As the last expressive word left his lips, the

door of the dining-room opened again, this time
to admit a small, fair-haired girl in a neat tailor-
made dress, wearing a straw hat, and carrying a
prayer-book under her arm.

"Good-morrow, Daisy! Good-morrow, Stephen!
How awfully late you are!" With an absolute
lack of ceremony she came forward, threw her
prayer-book on the table, and began to pull off her
gloves.

"I'm too early for the ten mass," she announced,
"so I thought I'd come in for a minute."

Daisy looked up. "How is father's cold?"

"Oh, gone, or as good as gone. He had a
Turkish bath last night."

Carey raised his head. "Frightfully dangerous
for a man with your father's weak heart."

Mary Norris sniffed disdainfully. "We'd all have
weak hearts if we had time for them. I'd have
one myself if I hadn't to do the housekeeping.
Daisy, do you know who I met while ago?"

"No. Who?"

"The Costello girl and the aunt!"

Daisy almost started. "Oh, Mary! And did
you speak to them?"

"Speak to them? Of course I did. I was simply
dying to see her properly."

"Well, and what is she like? Do tell us!" In
the keenness of her interest Daisy pushed back
her chair, leaving her tea unfinished.

Mary waited a moment, with the lingering enjoyment of the adept in relating a piece of gossip.
"Well," she said judiciously, "to begin with, she's
as different as anything from the lanky little thing

she used to be before she went to school. She's
awfully curious-looking, and yet she's awfully taking.   She has lovely teeth, and a queer sort of
light in her eyes, different from other people. Oh,
and do you know what?"

"No."

"She's asked to the Fair Hill dance—and she's
going to come out at it! I believe Mrs Burke
knew her father long ago: the Costellos were a
good family in Wexford, you know, though they
were as poor as church mice. I wonder if she'll
give Isabel a dress. 'Twould be a charity if she
did, for I'm sure she has to wear the aunt's old
clothes."

Before she had finished, Daisy turned impulsively
to Carey. "Oh, Stephen, isn't that lovely! I'll
see her splendidly at Fair Hill."

Mary's sharp green eyes followed her sister's.
"Surely Stephen isn't interested in the dance?"

"No, Stephen is not interested," Carey replied,
rising from the table and walking across the room.
At the door he looked back. "Daisy, remember
that that letter is private."

Daisy said nothing; and as soon as he had disappeared into the hall, Mary came quickly round
the table and perched herself on the arm of her
chair.

"What on earth is the matter with him?" she
asked.

Daisy looked behind her with a certain furtive-
ness. "Wait a second and I'll tell you."

"It's all right. He'll be ages getting his coat."

"Well, you'll be most *fearfully* surprised!"

"What at? Do tell me!"

"Am not I telling you? Oh, you *will* be surprised!"

"Go on, go on!"

"Stephen has had a letter from Frank, saying that he met the Costellos in Paris."

"Good gracious! And they never said a word about him, though I told them I was coming in here!"

"Didn't they? That was deep!"

"Why deep?"

"Because Frank says——"

"Oh, hurry!"

"I *am* hurrying! It's you that keep on interrupting. Frank met them ten days ago in Paris, and ever since he's been with them morning, noon, and night; until the end of the whole thing is that he has fallen head over ears in love with Isabel Costello—and actually wants to marry her! Now, what do you say to that?"

Mary stared at her sister. "I never in all my life heard anything to equal it!" She gave each word its full and separate value. "Why, she hasn't a penny to bless herself with!"

"Not a farthing."

"Stephen must be simply——"

"Ssh! I hear him. Don't for your life pretend that I told you."

Mary gave her a withering glance. "Do you think I'm a fool, Daisy?" She picked up her gloves and prayer-book, and was sauntering slowly towards the door when Carey entered.

"Hallo! Going?" he said.

"Only up to the nursery." She swung out of the room, and they heard her run upstairs.

Carey advanced a few paces. His overcoat was on, and he was carrying his hat in his hand. "Daisy," he said, "have you answered that invitation of the Burkes' yet?"

Daisy raised her eyebrows, for all social matters usually lay within her undisputed demesne. "No. Why?"

"I suppose I'm included in it?"

"Of course! But they know you never go to dances."

Carey slowly buttoned up his coat. "I have been thinking," he said; "and it seems to me that it's very little good tackling Frank until I've seen the girl. It's the girl who must be squared first of all. I've thought it out, and you may as well accept this invitation for me as well as for yourself."

Once again in this morning of surprises Daisy's blue eyes opened widely. "But, Stephen——" she exclaimed.

No answer was vouchsafed by Carey. Having given his commands, it was not his way to justify them by reasons. Without looking again at his wife, he passed out of the room and down the hall; and a moment after, the closing of the outer door announced to all whom it might concern that the master spirit had left the house.

CHAPTER III.

A MATTER of small significance, one would say, that a man should announce his intention of going to a dance! But we are dealing with a small world. To the ant a grain of sand represents an appreciable portion of its own environment; and in his family circle, Carey's acceptance of Mrs Michael Burke's invitation made a definite stir of excitement.

The hall door had barely closed upon him when Daisy had flown up the stairs to impart the news to her sister; and Mary, in the intervals of swinging the second child, Francis, to and fro on the rocking-horse in the nursery, had replied with the terse comment, "You take my word for it, Daisy, he's got his back up!"

There had been a good deal of unvarnished truth in this blunt sentence, for in her way Mary Norris was a person of discernment. She shared with Daisy—indeed, with the whole female section of her set — an extraordinary and far-reaching curiosity; but with her, inquisitiveness was supported by a moral courage and an instinct for a secret so marked that mere love of scandal was raised to a fine art. Women feared her,

and yet leaned upon her; but men feared her
and fought shy of her, for there was a satirical
humour in her smile and a sharpness in her eye
that made her a very lively companion, but left
you with an uncomfortable suspicion that, having
amused you at the expense of your neighbours, she
only awaited your departure to pillory you for the
benefit of others. All things are grist to the mill
of such professed gossips as Mary Norris — the
meanness of so-and-so's husband, the neglected
condition of so - and - so's children, the terrible
stories that so - and - so's servants have told in
their new situations. Petty and contemptible,
perhaps! And yet for the class in which it
thrives, this network of scandal has a meaning
and a result. Life carried on under the micro-
scope has a curiously restraining effect upon the
units that compose it: by a high moral standard
you may influence the man whose aims and ideals
are already elevated, but by the wholesome tonic
of his fellow-man's criticism you touch every class
of human being. This knowledge that other eyes
are for ever peering into his holy of holies is a
factor to be reckoned with in the life of the
Irish townsman; and it may be a question for
the sceptic whether his indisputable moral in-
tegrity would flourish as notably elsewhere as
it does in its present restricted atmosphere.

A fortnight went by, during which Stephen
Carey never once alluded to the coming festivity,
and Daisy lived in a ferment of excitement con-
cerning her new dress; the question of whether
she would have her hair done at the hairdresser's

or at home; the continuous speculations as to who had, or had not, been included in the Burkes' invitation list. The actual moment of fruition—when all doubts were to be set at rest, all conjectures dissolved into certainty—found the Lady Lane household in the usual excitement that such an event provokes. Mary Norris, who was to accompany the Careys to the dance, arrived with her portmanteau at five o'clock, and retired at once to the large back bedroom that was to be her property for the night, and in which Daisy's new red dress was already laid out upon the bed, flanked by a pair of high-heeled slippers, open-work stockings, and a fan,—for the sisters still retained the habit, borrowed from their childish days, of dressing together for any noteworthy entertainment.

Mary entered the room followed by Julia, and paused at once to examine the finery.

"It's lovely, Miss Mary, isn't it?" Julia hazarded, setting down the portmanteau.

Mary said nothing.

"The mistress is afraid 'tis the way 'twill be too bright. But sure, as I was sayin', there's no tellin' colours by gaslight!"

"No!" Mary agreed, mentally considering the effect of the red next her own forget-me-not blue dress.

"Will you be havin' a cup of tea, Miss Mary? And will I put a match to the fire?"

"Oh yes, do, Julia. I have to crimp my hair! But I don't know about tea. What time will the mistress be in?"

She took off her gloves, threw them on the table, and began in a businesslike way to unpack her things.

"Oh, she can't be long now, miss. She's gone this good while."

Julia knelt down before the fireplace, applied a match to the sticks, and blew vigorously upon the flame. "'Tis the way this kindlin' is damp!" she added to herself. "And sure I'm tired of tellin' Bridget to put it over the range. Miss Mary, I suppose 'twill be a grand ball?"

"Oh, yes, 'twill be a splendid dance. There are over a hundred asked, and there's to be a band and a sit-down supper. I hope 'twon't rain, though!" Mary glanced anxiously towards the window as she drew her dress from its wrappings.

"I suppose 'tis the garden you're thinkin' of? There's a grand garden at Mr Burke's."

Mary reddened. "Nonsense, Julia!"

But Julia had the privileges of eight years' service in the Norris family, so she looked back over her shoulder without perturbation. "Ah, go on, Miss Mary! Sure, 'tisn't dancin' the whole time you'd be on a fine spring night like this!"

"Indeed, I hope it is, if I have partners."

Julia smiled knowingly to herself as she rose, previous to departing; then she made a sudden gesture of delighted admiration, as she caught sight of the glories of the blue dress.

"Oh, Miss Mary! But that's somethin' like! And the lovely little silver bow-knots on the blue silk! 'Tis like a blessed virgin's altar, it is!"

"Yes, I think it's nice," Mary agreed, not quite certain that the simile was flattering; then she looked quickly round, as the door behind her opened. "Oh, here's the mistress! Well, Daisy, I'm waiting ages!"

Daisy came into the room laden with little tissue-paper parcels, which she deposited on a chair before kissing her sister. "I'm just dead!" she announced. "I tried five shops for a black aigrette for my hair, and had to get a bit of tulle in the end. Waterford is a terrible place! But what do you think of the dress? Is it fearfully bright?" She twisted round eagerly towards the bed.

"N-no."

"You think it looks brighter than it did at Mrs Walsh's yesterday?"

"Well, you can't even see yourself properly at Walsh's, to say nothing about colours! I don't know why you go to such a dingy old hole."

"She cuts very well!"

"Not at all! That's your imagination."

"Indeed, it isn't! You said yourself my brown was the nicest dress I ever had. And anyway, Mary, I think it's rather mean of you now, when it's too late, to be making me dissatisfied. I suppose the dress is awful!" Her voice trembled a little with a mingling of disappointment, annoyance, and fatigue. "Perhaps I'd better wear my old pink!"

"Don't be silly, Daisy!"

"I'm not silly! You'd be sillier if you were in my place! I don't think I'll go at all!"

Silence reigned after this announcement, while Mary began to take down her long fair hair.

"Lilly O'Farrell has a dress exactly the same colour as yours!" Daisy announced at last. "I saw it yesterday at Walsh's."

Mary looked round, her mouth full of hairpins. "I'm sure I don't care how many people have the same coloured dress!" she said indistinctly. "I hate to be remarkable!"

Daisy coloured at the thrust. "It's better to be remarkable than dowdy. Julia, what are you waiting for?" She turned suddenly on the servant.

"Nothin', ma'am! Only to hear when you'll be takin' your tea."

"Oh, bother tea! I don't want any."

Mary hurriedly took the hairpins out of her mouth. "Nonsense, Daisy! Don't be absurd! You know we'd like tea—unless, of course, you want to have dinner with Stephen!"

"You know very well I'd hate to have dinner with Stephen!"

"Well, for goodness' sake let us have the tea!"

Daisy's attitude relaxed a little. "All right! Very well!"

"And what'll we have?"

"Well, we could have some ham — and there are cakes——"

"That would be lovely! Ham, Julia—and cakes —and, Julia, don't forget the mustard!"

"All right, Miss Mary! And when will you be wantin' it, ma'am?"

Daisy looked at her sister. "In half an hour?" she suggested.

"Or now?"

The expressions on both their faces wavered, until finally they laughed. "Very well!" Daisy said. "Now, Julia, please!"

In silence they watched her go; then Mary shook out her long mane of hair and, taking up a crimping-tongs, carried it to the fire and placed it between the bars.

"I wonder who'll be there?" she said for the fiftieth time.

"Owen Power will, anyway!"

Mary bent forward, and busied herself rather unnecessarily over the position of the tongs. "How do you know?"

"I met Josephine Power when I was trying Sheehy's for the aigrette, and she told me Owen and Jim are both going."

Mary took out the smoking tongs and, carrying it to the dressing-table, began to pass it through her hair. "A great condescension on Owen's part, I'm sure! Oh, bother! I've singed my hair."

For a while Daisy remained silent, watching her sister as she made a succession of journeys between the table and the fire; then at last, as Mary knelt down once more before the hearth, she walked across the room and suddenly put her arm about her shoulder.

"Polly, do you like him still?"

Mary turned and looked up at her, her face flushed and half aggressive. "I'd be very sorry to trouble myself about any man!"

"I know! But, still——"

"What?"

"Well, you know he likes you."

"Indeed I don't!"

"Nonsense! You know it right well. What about the picnic at Woodstown in October? 'Twas ten o'clock when you and he got back."

"Well, I had a puncture—and we had to mend it."

They both laughed, but almost immediately Mary became serious again. "I wonder if he'll ask me for a dance, Daisy? 'Twill be so horrible if he doesn't."

Daisy's more malleable nature bent instantly to the softer tone. "As if he wouldn't!" she said.

"Oh, it's never safe to be sure."

"Nonsense!"

Mary stared hard into the fire, as though the riddle of her future was open and readable in the heart of the coals. "Men are awfully queer, Daisy," she said at length. "You can never be sure of a man."

"Nonsense! All men marry, if they can afford to; and—and if they like any one."

A frown of impatience crossed Mary's white forehead, and a little tinge of contempt lifted the corner of her mouth. She shook back her hair, as if about to retort with some scrap of the worldly wisdom she had acquired, no one knew where; but on the spur of the moment her impulse changed.

"Ah, well!" she said. "'Twill be all the same in a hundred years! Here's Julia—and the tea!"

CHAPTER IV.

THE dance was to begin at nine—an hour unusually late and fashionable for an Irish town; and at half-past eight the hired car that was to convey the Careys to Fair Hill was already drawn up in Lady Lane.

It is a peculiarity of the town of Waterford that no closed vehicle plies for hire in the streets; so when those of its inhabitants who are not blessed with carriages fare forth after dark on duty or on pleasure, they resort by necessity to the livery stables, from which issue vehicles that for the most cogent of reasons avoid the searching eye of day. It may be a brougham that answers to the demand —a relic of former glory, moth-eaten and tottering to its fall, or a hansom-cab that has drifted like a piece of flotsam from the sea of London life, or perhaps it may be a "covered car" that can trace its antecedents to Limerick or to Cork. To those who have not actually travelled in such a vehicle, the name "covered car" is a mere figure of speech, conveying nothing, and demanding definition: outwardly, it has the appearance of a large square box, one end of which has been knocked out and replaced by a low door, a step, and a pair of funeral curtains; inwardly, it is possessed of two seats, upon which the passengers sit *vis-à-vis*, clinging to straps that depend from the small windows set like port-holes on either side of the driver's seat. A drive in a covered car is never likely to be forgotten, for a haphazard abandonment of life and limb marks it from the first moment to the last, when by an ingenious movement of the jarvey the horse is pulled round, vigorously backed, and the wheels of the car collide with fearful violence against the kerb.

Such a conveyance Daisy and Mary found awaiting them when they emerged from the house at a quarter to nine, arrayed in long, light dust-coats and wearing woollen wraps over their heads; and immediately the hall door was opened, the driver— a disreputable individual in a tall hat several sizes too large for him and a coachman's coat from which most of the silver buttons had disappeared— hurried forward, thrusting a lighted pipe into his pocket.

"Wait a minute, ma'am! Wait a minute! I'll back her!"

"Oh, don't!" Mary cried. "Don't back at all! We'll get in as it is."

"Oh, sure, whatever you like, Miss Norris! 'Tis equal to me. I'm on'y thinkin' of ye'er feet on the muddy road—though, after all, 'tis more dust than mud it is."

Neither took any notice of this mixed statement, but as hastily as possible beat past his dirty assisting hand, and seated themselves high up under the windows of the car, to protect their skirts as far as might be from subsequent contact with Carey's feet.

"I feel awfully nervous!" Daisy announced, when at last the driver had reluctantly returned to his horse's head, to tie up a broken piece of harness. "I wonder if my hair is straight? I wish to goodness I had gone to Davitt's after all. I'm sure it's hideous."

"Not at all! It's all right!" Mary said without looking at her.

"I wonder if I'll have any partners?"

"You will, of course! Anyway, it doesn't matter to you. You're married."

Daisy turned round indignantly. "Oh, indeed, doesn't it?" Then she paused, as Carey appeared in the open doorway, and in the diversion of interest her anger died. "How well Stephen looks in evening dress!" she exclaimed involuntarily.

"That's a matter of taste." Mary stooped to gather in her frills; and as she raised her head, she added in a louder voice, "For goodness' sake, Stephen, hurry! We won't get a single partner."

Carey came slowly across the pavement, buttoning up his coat. "All right! Go on now!" he called to the driver, as he placed his foot on the step.

With his added weight, the shafts rose and the car dropped back to what was its typical angle.

"Good heavens!" Mary exclaimed. "You're a frightful weight!"

"Twelve stone! Why aren't you sitting at the same side?"

She looked at him with scorn. "On account of our dresses, of course!"

Further controversy was cut short by the starting of the car, which was accomplished by much noisy admonition from the driver and sundry backings and false starts on the part of the horse, before they could pass triumphantly down the street at a respectable trot. For the first ten minutes a cramped and uncomfortable silence reigned; then at last, as they came within appreciable distance of the steep ascent that led to Fair Hill, Carey spoke again, moving his legs painfully.

"Of all the abominable tortures man ever invented," he said, "covered cars are the worst! This decides me. I'll have that motor of Leader's."

At the tremendous announcement Daisy jumped round in her seat, forgetful even of her dress. "Oh, Stephen, you don't mean it? Will you really? How lovely! How perfectly lovely! I don't know how I'll sit in it, the first day we go out; I'll be so terribly proud!"

Mary lifted her chin. "They say it nearly beggared Leader!"

"So much the better for me! He paid a thousand for the car, and now he'll be glad to get four hundred for it."

"Oh, but the buying isn't all! Old Mr Hayse told me the other day, as a dead secret, that it costs him five hundred a-year, with petrol and repairs and things."

"Well, old Hayse is as blind as a bat and drives at fifty miles an hour. If you knew the compensation cases I've settled for him out of court, you'd say five hundred was doing it rather cheap. Here we are at the hill! I'll walk up, Daisy!" He opened the door of the car without calling to the driver, and let himself out.

As the horse started forward in appreciation of the lightened weight, Daisy thrust her head out of the car.

"Stephen! Stephen!"

"Yes! What?"

"You'll meet us at the door of the dancing-room?"

He assented, and stepped back to the side of the road, as a large one-horse carriage, crowded to its fullest extent, dashed proudly past the hired car; and, at the same moment, Mary caught Daisy's arm and drew her back into the shadows.

"Don't hang out like that, Daisy! It looks so badly!"

"Why? Whose car was it?"

"The Powers', of course! Didn't you see?"

When Carey's foot dropped from the step of the car to the hard roadway, he drew a breath unmistakably pregnant with relief. Whether the relief depended entirely upon a release from a cramped position, or whether it had for inspiration a subtler sense of loosened bonds, it is for the psychologist to say. Certain it is that he felt more free of outlook and more individually independent after Daisy's appeal had melted into silence and Daisy's pretty anxious face had been merged in the darkness of the car. Not that he cherished an opinion of himself as a man shackled by matrimony; nor that we, who would follow his story, must think of him as such! Love, and the conditions engendered by love, had never loomed large enough upon his horizon to be considered as factors capable of mending or marring his existence. His feelings, as he stiffened his shoulders to the ascent of the hill, were simply the feelings of a man who has been freed from a position that wearied him, and who, as a matter of reaction, turns with zest to his personal concerns. A task awaited him to-night,—a task self-set and therefore acceptable; and all action— even action so tame as that which he anticipated —had its own incentive power. He reached the summit of the hill almost as soon as the covered car; but, jealous of his stolen solitude, he did not follow it up the avenue of chestnuts that glinted a faint green against the April night sky, but paused outside the gates to look back over Waterford, lying half-veiled in vaporous fog.

The scene was eloquent, as are all Irish scenes— touched with an unnamed pathos, wrapped in that mystery from which memory can draw such innumerable and binding threads; and as he looked down upon the clustering roofs and pointing spires, he stepped unthinkingly into that region of sentiment to which, by right of birth, every Irishman holds a key, and into which his feet turn instinctively the moment the rein of self-restraint is loosed.

As in the windings of a dream, his mind sped back over the years of his youth to the days when, as a little red-haired boy, he had followed his father's workmen up their scaffoldings, and had looked out over this same city of roofs and spires, weaving with a child's imagination picture upon picture of the world beyond the confines that formed his home. The subject of these pictures had always been the same,—always the wonderful, fabled world where name and fortune awaited the adventurous.

But fate and time between them had clipped the wings of the soaring dreams; the boy, with his ugly, clever little face and preternaturally observant eyes, had slowly grown to manhood without sight of that great Beyond: had slowly grown to manhood, and to the conscious compromise with ambition that men of his country and of his class are daily and yearly driven to make. In Ireland, the bread of expediency is the staff of life, and Stephen Carey had early seated himself at the frugal board. If now, in these later days, a ghost of the lost ambition ever glided behind his chair, pointing a wavering hand towards the great market-place of life, where the fountains flow to quench all thirsts, only his eyes saw the passing of the shade : none guessed that for a moment his achievements shrank to their true proportion, and the good substantial bread became as ashes in his mouth.

Out of the vaporous mist the phantom rose with its train of stifled hopes pressing up against him, whispering inaudible words, proffering intangible embraces. But his mood to-night was aggressive rather than depressed ; he shook off the clinging presence, and set his face towards reality, pictured by the long line of budding trees and beyond them, by the large square house ablaze with light.

The hall door of Fair Hill was hospitably open
as he drew level with the house, and he saw as
on a stage the lighted interior—the fine square
hall, built within the last five years, and possessing
not a fragment of romance; the rugs of expensive
texture and vivid colouring; the palms standing
upon ugly pedestals of glazed pottery, each detail
significant, each betraying in its own proportion
the taste and the social standing of Michael Burke,
successful dealer in butter, justice of the peace
under the new *régime*, kindliest, most honest, least
intellectual of men.

Burke himself passed across the lighted hall as
Carey mounted the steps, and paused to greet him.

"You're very fashionable, Stephen," he cried,
"but better late than never! Where are the
ladies?"

"Oh, they're here! I walked up the hill. How
does this sort of thing suit you?"

Michael Burke made a comical face. "Well, to
tell the truth," he said, "there's great temptation
in the thought of my old pipe upstairs. But when
the young people begin to grow up, Stephen, faith,
pipes and the rest must go empty! You'll be in
the same boat yourself some day, when you have
three young men waiting to be settled."

Carey laughed indulgently, for he liked Michael
Burke, with his odd turns of speech, his homely
ways, and sterling character. "I suppose so!" he
agreed,—"I suppose so, indeed! Where am I to
leave my coat?"

"Oh, upstairs! Upstairs! My little snuggery
has been turned inside-out for a dressing-room.

Up with you! You know the way. There's the
first dance beginning, and Ellen will be wanting
me! Don't be long, though!" With a nod and a
friendly smile, the little man disappeared through
a velvet-draped doorway into a room from which
the first bars of a waltz were floating out into
the hall.

A very few minutes sufficed to relieve Carey of
his hat and coat, and presently he was back
again in the hall, following the direction his host
had taken. The dancing-room was already full of
whirling couples when he made his appearance;
and, pausing inside the door, he was compelled to
make one of a little group of young men and girls
who had hurried down from the dressing-rooms at
the first sound of the music, but who were reserv-
ing themselves for the second dance, while they
criticised their fellow-guests.

One or two heads were turned as he appeared,
and a couple of youths muttered a diffident "Good-
night, Mr Carey!" but the girls of the group
scarcely noticed him. In their world, the married
man hardly exists as an independent being, for he
is a thing appropriated, labelled, laid irrevocably
on the shelf. For the first few moments his presence had a damping effect, but very soon the animal
spirits of the party rose above the shy silence,
and set them chattering again like a band of
sparrows.

"I tell you what, though, she's awfully pretty!"
The man who spoke was Owen Power, a young
barrister of handsome face and consequential manners, who paid periodical visits to his people in

Waterford, and who was supposed to bring with him from Dublin an air of fashion and advancement not locally to be acquired.

"Owen is struck!" put in a heavy youth, in a dull, drawling voice.

"What'll somebody else say?" cried a girl of seventeen, with a dazzling complexion, and bright, impertinent eyes.

"Shut up, Amy!" The heavy youth had a brother's privileges, and used them ungallantly.

Amy laughed and tossed her head. "All right! I'll say nothing—but I'll think the more!"

The brother growled something unintelligible, and at the same time Power adjusted his pince-nez and leant forward.

"Here she is! And, I say, *doesn't* she dance!"

"Who is she dancing with?"

"I can't see."

"It's Willie Neville!"

"No, it isn't!"

"Yes it is, though!" The girls peered over each other's shoulders in a fever of curiosity.

"I say!" Power cried again,—"I say, doesn't she dance! She puts me in mind of the Spanish dancer we had in Dublin for a week last year."

"Oh, well, she's nearly foreign as it is!" Amy murmured. "Half the Wexford people have Spanish blood. Here she is!"

The word "foreign" attracted Carey, who had been absently trying to single out his wife's red dress in the crowded room. It touched him to interest, and instinctively he turned to find the object of the description.

Out of the heterogeneous crowd that twisted and reversed and backed in a frenzy of energetic joy, his eyes alighted upon one figure and remained arrested, while in his mind Power's words found a sudden and strenuous echo. She could dance! She certainly could dance!

By ordinary judgment, she was merely a girl of twenty; but in that moment she might have been a flower swaying in the wind, a young animal stretching itself to the sun, a bird in its first flight, —anything fresh from Nature's hand, pulsing with the delight of living and knowing itself alive. She skimmed down the room, unconscious of the partner whose arm encircled her; she saw nothing beyond the stirring perspective of light and colour, heard nothing but the swaying music of the waltz that swelled and faded in waves of sound. She swept past the little group in the doorway, totally unaware of its existence, and for one instant Carey looked down into her face. But it was only for an instant: immediately he drew back against the wall, with a curious, half-shamed sense of having looked upon something not meant for his gaze. For the essence of womanhood, intimate and unguarded, lay in the flushed cheeks, the half-closed eyes and parted lips.

To rid himself of the sensation, he turned abruptly to Power. "Who is that, Power?" he asked. "The girl in white?"

Power answered with his eyes upon the retreating couple. "That's old Miss Costello's niece—just back from school."

The last bars of the waltz crashed out, and a

laughing, excited crowd made a rush for the door. Carey stepped aside to let it pass; and then slowly, as though acting upon some half-formed thought, he walked down the ballroom to where Mrs Michael Burke was holding a little court.

CHAPTER V.

VERY slowly Carey walked down the room to where a group of twelve or fourteen elderly women, arrayed in dark silk dresses and wearing lace caps, were gathered about their hostess, closely observant of the scene being enacted before them. Every guest in the ballroom, with his or her genealogical tree, was accurately known to each of these spectators, and a running fire of comment and criticism kept pace with their various actions. A little tremor of interest and curiosity passed over the group when Carey's approach was signalled, and glances of speculation were rapidly exchanged, heads brought closer together, and voices discreetly lowered.

With a man's innate sensitiveness to observation, he made haste to single out his hostess and shelter behind her greeting. Not that he had any affection for Mrs Michael Burke; on the contrary, it was a never-failing source of wonder to him how kindly, commonplace Michael could ever have chosen such a mate, for Mrs Burke was what, in her particular set, is known as "very grand," which, literally translated, conveys the impression of a vast and unloveable superiority of manner, coupled with

definite social ambitions. In his feeling of vague
dislike Carey shared a common opinion, for not
even Burke's own relations had ever, in the twenty
odd years of his married life, arrived at the point
of feeling at home with Mrs Michael. Her invitations to Fair Hill were never refused, for such
invitations implied a certain social distinction, but
the uncultured band of relatives never outgrew
the nervous sense of the hostess's critical eye, and
a sigh of relief invariably escaped them when the
large iron gates, aggressive in their prosperous coating of white paint, clanged behind them and they
were free to breathe their own less rarefied air.

This same consciousness of cold criticism fell
now upon Carey as he clasped her long, thin hand,
encased in a well-fitting black kid glove, for her
actions and bearing could convey to a nicety the
precise esteem in which a guest was held. As the
daughter of a bank manager, she was obliged in
the present instance to look askance at Carey's
antecedents, though, as the wife of a successful
trader, she granted him the meed of praise due to
his self-earned position. In his case, circumstances
balanced each other. He had been unfortunately
brought up, but he had married well. Her fingers
closed round his with a certain degree of cordiality,
and her thin face relaxed into a smile.

"Good evening, Mr Carey! I have just been
talking to your wife; she danced the first dance
with my cousin, Surgeon-Major Cusacke. He's
stationed at the Curragh, you know. Such a nice
fellow! I must introduce you to each other." She
spoke in a high, clipped voice, from which the

brogue had been carefully eliminated,—a voice that, in its studied precision, had something in common with his wife's.

The similarity struck Carey, flashing across his mind with a slight, sharp contempt. Usually, he was not a little proud of Daisy's social advantages, but this reflection of them in a woman who was antagonistic to him jarred upon his senses, still tingling from contact with elemental things. Dropping Mrs Burke's hand, he answered quickly and indifferently. "Oh, Cusacke! I met him at the Tramore races last year."

Mrs Burke was sensible of the little slight, but she prided herself on being a hostess and a woman of the world; and, whatever her silent criticism of his manners, she gave no outward expression of it.

"And what about yourself, Mr Carey? Are you going to play cards? Or can we persuade you to dance? There are plenty of pretty girls here—but the men are always wanted."

Carey laughed. "Old married men like me?"

She smiled the chilly smile that was thought the essence of good taste. "Oh, you mustn't be running yourself down! Let me find a partner for you. But, of course, you know everybody here!"

"Indeed I don't! It makes me feel quite old seeing all these children who were in the nursery in my dancing days."

"What nonsense! There's nobody here you don't know — unless, perhaps, Dan Costello's daughter. You remember the Costellos? Dan was with my father in the bank in Enniscorthy before he was moved here."

"Oh, yes, I remember him. A dark, excitable little man."

"Yes. The greatest fool that ever lived. If you made a king of Dan Costello, he'd be begging in the streets the week after! He hadn't a grain of sense."

"Who was it he married?"

"Don't you remember? He ran away with a Miss Dysart of Derryvane. 'Twas the talk of the County Wexford for a year after. Her father cut her off without a penny; and, they say, she used to have to turn Dan's old coats for herself when he was done with them! But all the Wexford people are queer!"

Carey laughed. "And what about the girl?"

"Oh, Isabel! Isabel is pretty. Perhaps you saw her, though. She was dancing the first dance."

"I saw her, yes!" He was careful to answer indifferently.

"And what did you think of her? She's curious-looking, isn't she?"

He made no reply.

"Your wife and your sister-in-law admire her greatly. I must introduce you to her. I wonder where she's gone to!"

"She's half-way down the room, standing near the door." Carey still kept his voice studiedly unconcerned, for he dreaded Mrs Michael Burke as we dread all powerful influences, the workings of which we do not understand.

"Oh, is she? We'll go and find her, then." She excused herself to the nearest of the matrons, and sailed down the room, with Carey following in her wake.

As they drew near to Isabel Costello, she was standing by the wall, the centre of a group of men, her head thrown slightly backward, so that the light from the chandeliers fell full upon her rounded chin, her parted lips, and white, flawless teeth. More than ever, she suggested the young animal stretching itself to the warmth and comfort of the sun—to the caresses of life; and this subtle, indescribable impression came home to Carey interwoven with her physical being—lying like a shadow in the blackness of her hair, dancing like a will-o'-the-wisp in her hazel eyes.

At the moment that they paused beside her, she was holding up her programme, the pencil poised in her hand, her dancing eyes roving from one man's face to another, in transparent joy at the exercise of power. "Well, I can't give it to you all!" she was saying in a clear voice. "I can't give it to you all — unless I divide myself up into little bits! And, even then, only the person who got my feet would have a good dance!" She laughed, once more displaying her strong, white teeth.

"Isabel! Here's somebody I want to introduce to you!"

She turned at once at sound of Mrs Burke's voice, the laughter still on her lips.

"Mr Carey! Miss Costello! And don't dance too much, Isabel! Your aunt will be blaming me if you look washed-out to-morrow."

A flash of amusement shot irresistibly from the girl's radiant eyes to Carey's, and involuntarily he responded to it, as he acknowledged the introduc-

tion; but the opening bars of the next waltz came
swinging down the room as he bent his head, and
before he could speak the little group of men
became clamorous again.

"Well, Miss Costello, and who is to have the
dance?"

"I asked first, you know!"

"Indeed you didn't, Jack! 'Twas I! Wasn't it,
Miss Costello?"

"Well, I asked last. And the last shall be first,
you know!" Owen Power pushed his way to the
front with a confident smile.

Again Isabel looked from one face to the other.
"I tell you what I'll do!" she said suddenly.
"I'll give the dance to Mr Carey—and then none
of you can be jealous!" Like a flash she wheeled
round upon Stephen.

The demand in her glance was so strong, the
whole onslaught so sudden, that no thought of
resistance suggested itself to him. Without a word
he stepped forward and put his arm round her
waist, swinging her out into the circle of dancers
that was rapidly filling the room.

It was five years or more since he had danced,
but few Irishmen are awkward in an art that
comes to them more or less naturally. He guided
her carefully down the room, testing his powers,
exercising his memory, anxious not to do himself
discredit; then, as he gained the farther end, and
passed the group of matrons, the spirit of the
moment suddenly entered into him, as the music
quickened and he felt the strong supple body
of his partner brace itself in response. A thrill

passed through him, dispersing a long apathy;
his position and his responsibilities were moment-
arily submerged in the sense of sound and motion;
his arm instinctively tightened, drawing the girl
closer, and with one impulse they spun out into
the centre of the room.

For several minutes they danced in silence;
then at last they paused by the door where they
had first met. They looked at each other, and
she gave a breathless little laugh.

"How well you dance!"

"I don't! 'Twas you made me."

She coloured with pleasure. "Do I dance well,
then?"

"Well? You dance wonderfully."

"I learnt at the convent in Paris from a French
teacher. We weren't supposed to learn waltzes, but
she taught me. There's nothing so heavenly as
dancing, is there?"

Carey looked at her, engrossed in some thought
of his own.

Her face changed and darkened. "But perhaps
you didn't enjoy it?" she added, swift as lightning
in her change of tone.

"Didn't I?" His eyes were still upon hers.

The blood rose quickly to her face, chasing away
the shadows. "Then perhaps it's only that you're
trying to be nice to me, because it's my first
dance?"

The tone of the voice, the utterance of the
words, were charged with unconscious coquetry.
The sense of exhilaration swept over Carey afresh,
as though her light fingers had lifted the dry record

of his days and her light breath had blown the dust
from the pages.

"Could I be nice—even if I tried?" His tongue,
unused to the tossing of words, brought out the
question awkwardly—stupidly, it seemed to him;
and he looked to see her lip curl.

But, so fine is the net by which fate snares,
she liked the embarrassment in his voice; she liked
his evident unfitness for the game of give and take.
It was exciting to put it to the test—to step forward, sounding his interest—to retreat, daunted by
the mystery that shrouds the unknown personality.
Her feminine intuition recognised the essential—the
man—in Carey, and her feminine instinct rose to
meet it. Premature instinct, perhaps, in a girl of
twenty! But mentally, as well as physically, the
admixture of southern blood was marked by early
development. As her body was built upon gracious
lines, so her mind had already flowered, where others
lay folded in the bud.

"You *are* nice—even without trying." She felt
her pulses throb at her own daring, and the sensation
was delight.

Carey took a step forward. "You'll have to
justify that!" he said quickly. "You'll have to
give me another dance."

Without a word, she handed him her programme;
and as they bent over the little card, their heads
close together, their shoulders all but touching, she
was conscious that her heart was beating faster
than it had beaten all the evening, exciting though
the evening had been.

"Which would you like?"

"This!" He drew a line through a dance in the middle of the programme. "And now, where will we go?"

As he handed her back the card, some crashing chords came down the room, indicating the end of the second waltz, and in response, half a dozen couples stopped at the door, and hurried out into the hall. The first to halt were his sister-in-law, Mary, and young Power; and as they passed, Mary's keen eyes swept over his face and Isabel's.

"Daisy waited ten minutes for you!" she remarked as she went by.

Isabel looked after her in surprise. "Mary Norris didn't seem to know me!"

"Oh, you'll get used to that! It's a habit of Mary's to kiss people one day and cut them the next."

Isabel's surprise was turned upon him. His tone, his expression, his bearing had all changed as if by magic. He had drawn back into a shell of reserve, as though in the moment of expansion some antagonistic influence had blown across his mind.

"Let us get out of this crowd," he added in the same curt voice.

In the hall and on the stairs some chattering girls and their attendant youths had already found seats; but the hall door was open, offering a tempting view of dark trees and deserted pathways. Carey paused and looked towards it.

"I suppose you'd be afraid to go out?"

Isabel's momentary depression flared to excitement.

"Afraid? What would I be afraid of?"

"Oh, I don't know. Wet feet, I suppose. All girls' shoes are paper."

She withdrew her fingers from his arm, and, with her head held high, led the way across the hall and out on to the gravelled pathway.

A little titter of laughter came from the stairs; she heard it and stopped.

"Were those people laughing at me?"

"No. Why?"

"No reason. Only I could kill any one who laughed at me!"

Carey looked at her through the darkness—her graceful figure bent slightly towards him, her muslin skirt held high above her white satin slippers. "Do you always have such fiery sentiments?" he was drawn to ask.

"Oh, I feel things, yes!"

"Then I'm afraid you're going to dislike me, Miss Costello!"

There was no mistaking that his reason and his will forced him to snatch this opportunity, while his inclination stretched out detaining hands; and when such a conflict is waged in a man's mind, his expression is apt to be unnecessarily cold, his tone unnecessarily harsh.

At his words, Isabel's head went up again, with the action of a young deer scenting danger. "Hate you? Why?"

"Let us walk on, and I'll try to tell you!"

In silence they turned and passed down the

avenue—she brimming with uneasy curiosity, he girding himself to the attack.

"Do you mind if I smoke?"

"No, I don't."

He took out a cigarette, and lighted it with the care of a man whose thoughts are upon other matters; then he threw the lighted match away into the undergrowth, where it flared for a moment and went out with a little splutter.

"Miss Costello, I had a letter the other day from my brother Frank."

She stopped. "From Frank?"

"Yes. He wrote—and told me."

"Told you——?" Her voice faltered.

"Yes. Told me that you and he are engaged."

"Oh," she cried naïvely, "and he never said a word to me about having written! I suppose he was afraid you'd be angry. Were you angry?"

Carey tightened the buckles of his armour. "I was!" he said. "Very angry."

"And why?" Challenge and defiance leaped at him suddenly. He could feel her nerves quiver to her thought.

"Why? Oh, because a sensible man can't help being angry when he sees an act of folly; and this is folly, you know—utter folly."

Isabel's muslin dress slipped from her fingers and trailed upon the ground. "Why?"

"Oh, because Frank has no money, no influence —nothing in the world that could justify his marrying."

She looked down. "I suppose it wouldn't be so bad if the girl he wanted to marry had money of her own?" she asked in a very low voice.

Manlike, he walked into the trap. "It certainly would make things more practicable."

In a flash she was round upon him again, her pride and anger aflame, her sense of wounded dignity blazing in her eyes. "Oh, I see! I see! I'm not good enough for your brother!"

Involuntarily he put out his hand. "I never said that!"

She gave a sharp little laugh. "Didn't you? It sounded very like it. I'm not good enough—not rich enough for him! He must wait till he can make a better match!" With a little gasp, her voice broke.

"But, my dear child——"

"I'm not a child! I'm twenty—and old enough to manage my own affairs. And I can tell you one thing!—I can tell you one thing, and that is that I'd rather die now than break off my engagement! I'd rather die now than break it off—even if I didn't care a pin for Frank!"

Carey looked at her passionate face, in which the eyes gleamed black and bright; and again he was stirred, as though a current of electricity had coursed along the rut of his commonplace life.

"Very well!" he said. "Then I suppose we declare war? I have a will of my own, too, you know!"

She met his eyes, half curious, half amused. "Yes," she said with defiant seriousness. "We do. We declare war!"

He bent his head in acceptance of the defiance;

and, without another word, turned on his heel and began to walk slowly back towards the house, leaving her to follow as she pleased.

There was no chivalry in the action; it was a case of the elemental man following his instinct. But all human drama is built upon the primative; and the fewer the stage accessories, the sooner the arrival of the psychological moment.

CHAPTER VI.

THE noonday sun was streaming into Isabel Costello's bedroom when she woke to the world on the day following the dance. Under ordinary conditions one can comfortably lie abed in Waterford until ten o'clock; and when a crushed muslin dress, a broken fan, and satin slippers with soles worn shiny from dancing, testify to a night of wild activity, there is no limit to the thraldom of sleep.

She woke slowly, drawing in with each half-conscious breath the confused, agreeable sense of something vaguely exhilarating in the immediate past. Her first action was to raise her arms above her head and lazily stretch herself; her next, to sit up, shake back the great plait of black hair that had fallen over her shoulder, and look round the little room that still held the unfamiliarity of new surroundings. The curtains of the one window had been pulled back, and the spring breeze blew in, carrying with it the scent of wallflowers from the small front garden. There is magic in the scent of wallflowers—such magic as lies in spices and cedarwood—to call up pictures from the treasure-house of imagination, and Isabel closed her eyes to the ugly Victorian furniture that hampered the little room, to the grey wall-paper that even the sun could not fade into brightness, and in a moment she was skimming down the ballroom at Fair Hill, tingling again with the joy of movement and the intoxication of success. For this was her inheritance, her birth-right—this power to vibrate like a fine instrument to every passing touch; it was patent in the flash of her smile—in the sudden frown—in the threat and the caress that ousted each other continuously in the depths of her eyes. She was Irish, but Irish with the blood of Spain reliving in her veins from a forgotten generation. And of such a compound, what results? Throw oil upon water, and you induce pacivity; cast it upon fire, and the flames laugh back into your face! She was a Celt in imaginativeness, in fatalism, in pride; but in her recklessness, in her vitality, there was the beat of warmer blood—the call of a race, more intense, more tempestuous than Nature ever placed upon northern shores.

Still drinking in the soft, moist air filled with the subtle scent, she dropped back upon the pillows, lost in retrospect; then slowly and reluctantly her eyelids lifted, as her quick ear caught a step on the corridor outside.

A moment later, the handle of her door was turned, and her aunt, Miss Costello, walked into the room, carrying a tray on which rested some thick pieces of bread and butter, a brown glazed teapot, a milk jug, and a cup and saucer. She was a thin, dried-up little woman of fifty-five, with a brown and prematurely wrinkled skin, sharp black eyes, and wispy black hair. In her case, the alien blood had run to asceticism and a nervous unpractical activity that had worn her out before middle age. She came up to her niece's bed now with a haste that suggested a multitude of affairs claiming her attention, and set down the tray so quickly that everything rattled.

"Well, Isabel! Good-morrow! What hour was it at all when you got in?"

Isabel put up her mouth very graciously for her aunt's kiss. When her nature was submerged in pleasant or exciting recollection, she overflowed with affection towards the world at large.

"'Twas five o'clock, Aunt Teresa."

"Five! What on earth were you doing till five? It must have been broad day!"

"'Twas, nearly!" Isabel laughed at the remembered pleasure.

"Did you enjoy yourself?"

"Enjoy myself! I never in all my life enjoyed myself so much."

"And did you keep the car the whole time? I wonder what sort of a bill Loughlan will make out!"

"The car? Oh, the car was there at two, but they wouldn't hear of my going away. I came back with the Powers."

Miss Costello looked impressed, and, drawing herself up, smoothed the frill of the black alpaca apron she always wore.

"Oh, indeed! The Powers! That was very nice for you."

"'Twas, in a way."

"Indeed it was! The Powers are very well off; and Mrs Power is very good position. She was a daughter of Mr Knox-Nash of Gallybanagher."

"So she told me while we were driving back! But, Aunt Teresa——"

"What?"

"Do you know who I met last night?"

"No. Who?"

"Frank's brother."

"What! Stephen Carey! You don't say so! Why, I thought he never went to parties."

Isabel's thick black eyelashes drooped over her eyes. "Why shouldn't he go to parties?"

"Oh, because he's married and settled down."

"But he's not old."

"He's thirty-eight. Did he dance last night?"

"Of course he did! Why wouldn't he dance when he's able to?" Her eyes flashed up to her aunt's face.

"Oh, I don't know! Only a man with a wife and three children has generally something better to do than to be losing his night's sleep. Oh, but I forgot! There's a letter for you from Paris." She began to search hastily in her apron pocket. "Ah, here 'tis! I knew I put it in!"

Isabel took the thin foreign envelope and laid it unopened on the tray.

Miss Costello's sharp eyes caught the movement "Why won't you read it?" she asked.

"There's time enough!"

"Oh, is that the way? In my young days, a girl didn't take a man's letters as coolly as that. But perhaps I ought to go!"

Isabel flashed round upon her angrily. "As if I ever thought of such a thing! I know what's in the letter, that's all. And when you know what's in a letter you're not very excited to open it—at least I'm not!"

Her aunt's face looked disturbed. "Isabel, you don't tell me you're getting tired of him?"

"I didn't tell you so."

"Well, I only hope your head wasn't turned last night!"

"What on earth would turn my head?"

At her niece's darkening brow, Miss Costello was thrown into nervous confusion. "My dear child, nothing! Only I suppose you danced with all the young men—with—with Owen Power and the rest of them."

Isabel laughed, her good-humour restored by the absurdity of her aunt's idea. "Oh, no, Aunt Teresa! Mr Power didn't turn my head. I don't like beauty men. And, look! To please you, I'll open Frank's letter!" With an incredibly swift turn of the fingers, she tore the letter open and, before Miss Costello could remonstrate, began to read it aloud.

"Listen, Aunt Teresa! 'DEAREST ISABEL,—Thanks for your nice letter. I am still very lonesome, as you can understand; and I think of you every minute, and wish all our walks and talks could come over again. You are in my mind always. Do you often think of me?

"'I have written to my brother Stephen, telling him about you, but I'm afraid he is not very well satisfied, as I have not heard from him yet. Let me know if you meet any of the family. It worries

me a bit not to know what they think; but Stephen
is a queer chap, all for getting on in life, and not
giving way to sentiment——'"

Isabel stopped suddenly in her reading.

"Is that all? I hope there'll be no unpleasant-
ness with the Careys."

"Oh, that's all! It goes on for ages in the same
sort of way. Aunt Teresa?"

"What?"

"What has Daisy Norris grown up like? I
didn't see her last night."

"Daisy Norris! Oh, she's pretty—and, of course,
she's rich."

"Rich!" Isabel tossed her head. "As if that
mattered!"

"It mattered a good deal to Stephen Carey."

"Why?"

"Oh, because he had a hard enough life of it in
the beginning. Many a time his brothers would
have been in the workhouse only for the way he
slaved. Your poor father knew it through the
bank."

"And he married Daisy Norris for her money?"

Miss Costello looked shocked. No Irishwoman
likes her insinuations put into blunt speech. "I
wouldn't say that to anybody, Isabel, if I were you.
There's no doubt, of course, that Daisy's money
wasn't in his way; but, all the same, 'tis an ugly
thing to be saying about any man, that he married
for money."

"Well, was he in love with her?"

"Oh, how do I know? I suppose he was. 'Tis
hard to say those things."

" And was she satisfied ? "

" How satisfied ? "

" Satisfied with that sort of a bargain?   I know
I wouldn't be."

Miss Costello looked at her niece with that half-
pathetic perplexity that the old so often bring to
bear upon their study of the young.   In the long
tale of years that had made up her own life she
could find no key to the nature that looked at her
from Isabel's restless eyes.

"I can't make you out, Isabel!" she said at
length.

Isabel turned on her side, and the plait of black
hair fell again over her shoulder.   "What I mean,
Aunt Teresa, is that if I was rich, and was going
to marry a man like Mr Carey, I'd take very good
care that he didn't marry me for my money alone."

Miss Costello smiled uncertainly.   "Would you
indeed?   And how would you manage it ? "

"Oh, I can't tell how, but I would!"   Her eyes
turned to the window, and then flashed back again.
"What a fool she must have been!" she added
suddenly; then, seeing her aunt's shocked face,
she put up her hand in a pretty gesture of de-
precation.

"Auntie!   Auntie!   Don't look so shocked!   It's
only that I like fighting for things, and I can't
imagine other people not liking it too."

A look akin to horror tightened Miss Costello's
thin lips.   "Don't, Isabel, dear!   'Tisn't right to be
saying things like that.   Girls in Waterford don't
talk like that."

"Why?"

"Well, it wouldn't be thought nice. You'd get the name of being odd."

"But why?"

The repetition stung Miss Costello to annoyance. "Ah, don't be silly, child! You know very well that a girl must do what other people do—'specially if she has no money. Saying queer things is nearly as bad as doing them. If you want to make nice friends, and be taken up by people richer and in better society than yourself, you'll have to be particular."

"I don't care whether people take me up or not. I'm poor, I know; but I'm not a beggar to be patronised."

"Ah, there you are again! Running away with every word I utter! I never said you were a beggar. I don't know where you get such ugly words."

"Well, they're true words, aren't they?"

"Maybe! But it won't always be enough for you that things are true. I tell you people here have a certain notion of what other people ought to be, and if you differ from that, they just leave you where you are."

Isabel considered this statement. This, then, was what she had returned to from the long probation of school life, first in Dublin and later in Paris! This weighing of words! This bondage in a free world! Her restless spirit rose up, swiftly antagonistic and rebellious.

"Aunt Teresa, I'll never do it!" she exclaimed. "I'll never—never do it! I can't cut out my life on a sort of pattern. It must be what I want it to be, or nothing at all. Oh, I wish I had died

last night! The world is horrid the day after
things!" She put her hands over her face in an
impulse of despair as sudden and real as her excitement had been.

Miss Costello looked frightened and flurried. Life
had presented a new and unwelcome problem in
this grown-up niece, and she shrank constitutionally
from responsibility.

"Isabel, dear! Isabel, dear—don't!" she said
helplessly. "That's not the way to be looking at
things at all. Say a prayer to Saint Philomena to
help you to be sensible! Be a good child now, and
say a little prayer!"

Isabel dropped her hands, showing a flushed and
defiant face. "I'm not a child, Aunt Teresa! And
I've given up Saint Philomena: she never does
anything for me now." She almost trembled at
her own temerity as she made the statement, for
veneration of the saints and firm belief in their
friendly intercession is the very breath of life in
such places as convent schools; and, moreover, she
knew that she was treading sacrilegiously upon
Miss Costello's most sacred ground. But rebellion
was alive within her. "I don't think it's much
good praying against things like that," she added.
"How could the saints have time to bother whether
I'm sensible or not?"

"Isabel, I'm shocked at you! If your poor
father could only hear you! A man that said
his rosary every night of his life!"

The demon of insubordination stirred in Isabel,
prompting retaliation. "If he hadn't said so
many prayers," she said irreverently, "perhaps he

might have got promotion in the bank—and left me better off."

For one moment Miss Costello looked down on her in speechless anger; then, by an agitated exercise of the control her religion taught her, she turned and walked out of the room.

As the door closed, Isabel's bravado evaporated. "Aunt Teresa!" she called suddenly. "Aunt Teresa, come back! I'm sorry!"

But by keeping her indignation within bounds, Miss Costello felt that she had done enough. At the sound of her name in Isabel's quick, emotional voice, she paused on the corridor, murmured a prayer for her niece's spiritual guidance, and silently passed down the narrow stairs.

CHAPTER VII.

LAST mass, celebrated at twelve o'clock, is the important event of Sunday in an Irish Catholic town. Almost medieval in its pomp and pride, it presents a curious contrast to the drab-hued life outside the Church; for within the precincts there is colour for a dozen pictures, were there artists to paint them. Splendid vestments, cloth of gold, wax lights, and the glory of flowers are blent together in an atmosphere clouded with incense; while over the heads of the congregation, making the impression audible, the organ whispers or thunders the majesty of the Eternal.

It was Isabel Costello's fourth Sunday in Waterford, and in the bench nearest the altar she sat beside Miss Costello, who might have posed for the spirit of religious fervour as she knelt, rigid in her plain black dress, armed with long brown rosary beads, and a ponderous prayer-book.

It would mislead from the outset to say that Isabel was religious; yet it would be overstating the case to say that she was devoid of the religious sense. Every tenet of the Roman Catholic Church she accepted with unquestioning belief, because to her imagination those tenets were

fixed as the stars in heaven; but in her composi-
tion there was nothing of the ascetic. Pray she
could—and frequently did—with a passionate fervour of supplication; but she preferred the *prie-
dieu* of an oratory to the bare floor of her own
room, and her moments of devotion were usually
inspired from without rather than from within.

She sat now in the clouded atmosphere, and
her thoughts, freed by the music of the organ,
flowed out upon the stream of her fancy. Her
prayer-book lay open before her, but her eyes
were not following the prayers: she sat, as she
had sat a hundred times in the convent chapel,
weaving the dream that all youth weaves; but
with this difference, that in the convent chapel
the dreams had been tinged with the pearl and
silver of dawning things, and now the light of a
waking world was touching them to rose and
gold. There was life to be lived now! She no
longer stood expectant in a realm of ideals.
Vaguely moved by these imaginings, she stood
up and knelt down, mechanically noting the
chanting of the priests, the silences of the choir,
and the fresh bursts of music from the organ,
while her mind travelled back over the ground
she had covered, from this mass in the Waterford cathedral to the day in Paris when love had
confronted her in the guise of the first man she
had known. For it was love—the image, the
abstraction—that had broken down her defences
on the evening that she had stood by the
window of the hotel salon with Frank Carey,
and looked down into the narrow street, where

the asphalt shone like ice in the white light of
the electric lamps, and the stumbling of the cab-
horses and the cracking of whips rose mingling
with excited street cries. There had been a
sense of fate in the air that evening. She remembered looking across at the opposite houses
and thinking how like they were to painted
houses upon the stage, with their flat fronts and
shuttered windows; then that first recollection
was rent by the newer, stronger memory of
Frank's arm thrust suddenly about her waist,
and Frank's unexpected kiss upon her cheek.
Rough, untempered love - making it would have
been to the mind of the experienced, but to the
girl released a week before from a convent school
it had seemed the knowledge of life; and Frank
Carey, the freckled, sandy - haired boy, had taken
on the glamour of romance in that moment of
daring.

Reflected in the mirror of her thoughts, he had
appeared before her in that moment as the knight
storming the castle of his lady-love. And now?
The organ spoke low, dropping to the note of question, and her cheeks reddened as though human lips
had propounded a riddle. Now? She looked at the
figures of the three priests officiating at the mass
that was drawing to its close, and suddenly the
vision of the avenue at Fair Hill rose up before
her mind—the avenue with the chestnut buds
silhouetted against the night sky and the first
stars dappling the darkness.

The blessing was given, and the congregation
stood up for the last gospel. Isabel rose with

the rest, and knelt again for the final prayers; then at last, the service ended, the three priests disappeared into the mysterious regions behind the altar, the organist struck the first chord of the solemn march, and the stream of people began to pour into the aisle.

It was some time before Miss Costello had finished her private devotions, and the church was fast emptying when she and Isabel rose to depart. They were almost the last to emerge from the church and step out upon the flagged space guarded by railings that shuts the cathedral from the street and makes a tempting loitering place for those whose duty lies behind them. Isabel's first impression as she came out into the light was of a crowd broken up into little knots of two and three, and of a number of voices exchanging conflicting greetings; her next, the consciousness of Miss Costello pulling at her sleeve with nervous anxiety.

"Isabel! Isabel! Don't you see Mrs Power saluting you?"

Isabel turned sharply. "No, I don't, Aunt Teresa! Where?"

"Over there, by the steps. Look now! She's smiling at you."

Isabel turned, half-reluctantly, in the direction indicated, and then the blood rose hotly to her face, for Mrs Power was the centre of a party formed by Mary Norris and Daisy and Stephen Carey.

"Go on, Isabel!" urged Miss Costello; "she wants to speak to you. You ought to thank her for driving you home that night; 'twould be only polite."

Isabel didn't seem to hear her aunt's persuasion, and it is doubtful whether the pleadings would have met with any response had not Mrs Power made a forward movement, and settled the question for herself.

"Ah, my dear child, how are you? I haven't seen you since the dance!" she said, pushing a way though the intervening people, and extending a friendly hand. "What have you been doing these weeks past? And here's your aunt, too! How are you, Miss Costello? You ought to have been at Fair Hill that night: you really ought. There were no two opinions about it, your niece was the belle. She could have filled her programme twice over; even my own husband lost his heart. I can tell you I was quite jealous." She gave a pleasant laugh, drawing the girl into her favour with a motherly tone and glance.

Meanwhile a moment of indecision had fallen on the little group she had deserted. With many misgivings Daisy was asking herself whether she should or should she not make advances towards this possible disturber of her husband's projects? But as she hesitated between uncertainty as to Carey's views and the instinctive desire to stand in with Mrs Power in all social matters. Stephen decided the point by stepping forward and greeting Isabel.

"How are you, Miss Costello?"

Isabel started at the sound of her name; and turning, gave her hand in a silence born of sudden and uncontrollable shyness.

"How are you?" he said again, a little awkwardly. "We haven't seen you since the dance. Let me introduce my wife! I think you know my sister-in-law!"

For a swift second Daisy looked at Isabel, Isabel at Daisy, appraising each other sweepingly, as women do; then Daisy held out her hand.

"How are you?" she said. "We used to know each other long ago. I remember you as well as anything at a children's party at the Burkes' when I was ten; and you cried because I fell over you in 'Blindman's Buff.'"

"Oh, yes! I remember too." Isabel laughed. "I was only five, but I remember as well as anything that you and your sister had blue dresses and fair plaits tied with blue. I envied you fearfully."

Daisy echoed the laugh, and Mary Norris strolled slowly forward. "How are you?" she said, using the inevitable greeting. "How did you enjoy the dance? You seemed to be having a grand time, as far as I could see."

"The dance? Oh, 'twas splendid! I loved it!" Isabel looked straight in front of her, conscious that Carey's eyes were watching her with half-unwilling interest.

"And who did you like best?" Try as she might, Mary could not hide the half-malicious lifting of the corner of her mouth.

Isabel turned. "Oh, old Mr Burke, of course!" she said with native readiness.

Carey laughed. "Good! Take my advice, Miss Costello. Don't let them draw you!"

Mary's smile deepened as she saw Isabel colour; and Isabel, conscious both of the smile and of her own blush, glanced round confusedly. "We—we ought to be going," she said. "Where's Aunt Teresa?"

"Here! Here, my dear, gossiping with me! You're right to remind us how idle we are. Daisy, I'll run in with you to Lady Lane for a minute." Mrs Power wheeled round upon them with her large, placid personality and homely smile.

Daisy made a hasty little gesture of pleasure and gratification. "Oh, do! Do, Mrs Power!" Then, as she saw Mrs Power look promptingly towards Isabel and Miss Costello, she added in a less enthusiastic voice—"And you, Miss Costello! Won't you come in for a minute too?"

Miss Costello looked confused. "It's—it's very kind of you, Mrs Carey, I'm sure! Very kind of you!"

"Only we must go straight home," Isabel added promptly. Swift in the gaining of an impression as in the prompting of an instinct, she had heard the hesitancy and felt the doubt in Daisy's mind.

Miss Costello looked nervous, and Daisy slightly offended—"Oh, of course if you are busy——" she said.

"We are. We promised to be back. Didn't we, Aunt Teresa?"

At her niece's glance poor Miss Costello wavered hopelessly. "We are. We did," she said. "It's very kind of you, but——"

"Good-bye! You see we must go. Good-bye, Mrs Power! Good-bye!" In turn Isabel shook hands with Daisy, Mary, Mrs Power and, last of all, with Carey. For the one fleeting second that her hand rested in his, she glanced up at him—a quick, bright look difficult to read; then, leaving her aunt to follow as best she could, she turned and walked out into the street.

As Miss Costello beat a hurried retreat, Daisy, whose eyes were upon Isabel's straight, lithe figure, spoke her thoughts. "She's queer, isn't she?" she said in a slow, meditative way.

"Queer?" Mary cried. "I think she's the coolest person I ever met in my life. I can tell you I wouldn't like to be in the aunt's shoes."

Mrs Power put her hand on Mary's arm. "Ah, now, Mary, make excuses! What is she but a child!"

"A very wide-awake child, Mrs Power!"

"Ah, no, Mary! I don't think so."

"Don't you? Wait and see!" Mary turned, and began to make her own way through the crowd of loiterers.

"And you, Stephen? What do you think of her? I like a man's opinion on my own sex."

Carey turned, roused from a brown study. "I?" he said. "Oh, I don't pretend to understand women, Mrs Power."

CHAPTER VIII.

MEANWHILE, Isabel and her aunt were making their way up the hill that led to New Town, where Miss Costello's small house stood behind its patch of garden. For several minutes after they had parted with the Careys neither of them spoke; but at last, as their goal drew within sight, Isabel felt her sentiments no longer to be controlled.

"Aunt Teresa," she said suddenly, "I don't know —I really don't know how you can go on like that."

Miss Costello half paused in her hurried walk. "Like what?" she demanded.

"Oh, not having a bit of pride! Not seeing when people don't want you!"

"Don't want me? But the Careys wanted us— Daisy Carey herself asked us."

Isabel tossed her head contemptuously. "Yes. Asked us because Mrs Power was nice to us— and Mrs Power is good position. Do you think she'd have done it except for that? Indeed she wouldn't!"

Poor Miss Costello was crushed, nevertheless she made a fight for her own attitude. "Well, I think you ought to have gone in, all the same. You'll have to be friendly sooner or later, if you're to be one of the family."

"I may never be one of the family!"

"Isabel!"

"Oh, well, I didn't mean that."

Miss Costello heaved a sigh of relief for even this small mercy. "Of course not!" she said, to reassure herself. "Of course not. Not when you can count on Frank. I'm sure the poor fellow is devoted enough!"

Once more Isabel's chin was contemptuously raised. "Would you like to be going to marry a 'poor fellow'?"

"You're very absurd, child! You know I didn't mean it like that. I'm sure Frank is very talented."

"Talented, indeed! I'll tell you what Frank is. He's just a shadow of his brother. Only for his brother he wouldn't be there at all. I found that out since I came home."

"The shadow of his brother? Indeed, I don't agree with you. I think Frank Carey has plenty of cleverness of his own; and I'd much prefer him myself to Stephen. He's a great deal pleasanter in his manner."

"Weak people are nice to everybody, because they haven't courage to be anything else!"

Isabel made this pronouncement as they were passing through the garden-gate, and, having made it, she stepped aside into the small grass-plot, to gather a handful of violets, while Miss Costello hurried into the house, where the one servant of the establishment was awaiting her superintendence in the cooking of the early dinner.

The flowers gathered, Isabel made her own way indoors, passing up the narrow stairs to her cramped bedroom. Her first action on entering the room was to cross to the dressing-table, peer closely into the mirror at her own reflection, and, taking off her hat, to throw it carelessly on the bed.

She could not have explained her mood, but she felt restless and half angry. Nothing definite had happened to displease her, but it was precisely this negative condition of circumstances that left her disturbed. She would have everything fire or sun —battle or ecstasy; the calm, the uneventful she banished from her toleration with an unsparing definiteness.

Having thrown her hat aside, she lingered for a while by the dressing-table, her fingers drumming on the white cloth that covered its mahogany surface, her eyes dark and brooding; then, forced to action by some prompting thought, she slowly opened one of the table drawers and drew forth a blotter filled with odd sheets of note-paper and envelopes of varying sizes; and unearthing a pen and a pot of ink from some dark recess, placed the whole collection upon the table.

Her next move was to pull forward a chair and seat herself upon the edge of it, and this action was typical of her mood: the fact that she did not approach her task squarely showed that it was unwelcome, for to the things that were congenial she went straight as a bird in its flight, heart and soul, mind and body—one undivided impulse.

With her neck uncomfortably twisted and her elbow resting on the table, she dipped the pen into the ink, made a blot on the white cloth, and, drawing forward a sheet of paper, wrote the words "Dearest Frank."

For a long time she remained looking at this accomplished work and striving to connect it with herself. She looked at the words and wondered—looked at them again, and wondered again. Why had the writing of a letter become a thing so irksome? She recalled her first note to Frank—how the blood had flooded her cheeks at the mere fact of putting a man's name upon paper—how every shy and halting expression had meant a separate sensation. Why had all this changed? Why had the excitement, the glamour fallen from the whole idea, as colours might fade from a picture? A wave of impatience trembled across her mind. She felt angry—she felt cruel. Suddenly seizing the paper, she tore the letter in two, as though by the act she could inflict some punishment upon the unconscious author of her disaffection; then with equal suddenness she lifted her head in a listening attitude, for her quick ears had caught the sound of footsteps on the little gravel-path, footsteps that were followed almost immediately by a knock on the hall door.

Visitors were few and far between at the little house at New Town, and involuntarily she rose and ran to the window. She pulled back the starched and torn lace curtain, and leant forward curiously; then as precipitately she drew back again, all the anger, all the waywardness gone from her face, every feature lighted up with sudden interest.

She sat down on the side of her bed, her hands clasped, her heart beating quickly, as she heard the slipshod steps of the servant shuffle down the hall, heard the door open, and heard the visitor's peremptory demand for Miss Costello. Next, she was conscious of two pairs of feet going down the passage and of the shutting of the parlour door, followed by a perfectly audible and flurried explanation between the servant and Miss Costello in the back regions of the house; then lastly, she distinguished her aunt's steps on the creaking stairs, and a moment later saw her excited face round the corner of the bedroom door.

"Isabel!" she exclaimed, almost before she had entered the room. "Isabel, do you know who's below?"

Isabel sprang to her feet. "S-sh, Aunt Teresa! He'll hear you."

"It's Stephen Carey."

"I know."

"What on earth can he want? What do you think he can want?"

"How do I know!" Isabel hid the light that was dancing in her eyes.

"Am I an awful object? I was just in the middle of making the apple-dumpling. It's a queer hour, indeed, for a person to be calling; he might have waited till three o'clock!" She came forward into the room, her hair a little more untidy than usual, a check apron covering her black dress, and a dab of flour on her cheek testifying to her recent labours. "Let me look at myself!" she added, going up to the dressing-table, and pro-

ceeding without permission to smooth her hair with
Isabel's brush.

At any other moment this would have called
forth an indignant protest from the owner, but
Isabel was too excited now to give heed to the
niceties of property, and, coming forward graciously,
she even helped to pull down Miss Costello's sleeves,
and herself untied the apron strings and dusted the
flour from her face.

"Will I do now? I declare I am as flurried as
anything, being called away like that in the middle
of the dumpling! I only hope Lizzie will be able
to go on with it."

To this string of words Isabel paid not the
slightest attention; but, having made her aunt
presentable, pushed her unceremoniously towards
the door.

But Miss Costello refused to cross the threshold.
"You'll come with me, won't you? Oh, Isabel,
you'll come with me?"

Isabel looked down, coquetting with herself. "I
don't know."

"Oh, Isabel, do! Be a good girl, and do!"

"Very well, I'll come after you."

"Ah, come now!"

"No; afterwards."

"Very well! Will I do?"

"You're splendid."

"Well, don't be long!" She nodded a last
injunction; and, still full of nervous trepidation,
made her way downstairs.

Isabel stood on the tiptoe of interest as she heard
her descend the stairs and open the parlour door,

but her strained ears caught only the confused murmur of a greeting, followed by the closing of the door; and at this sign of privacy she turned back into the room, and for the second time since her return from mass walked up to the mirror and studied her appearance. This time the face that looked back into her own was alive and joyous, and as she brushed her ruffled hair, the sense of power and energy rose within her.

Money was scarce in the small household, and in consequence her wardrobe was of the scantiest; but with the unquenchable instinct of adornment, she took a bow of cherry - coloured tulle from a drawer and pinned it at the neck of her pink muslin dress. As she was in the act of arranging it, steps sounded again upon the stairs, this time awkward and shuffling, and presently a knock fell timidly on the door.

"What is it? Come in!" she called.

The door opened an inch or two, and the face of Lizzie the servant appeared at the aperture.

"Miss Isabel," she gasped, "Miss Costello is wantin' you below in the parlour; and she says you're to be as quick as you can." Lizzie was newly from the country, and as yet raw material.

"All right! Only I wish you'd come into a room, Lizzie, when a person tells you to."

"I will, miss! Yes, miss!" Lizzie backed incontinently down the stairs, overcome by embarrassment.

Isabel, very nearly as agitated as the maid, put another pin into the tulle bow and hurried across the room and out into the corridor; but pride would not allow her to run down the stairs, though her feet danced to be off, and she reached the parlour door with a very dignified demeanour.

As she turned the handle and entered, however, a little of the dignity evaporated, for the scene was not quite what she had anticipated. At the mahogany table that wellnigh filled the little room, Miss Costello and Carey were seated upon two of the stiff horsehair chairs that had come, with Isabel herself, as a legacy from the improvident Dan. Carey was sitting bolt upright, looking resolute and uncomfortable; while his companion, in a condition of obvious perturbation, was nervously plaiting and unplaiting the fringe of the table-cloth.

As Isabel appeared, Carey rose. "I suppose you are rather surprised to see me again," he began.

Isabel said nothing: if there was a difficult moment to be faced, she decided that he must bear the brunt of it.

Miss Costello stirred agitatedly in her seat. "I'm afraid Mr Carey hasn't come on a very pleasant mission, Isabel."

"No. No, I'm afraid I haven't. But won't you sit down?"

In the same determined silence Isabel accepted the chair he drew forward for her; and resting her elbows on the table, clasped her hands under her chin.

Carey, still obviously ill at ease, dropped back into his own seat and made a fresh essay. "I hadn't intended to do this — to come here like

this," he said; "but I realised in the last three
weeks that it mightn't be very easy to find an
opportunity of seeing you, and so I decided to—
to make the plunge."

Isabel bent her head in acknowledgment that
the words were meant for her, and Miss Costello
gave a fluttering sigh.

The difficulties placed in his way seemed to brace
Stephen, for he suddenly cast aside his conciliatory
tactics, and made a headlong rush for his point.
"Of course you know why I have come," he said.

Isabel, offended by this bluntness, opened her
eyes. "How could I know?"

At the little touch of artificiality he lost patience.
"Oh, don't make light of the matter!" he said
quickly. "Frank is serious to me."

In an instant Isabel was as angrily sincere as
he. "And do you think he's not serious to me?
Have you any right to suppose that?"

"Not serious, indeed!" Miss Costello murmured.
"When I think of the prayers I have said and
the candles I have lighted, that we might all be
guided to do right!"

Isabel gave her a withering glance and turned
again upon Carey. "After all, it must be more
serious to me than to anybody——"

"Except Frank himself."

"How do you mean?"

"Well, I mean that marriage must be more
important to a man than to a woman—not in the
sentimental sense, perhaps, but in the ordinary,
practical, everyday sense. After all, if a woman
likes to make a poor marriage she does it with

her eyes open and she finds compensations; it's the man who does it blindly, and it's the man who sinks under it. I know what I'm talking about."

"Some of the happiest couples have been poor!" ejaculated Miss Costello. "Look at my poor brother!"

Carey refrained from making use of the weapon placed in his hands, and merely said: "Don't forget that your brother is dead, Miss Costello, and that death casts a sort of glamour over things."

She heaved a sigh. "Ah, Dan was a saint!" she murmured to herself. "A saint!"

"But poor people *can* be happy," Isabel cried. "Poor people *can* be happy. I'd rather be a beggar ten times over, than make what they call here a 'good match.' I think it's much more to be despised to sell yourself as if you were a sheep or a horse than to marry because you care."

"Isabel! Isabel!"

"Be quiet, Aunt Teresa! I will say what I think. You hate me to marry Frank because I have no money; but if I was rich you'd let us get married to-morrow, even if I was lame or blind. You think of nothing but money—money and position. You live in a little, little world, where if people ever do feel anything, they're afraid to say so!"

Carey, watching the expressions darkening and lighting her face, leant suddenly across the table. "Miss Costello," he said, "I thought exactly the same as that, when I was your age. When I was twenty I thought Waterford the narrowest

hole on God's earth, and myself the one man
who was going to step outside it. But—" he
gave a quick, despondent shrug of the shoulders
—"I went under when the time came. I went
under like the rest. There's a big machine called
expediency, and we are its slaves. We oil it
and polish it and keep it running, every man
and woman of us; and if by any chance one
of us puts his hands behind his back and says
he won't feed the monster any more, what happens? Does the machine stop? Not at all!
It's the deserter who goes under; the machine
roars on louder than before. It's only by
pandering to it that we live; and the man who
has oiled his own particular wheel is in duty
bound to see that those dependent on him learn
to oil theirs. This brother of mine belongs to
me: I've fathered him and trained him and
educated him, and I'll see him have a fair start.
You must understand my position! You must
see my point of view! I'm writing to Frank
to-night; let me tell him that you have accepted my decision?"

Isabel kept her hands obstinately locked, her eyes
obstinately lowered.

"Let me write that to-night? Frank isn't a boy
with a great deal of character; he's not the boy
to make a way for himself."

"He cares for me."

"I have no doubt he does. But no romantic
man ever made a fortune."

Her eyes blazed again. "I don't want a fortune.
I told you that."

"I see! Then it's no use? The sensible thing doesn't appeal to you?"

"No, it does not. I hate the sensible thing."

"All right! I'm sorry! You force me to do what I don't like to do."

"What's that?" Isabel stood up.

"You force me to tell Frank that unless he breaks off this engagement I must stop supplies. It's very unpleasant, but there's nothing else for it. I've done what I could." He rose rather stiffly from his chair.

Isabel paled, then reddened violently. "You—you would do that?" she said.

"For his own good, yes. I told you the matter was serious to me."

" Oh, Mr Carey, you wouldn't!" cried Miss Costello. "You surely wouldn't! Think of the poor fellow's feelings! Young people will be young people, you know!"

"Stop, Aunt Teresa! Mr Carey, do you think that when you write to Frank, he'll break off our engagement?"

Carey hesitated. "Frank is not strong-minded."

"That means you do think it? You think he'll give me up at a word from you?"

"Certainly not that. But he is dependent on me; he hasn't a penny of his own—and a man must live."

"And suppose he writes back that he doesn't care a pin about your money?"

Carey began to move slowly towards the door. "On his own head be it, then!" he said. "I'll have done my best. I'm sorry I should have had to offend you." He hesitated and looked back at her.

But Isabel would not meet his eyes.

"Won't you say good-bye? I am sorry—though you may not believe it."

"Good-bye!" She did not look up or hold out her hand.

"Good-bye, Miss Costello!" He turned to the older woman.

"Good-bye, Mr Carey! I suppose you're acting for the best; but indeed I must say you're hard—very hard."

He did not attempt to shake hands with her; and, passing out of the room in silence, he went quietly down the hall, and let himself out by the small front door.

Instantly he was gone, Miss Costello's feelings broke all bounds. "Oh, Isabel," she cried, "what a frightful thing! What a terrible thing! A good match like that slipping away before our very eyes! What a pity your poor father wasn't more saving —not that he had anything to save! But if only you had a little money now, how different things would be! To think that a son of old Barney Carey the builder should have it in his power to despise one of the Costellos!"

Isabel stood for a moment listening to her aunt with pale lips and eyes black with passion; then all at once she brought her hands together with a fierce gesture. "Aunt Teresa," she said, "if you say one word more you'll drive me stark, staring mad!" And before Miss Costello had time to recover from her surprise, she had vanished from the room.

CHAPTER IX.

FOR a week inaction oppressed Isabel's life; then the atmosphere lifted. A letter arrived from Paris.

With the arrival of this letter everything was altered; it was as if a cloud had been dispersed, permitting the sun of activity to shine forth again and fill her world. She read it in the morning, while Miss Costello was at the ten o'clock mass; and, armed with sudden decision, she did not wait to peruse the pages a second time, but, pinning on her hat, sallied forth from the house, on fire with the sense of adventure.

The Waterford streets are not very remarkable either for business activity or beauty at ten o'clock in the morning, but romance is a matter of soul, not of surroundings; and as she threaded her way down the incline of streets from New Town to the Mall, her senses were attuned to the lilt of her thoughts, and her heart kept time like a dancer's feet.

At the corner of the Mall she stopped to give a penny to a blind beggar, and the man's eloquent flow of blessings seemed the last note in the pæan of triumph. For she was about to commit an act of daring, she was about to outrage that conven-

tionality in which the members of her set moved
and breathed; and as she swung along the streets,
she recalled Carey's outburst in the little parlour,
his simile of the great, insistent machine of expediency; and as added stimulus the vision of herself
rose up—one of the fearless few with hands met-
aphorically locked, refusing to feed the monster.

Crossing one or two of the more important
thoroughfares, she passed at last into one of the
quieter, narrower streets that in every town are
stamped with the seal of the professions, and over
which an air of privacy is gathered like a garment.   With eager and yet hesitating steps she
threaded her way along the deserted footpath,
taking quick, sidelong glances at the windows
carefully screened from the vulgar gaze, until
at last the name of "Stephen Carey, Solicitor,"
displayed in black letters on grated ironwork,
brought her to a standstill.

With an involuntary impulse she glanced up
and down the silent street; then, with slightly
nervous haste, she turned in at the open doorway.

A dark and dusty passage confronted her as
she stepped in out of the daylight, but a door
at its farther end gave renewed hope, for there
again Carey's name was blazoned forth, and,
hurrying forward, she knocked twice on the glass
panel.   For a moment she waited, listening in-
tently; then, as no sound reached her, she spurred
her courage and turned the handle.

The room into which she stepped was Carey's
outer office, and to a first glance it looked almost
as unattractive as the passage that led to it.

The ceiling was high; the walls bare, save where they were fitted with shelves; the only pieces of furniture two high desks placed in the middle of the room. A reedy youth of eighteen or nineteen was seated at one of these desks, a pen behind each red ear, his long legs twined round an office stool; at sound of the opening door he looked round casually, only to be transfixed with surprise at sight of the intruder.

Isabel coloured angrily at his open-eyed stare. "I want to see Mr Carey," she announced promptly. "Is he here?"

The youth took a third pen from between his teeth. "You can't see him," he said in a drawling voice that seemed to part grudgingly with its words.

"Is he here?"

"Yes, he's here."

"Then why can't I see him?"

"Well, you can't, for he's engaged."

Isabel, who was no respecter of persons, made haste to probe this statement. "What is he doing?" she demanded.

The youth, nonplussed by such directness, was drawn to answer directly. "Well, he's talking to the head clerk."

At this, Isabel's assurance flowed back in full measure. "Is that all!" she said contemptuously. "Go and tell him at once that somebody wants him!"

The youth wriggled on his stool. "Oh, I don't know that I can do that," he demurred. "Are you a client?"

Isabel ignored both the objection and the question. "Where is he?" she asked.

He indicated a second door. "In there, in his private office."

She acknowledged the information by a nod of her head. "Very well! Then I'll tell him myself," she said; and, leaving the youth too amazed for protest she crossed the room, and without more ado knocked peremptorily on the inner door.

There was a slight pause; then came a sound of steps, followed by the opening of the door, and the head clerk, a fair man with a short beard and near-sighted eyes, looked out impatiently.

"What do you want, Thomas?" he said, but seeing the intruder, he broke off. "Oh, I beg your pardon! What can I do for you?"

"Can I see Mr Carey? My name is Costello. Perhaps you'll tell him that I'm here."

"Certainly, certainly I will." The clerk glanced behind him hesitatingly, then stepped aside, as he saw Carey rise quickly from his desk and come across the room.

The surprise that had crossed Stephen's face at the sound of Isabel's voice was still visible as he pushed past the clerk and threw the door wide; and in that first unguarded second she seized upon the certainty that the surprise was not un-pleasant.

"I suppose I oughtn't to have come! But I wanted to see you, and I couldn't think of any other place."

Carey laughed, as he took her hand and drew her into the office. "You can go on with that deed, Allman!" he added; and the head clerk withdrew, closing the door.

She had taken him unprepared, and in the moment of surprise it seemed that he was once more the Stephen Carey of the Fair Hill dance—the real man, unshackled by convention.

Her spirits soared high. She looked into his face, echoing his laugh.

"But I shouldn't have come, should I?"

"You shouldn't—unless you want legal advice!"

She took the chair he pushed forward for her, watching him seat himself at the large flat-topped desk where he transacted all his work.

"You can guess why I came, can't you?"

"Another battle?"

She made no reply; but, smiling under the half-quizzical, half-questioning gaze of his eyes, slipped her hand into her pocket and pulled out a thin foreign envelope.

"'Twas for this. I wanted to show you this."

She held out the letter, and, as it passed from her hand to his, she sank back again into her chair, apparently absorbed in a study of the black tin boxes lining the walls, in reality listening with sharp intensity to the rustle of the paper between his fingers. She stayed quite motionless while he drew the sheet of paper from its envelope, and while he turned the first page; then, unable to restrain her curiosity, she moved in her seat and shot a swift glance at him as he sat with head bent and body leaning forward.

As if conscious of the glance, he looked up.

"So you wanted me to read this?"

She nodded.

He folded the letter and refolded it, drawing out the creases mechanically, while his eyes fixed themselves upon the papers crowded on his desk.

"So this is Frank's answer to me? He cares nothing for me or for my money, so long as you stick to him!"

He spoke in a low voice, so low that it was impossible to follow its expression; and Isabel, watching his immobile face, felt her courage falter.

"Are you very disappointed?"

He looked up at her again, and his glance was the hard, cold glance with which he had always scanned his failures. "Oh, I acknowledge myself beaten!"

The colour leaped into her face—the red banner of success. This was the moment for which she had lived as she swung along the streets, and her whole spirit rose now to meet it. With one of her swiftest gestures, she stood up and walked across to him.

"Mr Carey," she said, the nervous note of tense excitement thrilling in her voice, — "Mr Carey, why do you treat me as if I was a sort of enemy? Why do you speak to me as if I was trying to bring Frank to ruin, just out of spite? Why have you never asked me to break off with him as — as a sort of favour — as a sort of kindness?"

She looked down at him, her finger-tips resting on the desk, her face brimming with expression.

"Why haven't you ever thought that I might do it to help you—to please you?"

Carey glanced up. "I suppose I only know one way of getting things."

She threw back her head. "And you think women like that way?"

He was silent. It did not come to him to tell her that all his life he had commanded, not asked of, women.

"Don't you think if you had asked, things might have been different?"

"I never ask."

"Ask now!" The words were almost a whisper —a whisper in which he could hear the catch and quiver of her breath.

He twisted round in his seat. "What do you mean by that?"

"What I say. Ask now!"

Native suspicion ousted the surprise in his face. "I don't like being made a fool of!"

Isabel drew herself up. "And do you think I came here to make a fool of you? I'll tell you why I came! I came to tell you that you can keep Frank—that I don't want him—that I'm done with him."

In the immeasurable relief of the moment Carey jumped up. "You mean that?" he cried. "You actually mean that?"

"I do mean it; yes."

They stood for a moment looking at each other in the quiet office—he absorbed by the news, she observant of him. In the crucial moments of life it is always the woman who puts the eternal

"Why?" Man, the active, the unanalytical, who deals in results. It never touched Carey's mind to question the motives that had prompted this act of renunciation, the tangled feelings that had prompted this change of front: if he saw Isabel in the affair at all, it was merely as the exponent of an unlooked-for generosity—a creature who had proved herself strangely sensible by falling in with his own views. The subtler compliment went altogether unobserved.

"It's—it's very generous of you," he said at length. "What can I say?"

"I don't ask you to say anything. I'm not doing it for thanks."

"And Frank? Have you thought of Frank?"

"I'll write to Frank to-night."

Carey's face changed. "He'll be very much cut up, remember! He'll do all sorts of things. He'll probably threaten to kill himself when he first hears this."

Isabel smiled. "First? You're not very complimentary."

"Oh, it has nothing to do with you. It's only that I know Frank. As for compliments, I can't pay them, but I'd like to ask you to forgive me for—a lot of things; and I'd like,—I'd like, if it's possible, to be friends."

Her glance, quick and warm, flashed to him. "You're sincere when you say that?"

"Yes. I am."

She held out her hand in a swift, free gesture. "Then I'll go. I wanted you to say it. Good-bye!"

He took her fingers in his hard, strong grasp.

"Good-bye! And thanks!"

This was their parting. No promise of a future meeting, no suggestion of all that was yet to come. A favour given, a favour received; a clasp of the hands, and an inarticulate sense of mutual understanding.

CHAPTER X.

HAD Isabel been the most industrious weaver of
plots, instead of the most heedlessly spontaneous of
beings, she could not have fitted impulse to action
with better social results than when she decided to
renounce Frank Carey; for on the fourth day after
her visit to Stephen she received an almost affectionate note from Daisy, asking her to excuse a
short invitation and dine at Lady Lane at six
o'clock. The consciousness of a calamity averted
breathed in every line of the commonplace little
letter, although outwardly it expressed nothing
beyond an effusive regret that they had only met
once since Isabel's return to Waterford.

Isabel was going through the last stages of a
trying scene with Miss Costello on the subject of
her great decision when the letter was brought in;
and, having read it, she tossed it across the table
with a little smile of malicious satisfaction.

"You wanted me to get on with the Careys, so
you ought to be satisfied now! I couldn't have
done the two things!"

Miss Costello sighed heavily. "Easy for them to
be nice to you now!" she said, as she put the note
down. "Indeed, when I was a girl, it wasn't to be

taking things into my own hands like that I would!"

Isabel gave a still louder sigh. "You've said that ten times, Aunt Teresa! I don't suppose you were ever like me, or that I will ever be like you."

"Indeed you won't! No one but your father's daughter would have thrown away such a chance as that!"

"Well, would you rather I didn't go to the Careys'?"

"I didn't say so. I suppose half a loaf is better than no bread—though indeed 'twas very different society your grandmother was in in the County Wexford!"

Isabel rose from the horse-hair arm-chair in which she was sitting huddled up. "Is it evening dress, I wonder!"

"Evening dress! What for?"

"Nothing! I was only wondering! At school, the girls used to dress for dinner when they were home on the holidays."

"Well, you won't find many in Waterford dressing for their dinner. I suppose old Barney Carey would turn in his grave with pride if he saw people sitting at his son's table in evening dress!"

"Well, what'll I wear then?"

"Your white blouse, I suppose."

"Oh, auntie, it's awfully dirty!"

"Wear your pink, then."

"But he saw me in that on Sunday!" She said the words unthinkingly; then paused, blushing.

But Miss Costello was not observant. "Is it Stephen Carey?"

"Yes."

"And do you think he'd see what you had on? He's not a bachelor, that he'd be noticing girls' clothes! Wear your pink!"

Isabel accepted the decision, not because she had nothing further to urge upon the subject, but because the scanty condition of her wardrobe was eloquently present to her mind. So in her pink muslin dress, with a sailor hat covering her hair and a dark ulster hiding her finery, she started that evening from New Town as the city clocks were striking half-past five.

There is no necessity for a chaperon at any hour in an Irish town, and it would be looked upon as extravagance for a young girl of Isabel's position to drive to a dinner-party. On foot, therefore, and alone she started for Lady Lane, and with the cool evening air blowing up from the river, and the thought of the enterprise acting as a stimulus, it was an undertaking full of interest. Much of portent centred round this invitation, for in the Careys' set young girls are not usually asked out to dine; they have their allotted place at dances and at evening parties, but dinners are generally dull affairs reserved for the married of the community, and this invitation of Daisy's was a mark of special and premeditated grace — at once a balm for previous coldness and a promise of future favour.

As Isabel approached the house, her steps became slower; and as she crossed the road she looked up at the windows, wondering which was Carey's—the place where he smoked, where he read, where he thought those strange, circumscribed thoughts that he had expressed in her aunt's parlour. Slowly, and with her mind full of question, she mounted the steps and rang the bell.

The door was opened to her by Julia, whose face was red from excitement and services rendered to the cook, and whose cap and apron were aggressively starched in honour of the evening's festivity.

"You'll take off your hat and jacket, won't you, Miss Costello?" she said, proud to display her recognition of the guest.

"Thanks! Yes."

"All right so! You can leave them in the spare room. I'll show you the way up."

She piloted Isabel up the wide staircase, where the walls were devoid of pictures but betrayed the ostentatious prosperity that new paint and paper argues in Ireland. On the first landing they passed the door of the drawing-room, which was half open, and through which the loud sound of laughter and voices came rather dauntingly to the visitor. On the second floor Julia opened the door of a bedroom —the same bedroom in which Daisy and Mary had dressed on the night of the dance—and Isabel looked round curiously as she stepped across the threshold and began to unfasten her coat.

It was a large room, bare of wall and high of ceiling, as are so many Irish rooms, possessing the lofty, square-paned windows of another generation, that rattle to every passing wind and permit the daylight to search out every cranny and recess with merciless rigour. Here, too, as in the hall down-

stairs, there was a veil of ugly modernity thrown
over the character of the place: two or three
pieces of fine old furniture stood against the walls,
but in glaring contrast to their dark solidity, a new
brass bedstead flaunted its existence, while curtains
of limp art muslin hung from the massive cornices
of the windows. Isabel condemned the taste that
had conceived these decorations, as she handed her
coat to the servant and went across to the dressing-
table to take off her hat. "If I had her money!"
she thought; and she heaved a sigh.

"Would you like a comb, Miss Costello? Though
indeed 'twould be a sin to touch your hair."

"No, thanks! I don't want a comb." Isabel
looked into the glass, twisting up a stray lock or
two, while Julia watched her with burning interest.

"I suppose you're glad to be back again, miss?
You were a long time away at school," she suggested, unable to suppress her curiosity.

"Oh, yes; I'm glad."

"I suppose you don't remember me, Miss Costello,
though I remember you?"

Isabel looked round. "How do you remember
me?"

Julia was satisfied, having at last drawn forth
some expression of interest. "Oh, indeed 'tis well I
remember you when you were a little thing. You
were like a gipsy, I remember—so dark. Me and
the other girls at Mr Nagle's used to be admiring
you that time."

" Did you live at the Nagles'?"

"Indeed I did, miss. I lived there seven years
before I went to Mr Norris's."

Isabel looked reflective. "I remember the Nagles' big gate just opposite our house," she said. "Fancy your being there!" Then a new look crossed her face. "Did you ever see my mother?" she asked in a lower tone.

Julia's face became sympathetic at once. "No, miss; God be merciful to her! I never saw Mrs Costello, though many a time I remember Mary Ahern, the cook, telling me the handsome-looking lady she was, and the terrible way poor Mr Costello was broke up after her. I believe 'tis walking the roads all night he used to be, till they were afraid his mind wouldn't hold out. But, God bless us, there's the hall-door bell again! I must go. Are you ready, miss?"

Silenced by the thought of the shadow that had darkened her house, Isabel followed the maid out of the room and down the stairs; but at the door of the drawing-room the moment with its immediate demands ousted the past, and her mind swung back to the thought of the ordeal to come.

With the flurried consciousness of the unanswered bell, Julia threw open the drawing-room door, made an unintelligible murmur that might have been taken for the guest's name, and hurriedly withdrew, leaving Isabel alone upon the threshold.

For a moment she stood uncomfortably aware of a very large room, filled with a multitude of chairs, cabinets, mirrors, and small tables, and of a group of three men and three women gathered round the fireplace at its farthest end: then, to her intense relief, Daisy Carey separated herself from the little circle and came forward with effusive haste.

"Oh, Isabel! How are you! How nice of you to come. Stephen isn't here yet—he telephoned from the office that he'll be a little late. You know Mrs Power and Mary! Let me introduce Father Cunningham and Father Baron and my brother, Tom!" With a friendliness in striking contrast to her previous manner, she took Isabel's arm and drew her into the party.

Isabel herself, rather confused by this change of attitude, bowed vaguely to the two priests and to a fair-haired boy of twenty, and suffered Mary, who was evidently following Daisy's lead, to touch her cheek with the semblance of a kiss.

"How are you, Isabel! Were you in time for your appointment on Sunday?"

Isabel coloured, and was glad to sink into the chair that Tom Norris pushed forward for her.

To her great relief, nobody took any further notice of her, and presently the little group dropped back into its former order, and the conversation she had interrupted was taken up again.

"What we want in this movement is organisation!" said Norris.

"What you want in every movement is money, if you ask me!" said Mary.

"Oh, you mustn't bring in a mercenary spirit, Miss Norris," objected Father Cunningham, the younger of the two priests, who had a pale, eager face and wore the gold cross of the total abstinence pledge on his black watch-chain.

"Oh, you needn't remonstrate with her," Norris broke in. "It's sickening to think of what women could do—and don't, just because the thing isn't fashionable!"

"I think it's sickening to be called a 'woman' by your own brother!"

Norris laughed involuntarily. "But seriously, Polly," he said, "look what you and Daisy could do, if you cared a straw! You could start classes in private houses, like they do in London."

"Public houses suit the scholars here ever so much better. Don't they, Father Cunningham?"

"Oh, well, of course, if that's your attitude——" Norris shrugged his shoulders.

"But, Tom," Daisy put in plaintively, "how on earth could I do anything—with Stephen and the children?"

"Well, Mary hasn't any children!"

"I like that! As if I hadn't a father—worse than thirty children! I'd like to see how many lectures you'd give, and how many classes you'd attend, if you had to mend father's socks! Here's Stephen, Daisy! I heard the hall door shut."

This announcement put a stop to further argument, and a few minutes afterwards Carey himself entered. He looked very tall and strong in the fading daylight that filled the room, and as he joined the little circle it seemed that he brought with him a breath of the outer air, the vitality and energy of the outer world.

He took Isabel's hand first of all, and although his greeting was ordinary, the friendly pressure of his fingers banished her diffidence, and she unconsciously lifted her head, looking out upon the scene with renewed self-confidence.

There was a moment or two of fragmentary talk, then Daisy rose; and, without preserving any particular order, the party straggled out of the room and downstairs. In the dining-room the big gasalier above the dinner-table was blazing with light, and on the table itself a display of the old cut glass for which Waterford is famous cast back the light from its facets, while the silver, of which Daisy was justly proud, was burnished to look its best. The higher refinements of civilisation may not be found in such households as the Norris's and the Careys', but an amazing number of valuable articles are handed down from generation to generation in these middle-class families, and the pantry of many an Irish housekeeper would fill the collector with envy.

When the party had sorted itself out and the seats round the large table were all occupied, it proved that Isabel's place was between young Norris and Father Baron. Very little was said while the soup and fish were eaten, for a meal in Ireland usually means a meal; but when the cover was removed from a joint of beef, and Carey entered on the task of carving, ideas began to stir again and the hum of opinions to make itself heard.

"Well, Father James, you were very silent up in the drawing-room!" Norris remarked, leaning across Isabel. "How is the movement going on down at Scarragh?"

Father James Baron was a man of sixty-eight, with a high colour, grizzled hair, and a wide mouth tempered with the love of his kind. He was priest of the smallest and most insignificant parish in his diocese, and a man of little worldly polish; but something deeper than the learning of books looked out of his small eyes, and when he spoke his listeners attended, however homely the words might be. There was true metal in the man, and it could be felt without explanation that it had been tempered in the furnace. He turned slowly now, and looked at Tom with the humorous indulgence of a father to his child.

"Well! well! well!" he said slowly. "And is it a little place like Scarragh you're going to turn your hand to now?"

"We must have every place interested, Father James," Norris retorted quickly. "No place is too small. What we want is undivided interest."

Isabel could restrain her curiosity no longer. "What is it you're talking about?" she said. "I'd simply love to know!"

Norris's face lighted up, full of enthusiasm at once. "Why, the great new movement," he said. "The Gaelic movement. Haven't you heard of all it's doing?"

"The Gaelic movement?"

"Yes," put in Mary across the table, "all the children in the National Schools can say their prayers in Irish now, and in a lot of the towns they've written up the name of the streets in Irish. It gives them quite a nice foreign look for tourists!"

"Indeed, Mary, you're too hard on them," said Mrs Power amiably. "You ought to be very glad that your brother has such nice quiet tastes, instead of betting and playing cards like so many of the young men." She heaved a placid sigh, recalling her own son's peccadillos, which she was far too lazily indulgent to check.

Carey looked up from cutting the last piece of beef. "Take a hint from that, Mary," he said. "Marry a man with nice quiet Gaelic tastes!"

Mary coloured with annoyance, and was about to make a sharp retort, when her brother seized the silence to urge his own opinions. "Don't listen to them, Miss Costello!" he said earnestly. "It's people like them that have kept Ireland where she is. We'd have been a nation long ago—a nation in the commercial and intellectual sense—only for the poisonous spirit of depreciation that's spread over every honest effort to raise the country. Look at Stephen! He's an intelligent man, and yet he wouldn't raise a finger——"

"Steady, Tom! I had both my hands to the plough once—only we called it the Land League then, not the Gaelic movement. You'll always have young men, you know; but Ireland won't be changed by that."

"I don't think you're right, Mr Carey," broke in Father Cunningham with the quick heat of the zealot. "The Land League, of course, was purely political. This is altogether different. It's when you begin to educate a country that you begin to progress."

"No doubt!" said Carey. "But are you prepared to educate Ireland? You might teach the new generation to talk in German, as far as that goes, but unless you allowed its mind to run in German grooves, you'd be leaving it exactly where it was. Are you going to teach the new generation to express itself in different sounds, or are you going to give it new ideas to express? That's the question, as I see it."

"The proper vehicle of expression must be the native tongue," said Norris hotly. "Once teach the people to speak and write in the natural language of the country, and you'll soon have the national spirit waking up. Why has Ireland—one of the most poetic countries in the world—no modern national literature? Simply and solely because she was thrown back again into infancy by being made to think and speak and write in a new language, when she was practically a fully developed nation!"

"Wait a minute, Tom!" Carey paused in the cutting of his own dinner. "You people hold that when England robbed us of our language, she threw us back into a sort of national childhood—out of which we are now slowly struggling?"

"Certainly! Certainly, we do! I'd like to know if any one can refute it!"

"Very well! And what are you trying to do yourselves? You're trying with might and main to do what England did in the penal days! You're sending Ireland back to school!" He took up his tumbler and drank some water with the hasty manner of a man whose temper is stirred. "Now that she has been trounced into learning her English, for goodness' sake, let her do what she can with that, instead of setting her down to a dead language! If you want advancement, let it be educational by all means; but let the education be modern! Souse the country with modern thought

—Spencer and Huxley, Haeckel and Kant—and be
hanged to sentimentality!"

There was silence after his outburst. Daisy looked
frightened; Father Cunningham excited; and the
older priest anxious.

"Those are dangerous writers, Mr Carey," said
Father Cunningham. "I'd be very sorry to see
Catholic Ireland reading such men as Haeckel."

"That sounds like weakness! If you are
sure of your flock, you shouldn't be afraid of new
pastures."

"A dangerous doctrine!"

A retort rose to Carey's lips, but on the instant of
its utterance his eye caught Father Baron's, and,
with a curious change of attitude, he shrugged his
shoulders and dropped the aggressive tone.

"Well, Father James, and what's your opinion?"
he substituted.

Father Baron looked infinitely relieved. "Well,
Stephen," he said slowly, "I think, after all, 'tis
good for young men to be at something, so long as
it isn't mischief; but I'm inclined to agree with you
that whether it's Young Ireland or the Land
League or the Gaelic movement, 'twill all be the
same in a hundred years!"

Carey laughed, half despondently, half sarcastically. "That's it!" he said. "That's it! 'The
brave days when we were twenty-one'!" His voice
dropped; and Isabel, who alone among the party
was listening to his words and not to his opinions,
shot an involuntary glance at him from under her
lashes, and by a swift flash of intuition it seemed
to her that in imagination she could hear the

whirr of the great machine of which he had discoursed in the room at New Town.

Except for a feeble murmuring of gossip between Daisy and Mrs Power, conversation flagged after this, while the meat was removed and a pudding placed upon the table, for no Irishman can be impersonal when his feelings are seething; and under the outward appearance of conviviality, one could feel Father Cunningham and Norris thirsting to break bounds.

At last the pudding gave way to dessert; the cloth was removed, fruit and port were placed upon the table, and Julia withdrew for the last time.

As the door closed upon her, Tom took a handful of walnuts from a dish, and began to crack them ostentatiously. "I'd like to know, Stephen," he said in an aggressive voice, "what exactly you mean when you talk about sentimentality?"

Daisy made a hasty little movement, and looked appealingly at Mrs Power.

"They're going to begin again!" she said in a whisper. "I think we'll go upstairs, unless anybody wants fruit."

Mrs Power and Isabel disclaimed all wish to eat, and the three stood up simultaneously, while Mary, who was nothing if not leisurely, rose last of all, picked up a handful of raisins, and strolled slowly after them to the door.

CHAPTER XI.

"What fools men are!" said Mary, as she calmly mounted the stairs in Daisy's wake, putting one raisin after another into her mouth. "Look at Tom! He's really awfully clever, and father spent a fortune on educating him; and what does he go and do now—just when he might be of some use to Daisy and me—but take up this Gaelic thing! Teaching the people, indeed! As if they didn't know far too much as it is! I'm sure it's harder to get servants every year."

"Indeed, that's true," Daisy agreed, as they passed into the drawing-room. "Only yesterday nurse actually refused to take baby out, because she had been kept awake the night before. And I pay her eighteen pounds a-year!"

"My dear, much too much! I never gave a nurse more than fourteen—and never would."

"But what's the good of that, Mrs Power, when they won't come for less?"

"You should be firm," advised Mrs Power, whose management of her own establishment was lax in the extreme.

Daisy sank into a low chair, and began to twist the rings on her pretty, useless-looking fingers. "I do try," she murmured, "but really, you know, they're awful—and children are such a responsibility."

Mrs Power laughed, as she sank into a seat. "Three children a responsibility! Look at me, with nine! But we mustn't be talking about responsibilities, or we'll be making the girls afraid to get married at all!"

Mary, who was eating her last raisin, glanced round at this. "Indeed, you won't find me marrying, Mrs Power."

Mrs Power smiled with superior wisdom. "We all said that once, Mary. But you'll be caught one of these days, all the same."

"Well, then, I have still to meet the man!"

Daisy and Mrs Power exchanged a swift glance, to which Mary considerately pretended to be blind.

"Isn't that a bad compliment, now, to the Waterford men, Miss Costello?" said Mrs Power, turning to Isabel and drawing her into the conversation. "I hope you aren't going to be so fastidious."

The suggestion was a little awkward, considering the secret shared by three of the party as to Isabel's broken engagement, but Isabel received it frankly and without embarrassment. "I don't know that I'll ever marry anybody, Mrs Power."

Mrs Power looked up at her, as she stood behind Daisy's chair; and something a little lonely, a little aloof in the solitary figure and the uncommon face, touched her motherly nature.

"Ah, my dear, I won't have you saying that!" She put out her hand and took possession of Isabel's. "I'll find a husband for you—whether you like it or not!"

Isabel flushed, her expression softening, her eyes lighting at the kindly thought for her welfare. "Oh, thank you!" she said. "I mean, thank you for caring whether I get married or not!"

Mary gave a faint little laugh.

Isabel's flush deepened, but from a new emotion. "Why did you laugh?" she said, turning quickly round.

Mary looked at her coolly. "Oh, no reason! It just amused me."

"Why?"

"No reason!"

Mrs Power felt the hand she was holding tremble, and she pressed it soothingly. "Don't mind Mary!" she said. "She doesn't mean half she says. And, indeed, if you don't marry, it won't be the men's fault. I'll venture to say that."

"I'd only marry for one reason," Isabel said suddenly, "and if I hadn't that reason, all the people in the world couldn't persuade me."

"And what's that?" Daisy asked curiously.

"The reason of caring for the person."

Daisy laughed. "Love in a cottage?" she suggested a little patronisingly.

Isabel's dark eyes flashed. "If I cared, I'd marry a beggar; and if I didn't care, it wouldn't matter to me if the person was a king."

The three listeners fell silent for a moment. To Mrs Power, with her long life and superior experience, Isabel's declaration seemed merely the folly of a young girl just out of school; while to Daisy it appeared the cunning of one who had lately been worsted in a vital social encounter; to Mary alone out of the party, it suggested something more—offering sudden glimpses into the depths and shallows of the nature behind the words.

Isabel looked round from one face to the other. "I suppose I oughtn't to have said that!"

Mrs Power laughed and patted her hand. "My dear child, say anything you like! But you have plenty of time to be thinking of love! And that reminds me, I told Josephine to write you a little note, asking you up to tennis. You have seven boys of mine still to meet, you know."

Isabel thanked her by a look; and Daisy, influenced at once by the fact of the invitation, drew her chair nearer.

"Indeed, we all want to see more of Isabel," she said. "She mustn't be a stranger any more. Mary, will you ring for tea? I don't know what they can be doing downstairs."

And so the talk became less personal; and with the arrival of tea, the two married women drifted towards the table on which Julia placed the tray. As Daisy filled up the cups, their voices imperceptibly dropped to the gossiping key, and Isabel and Mary found themselves shut out into an undesired companionship.

Taking their cups from Daisy, they wandered away, as in duty bound, towards the other end of the room. Mary was the first to break the silence. "I'm sorry if I was nasty while ago," she said, laying her cup on the top of the piano. In the few moments that had passed since Mrs Power's invitation, she had decided that a little trimming of sails would be necessary if her boat and Isabel's were to float upon the same waters. "Everybody is a bit cross now and then, don't you think?"

Isabel, fully conscious of her own erratic moods, saw an impulse of remorse in the words, and met it generously. "'Twas nothing!" she said. "I was nasty, too. Let us forget about it!"

"Yes; I want to. Do you play?"

"No."

"Do you mind if I play?"

"Oh, no! I love music."

Mary seated herself at the piano and began to play—passing carelessly from classical music to the newest comic song. She played well, almost brilliantly, with a hard, sharp touch; and as she played, she looked up at Isabel, who was leaning over the piano and watching her with interested eyes. "Is there anything you'd like? I can play most things by ear."

Isabel hesitated; then she said, "Play that waltz, 'Amoreuse.'"

Immediately Mary complied, and after a few bars looked up again. "They played that at Fair Hill. 'Twas the waltz you danced with Stephen."

"Yes, I know."

There was another pause, and again Mary's quick green eyes were lifted. "How do you get on with Stephen?"

Isabel drew back a little. "Get on with him? Oh, I don't know! All right, I think."

"And what do you think of him?"

"Think of him? How?"

"As a person."

"Oh, I—I don't know."

Mary looked down at the keys, and the waltz became slower. "He's a queer fish—Stephen! He hates the very sight of me."

"Why?"

She shrugged her shoulders. "Perhaps I see through him more than other people do—and he hates being seen through."

Isabel's lips parted in quick question, but they closed again at the sound of an opening door. "Oh, here they are!" she said.

Mary glanced over her shoulder at the four men entering the room. "Yes, here they are — when they want their tea!" And the waltz came to a conclusion with a few crashing chords.

The last words of the discussion were evidently hot upon the men's lips, and Norris and Father Cunningham made at once for the tea-table, where Tom, with a careless nod to Daisy, poured out two cups of tea.

"Well, I think we did for them!" he said in a low voice. "We didn't leave Stephen a leg to stand on."

The young priest stirred his tea thoughtfully. "I don't like your brother-in-law's views," he said. "They're dangerous views for an influential man."

Tom laughed. "Oh, Stephen doesn't mean all he says!"

"Perhaps not! I hope not!"

"Of course not! You're a regular pessimist sometimes."

Father Cunningham still stirred his tea absentmindedly.

"He's a very able man!" he said in the same musing undertone.

"Able? You may say that! There are few men the equal of Stephen, when he cares to show it. Hallo! They're not going, are they? Is it as late as that?"

"Indeed, it is, Tom!" Mrs Power caught the last words, as she rose to say good-bye. "It's time for all good people to be thinking of their homes."

"What nonsense, Mrs Power! The night is young!"

"'Tis, Tom—for young people. But 'tis time for me to be thinking of my family."

"Indeed you needn't trouble about your family! You'll find them all playing bridge."

She laughed good-naturedly. "All the more reason to go home and pack them off to bed. Good-night, Daisy! It's been a delightful evening."

Daisy protested prettily: "Oh, no, Mrs Power! You're not going! Please don't go!"

"I must, dear. I must, really. I promised to be back early. But don't let me break up the party!"

But the going of one guest set the minds of the others tending towards departure, and one by one excuses were made. Father Cunningham had a six o'clock mass to say next morning; Father Baron had to catch the last train to Scarragh; and finally Isabel pleaded that Miss Costello would be expecting her soon after ten.

In a very few minutes all the good-byes had been said, and the four women had left to seek the spare room and the guests' wraps.

"Your dinners are always such a success, Daisy!" Mrs Power murmured, as she tied her bonnet-strings.

"I don't know how it is, but somehow you have the knack of entertaining."

Daisy, who had no more knowledge of entertaining than a child of three, smiled delightedly at the harmless flattery. "Indeed, I don't know!" she demurred. "I don't think I do much!"

"Ah, you say that! But I must be off! How is Miss Costello going home? It would be nothing for me to drive round with her, if she hasn't told anybody to call."

"Oh, no!" Isabel protested. "It's altogether out of your way; 'twas too kind of you to do it the night of the dance."

"Not at all! The horse hasn't been out before to-day, and a little exercise would do him good."

"Oh, no, Mrs Power," Daisy expostulated. "Tom will take Isabel home."

Mrs Power smiled knowingly. "Ah, well then, I wouldn't take her for the world! Good-night, Daisy, dear! Mary, I think Josephine is expecting you up to-morrow! Good-night, my dear—I'll have to call you Isabel—Miss Costello is altogether too stiff!" She kissed all three in turn, and then bustled out of the room and down to the hall, where she had another effusive farewell with Carey, Norris, and the two priests.

When the door closed on her, Carey turned to Daisy. "Who's going to take Miss Costello home?"

"Tom is," Mary interposed before her sister could reply.

"Oh! All right!" Carey turned aside and joined Father Baron; while Mary's eyes, maliciously humorous, flashed over Isabel's face.

"It's too bad!" Isabel said quickly. "I could easily go by myself."

"Oh, Tom won't mind, I assure you!"

"What's that, Polly?"

"I'm saying that you don't particularly object to seeing girls home."

Tom laughed. "Not if Miss Costello is one of them! Are you ready now, Miss Costello? I won't keep you a minute." He disappeared into the recesses of the hall, and returned with his cap on and his arm through the sleeve of his coat.

"Now we're ready!" he announced cheerfully. "Give me a lift, Father John!"

Father Cunningham helped him into his coat, while Carey went forward to open the hall door.

Isabel kissed Daisy and Mary, shook hands with the priests, and then followed Tom, who had already stepped out into the street, humming a patriotic tune. On the threshold Carey put out his hand.

"Good-night, Miss Costello! We hadn't a word at all this evening."

Isabel said nothing.

"Next time, perhaps!"

"Perhaps!" She looked up and they both smiled.

"Good-night!"

"Good-night!" The hall door closed, and she was alone with Norris.

They turned out of Lady Lane in silence, but as they crossed the Mall he broke forth once more in his usual enthusiastic spirit. "Well, Miss Costello, and what do you think of your native town, now that you are back again?"

"Well, it seems rather strange," Isabel answered

thoughtfully,—"or I am strange,—I don't know which it is."

Tom nodded sagely. "Do you know, I felt just the same myself," he confided to her, "when I came home from college. There's no use denying it, you know, it seems a bit narrow at first."

"And you have to squeeze down to fit it?"

"Ah, well, no! Ah, no! I wouldn't say that. You know, we're an interesting people, Miss Costello, wherever we are—only it doesn't show up at first in places like Waterford."

Isabel did not at once subscribe to this, and Tom branched off into a new channel. "Tell me, now," he said, "weren't you at school in Dublin, before you went abroad?"

"Oh, yes, ever since my father died. I only went to France two years ago."

"And did they take any interest at all there in the new movement? Did they open your minds at all to the future of Ireland?"

Isabel laughed. "I don't know that they opened our minds to anything."

"There you are!" Tom threw out his arms in vivid despair. "There you are! How on earth are we going to form the nation when women are turned out in batches year by year with French and German at their fingers' ends, and no more knowledge of their own language than infants in arms!"

Isabel laughed again. "I don't know about fingers' ends!" she said. "I was able to say my prayers in French when I went to Paris, but that was about all."

"What a shame!" Tom cried, following his own

train of thought. "The most receptive years of
your life lost! But it's not too late, you know; it's
not too late! I wish, Miss Costello, you'd interest
yourself in the cause. If we could only induce the
educated women to take it up seriously, we could
move mountains."

"And do you think it will do any real good?"
Isabel ventured.

"Good?" He turned on her, aflame with enthusiasm in a moment—the enthusiasm that has
sent Irishmen down to death in the wake of lost
causes for more generations than one cares to count.
"Good? Why, it's going to make a nation of us!
It's going to lift us to the level of the rest of
Europe! It's the one movement that has really
touched the bed-rock of things—that has a sound
and true foundation. I'm not tiring you?" He
looked up, as he felt her steps slacken.

"Oh, no! It's only that we're here. This is my
aunt's."

His face fell. "Oh, I wish I could have told you
more! The walk was miserably short. But let me
ring the bell for you!" He strode up the little
path before her, and rang the bell loudly.

"Does it interest you at all?" he asked, as he
turned to say good-night.

"Oh, I think it's—it's most interesting."

"I'm so glad. I'm so glad. I must talk to you
again. Good-bye! And thanks for a most delightful walk!" He wrung her hand cordially, and
turned away, as they heard the chain being taken
off the door.

As he walked down the path, the door itself was

opened, and Miss Costello's face appeared in the aperture: almost before she had seen her niece, she broke volubly into speech.

"Oh, Isabel!" she cried. "I thought you'd never be back! Such a time as I have had! There's a telegram for you that came at eight o'clock. I half thought of sending Lizzie up with it to the Careys', but then I didn't."

"Thank goodness, you didn't!" said Isabel, as she walked into the hall.

"Well, here 'tis now, any way!" She held out the orange envelope. "Open it! Open it, and see what it is! I have an awful sort of a feeling that it's from Frank."

"From Frank? Nonsense!" But Isabel turned a little pale as she walked towards the gas-jet, tearing the envelope open.

For a moment she stood reading the message with a calm that reduced Miss Costello to despair; then she held out the thin pink paper.

"You're quite right, Aunt Teresa!" she said in a dazed voice. "It is from Frank. He's got my letter, and he's coming back to see me. He'll be here to-morrow."

CHAPTER XII.

THE arrival of this telegram from Frank Carey had something of the force and decimating power of a bomb exploding in peaceful surroundings. Under any circumstances the coming of a telegram causes excitement in such households as Miss Costello's; but when the fateful envelope holds within it such news as this, excitement cools before actual panic.

Isabel's first desire was to sink into the solitary chair that graced the hall; but that being already in possession of her aunt, she was forced to accept the nearest substitute, which proved to be the lowest step of the stairs; and from this coign of vantage she looked out blankly upon the situation.

"To-morrow!" she ejaculated. "To-morrow! That means he'll get in by the boat at some unearthly hour in the morning!"

Miss Costello, who was still scrutinising the telegram, answered from her own thoughts. "He handed this in just before the boat left," she said. "He's actually on his way now."

Isabel made a gesture of despair. "What'll his brother think!" she cried. "He'll think I didn't properly break it off. Oh, what on earth possessed him to do such a thing! What on earth possessed him!"

"Your letter, of course! I must say I feel for the poor fellow!"

"And why should my letter make him do such a thing? I think it's mean—I think it's downright mean—to come in on us like this! Never to give us a chance of writing—never to give us a chance of stopping him!" Her voice rose with her distress, and, urged to action, she stood up suddenly.

"I won't see him when he does come!" she announced. "I don't see why I should! You can see him for me, and tell him I meant every word I wrote, and that nothing in the world would make me take it back. Why should I have to see him? Why should he torment me like this, just because I don't want to marry him?"

Miss Costello, finding no pertinent answer, resorted to strategy. "If you really want to get rid of him," she said, "'twould be ever so much quicker to talk to him yourself. It's so hard for another person to get a man to see reason."

Isabel considered the statement. "Well, perhaps so!" she admitted reluctantly. "Perhaps so! I suppose so!" She crossed the hall, took up her bedroom candle, and, to her aunt's unfeigned surprise, walked upstairs without further remark.

That night she slept but little, tossing from side to side of her uncomfortable bed, and the early hours of the following morning found her waiting in the parlour, listening with high-strung nerves to every sound that might presage the unwelcome guest.

To those who would call Isabel cruel in the meeting of this crisis, one might point to the law of all created things. There is no cruelty in the cat that

crouches, all grace, all deft agility, to pounce upon a
bird; nor is there cruelty in the bird, hopping bright
and vigilant to destroy a lower life for its own
sustenance. Each is alive, and each to the utmost
limit of its power exercises its gift. Such was
Isabel—to be judged as such. As she sat on the
old horsehair sofa, her fingers nervously drumming
out a tune upon its slippery surface, there was no
regret in her mind—there was scarcely even pride
at the thought that her sentence could bring a man
hurrying across two countries to plead his cause
with her: her racing thoughts sped to one question
—how would this new contingency affect her own
life?

In the midst of her cogitations a car stopped
on the road outside, the garden gate clicked and
swung upon its hinges, and her fingers slipped inert
from the back of the sofa in sudden acknowledgment that the crisis was at hand.

She was standing when the parlour door opened,
her arms hanging by her sides, her head lifted in
nervous expectancy, and almost before her mind had
grappled with the situation, she caught a vision of
Lizzie's face, scared and inquisitive, and behind it
Frank's—colourless, jaded, unfamiliar from want of
sleep and lack of a razor. It is the details of a scene
that call to the imagination in critical moments;
and it was the detail of the unshaven chin that
sprang to Isabel's mind with the rapidity and force
of a lightning shaft. It might be subtly flattering
in its testimony of unsparing haste, but as a fact
it was revolting, chaining her feet to the ground,
making it impossible even to hold out her hand.

The door closed upon the servant; Frank hesitated for a moment, then took an uneven step forward.

"Isabel! Have you nothing to say to me? I've come all the way from Paris!" The words were pathetic, and there was pathos in the weak, emotional face—in the hollow eyes, in the protruding lower lip that seemed on the verge of quivering; but these things went down, marks as black as the unshaven chin, against the hapless lover.

"Isabel! What does it all mean? Haven't you a word to say?"

Then, and only then, did Isabel conquer her repugnance. "Oh, why did you come back?" she cried indistinctly. "Why did you come back at all?"

"Why? You know why!" He made an ungainly forward movement, and caught one of her hands. "Isabel, what is it? Don't try to get away!"

"Let me go, Frank! Let my hand go!"

"No, I won't let it go. I have a right to hold it. We're engaged still."

"We are not engaged." She wrenched her hand away.

"Isabel! What's the meaning of it all? It's Stephen who's done this!"

She flushed to her temples. "It is not! He has nothing to do with it!"

"Then who has?"

"No one."

"That's ridiculous! Something must have happened to change you like this. In Paris you

cared for me—in Paris you were willing enough to
marry me."

She stood with her eyes averted, an obstinate
line showing round her mouth.

"Isabel, some one has done this!"

Suddenly her glance flashed up to his. "Nobody
has done it," she said sharply. "If you want to
know the truth, it's because I don't care for you
any more—because I'm tired of you—because I'd
rather die than marry you now!"

This onslaught, so sudden and vehement, seemed
to sober him, as a shock might sober a drunken
man.

He turned very white and subsided into a chair
that stood by the centre table. There he sat for a
long time, huddled and inarticulate, until slowly,
imperceptibly, the Celtic flair for an emotional
situation prompted him to action. The prompting
was entirely instinctive, and his response to it
entirely unconscious; but a world of suggestion was
conveyed by the slow straightening of his body, by
the slow movement of his fingers, as they groped
cautiously towards his waistcoat pocket and fumbled
there in a blind, clumsy search.

Isabel, strung to emotion herself, and attuned to
receive the subtlest impression, felt her heart give
a hard, quick throb.

"Frank, what have you there in your pocket?
What are you doing?"

"Nothing."

"But I see you fumbling with something. What
is it? What is it?"

A gleam of satisfaction, overstrained and hysterical, flickered in Frank's eyes; he threw a glance of triumph at her frightened face. "All right so!" he said suddenly. "I'll tell you what it is. It's something that'll end the business for me, if you want to know. A fellow isn't a doctor for nothing." He pulled out a little phial containing half a dozen tabloids, and held it up before her.

It is impossible to tell in what spirit of bravado or youthful conceit he had provided himself with this weapon, but he launched it now with full effect.

"Oh, no, a fellow isn't a doctor for nothing!" he repeated. "I have only to swallow one of these, and I can tell you, women and the rest won't matter much to me!"

Isabel stared, then she made a little rush forward.

"Frank! Frank, don't be a fool!"

She had wrested the phial from him before he thought of resistance, and stood, half laughing, half panting.

"Frank, Frank, 'tisn't worth that!"

Then she paused again, newly dismayed, for Frank in a moment of acute reaction had thrown his arms out across the table, and burying his face in his sleeve, had broken suddenly into boyish hysterical sobs.

For a couple of minutes she stood petrified; then a sense of shame for him urged her to words.

"Frank, don't! Don't! I'm sorry!"

"But do you care for me, that's the thing? Do you care?"

She was silent.

"Do you care?" He lifted a face grotesquely marred by emotion, weariness, and tears. "Oh,

you don't! I can see you don't! I'm sick of life!"
His head dropped back again.

"No, Frank, you're not!" She girded up her
courage and slipped the little bottle surreptitiously
into her pocket. "It's only that you are worn out,
that you don't know what you're saying."

He buried his head still lower.

"Frank, look here! Wait till—till you have had
something to eat——" She looked distractedly
round for inspiration. "Wait till you have had
your breakfast, and you'll feel a different person."

He looked up indignantly. "Breakfast! Well,
if that isn't like a woman! Breakfast, when a
fellow's life is smashed!"

But Isabel glanced quickly behind her, at the
same moment giving his sleeve a jerk, to rouse
him to self-control. "Frank, here's Aunt Teresa!"
she whispered hurriedly. "Frank, pull yourself
together!"

But Frank had gone beyond the sense of shame,
and he turned towards the opening door without
attempting to wipe either the tears or the grime
of travel from his face.

"Well, Miss Costello, I suppose you are against
me too?"

At sight of him Miss Costello threw up her hands
in sympathetic dismay. "Oh, my poor boy! My
poor boy! Is it as bad as that?"

At the unexpected tone, Frank's self-pity welled
up anew. "I'm glad somebody feels the injustice
of it! Though, so far as I'm concerned, it's all
up with me! I'm done for!"

"Oh, don't say that! Don't say that, Frank!"

He shook his head. "'Tis the truth—and she knows it."

"Indeed, I don't!" Isabel broke in. "I hope you're more of a man than that."

Miss Costello looked from one to the other in tremulous consternation. "Oh, what an unfortunate business it all is!" she wailed. "And it was all so nice and settled, till that brother of yours interfered."

Frank flared up. "I thought so!" he cried, turning upon Isabel. "I thought so! So it is Stephen I have to thank for it."

Isabel stood mute and rebellious.

"I believe you weren't telling the truth while ago," he added quickly. "I believe you care for me all the time, and that Stephen worked on you and made you do it. Isabel, tell me! Miss Costello, ask her to tell me!"

They both turned on the girl, standing defiant and apart.

"Isabel, you cared for me in Paris! Miss Costello, you know she cared for me then!"

"Indeed I do. Indeed I do, Frank. Isabel, why can't you answer the poor fellow!"

Still Isabel stood obstinately mute.

"Isabel, was it Stephen? Did Stephen play on you?"

"No!" She shot the word at him with fierce vehemence.

"Then what was it? For God's sake, what was it? You can't throw a man away like an old glove, without any reason."

"I gave you a reason."

"It wasn't enough. You can't tire of a person in a few weeks—unless, of course,"—he stopped suddenly, and a gleam of suspicion lit his eyes,—"unless you fall in love with somebody else."

Isabel turned on him, swiftly furious, the blood mounting to her face. "How dare you say that!"

"I didn't say it. But I believe now that it's the secret—or why should you get as red as that? I believe you're throwing me over because there's another man."

The two looked at each other aggressively, while Miss Costello turned aside to mutter an ejaculatory prayer.

"Some other man has been making love to you."

"No other man has made love to me."

"Oh, Frank, don't now!" put in Miss Costello agitatedly. "Sure, what other man could she meet? We're like nuns in a convent here."

"Be quiet, Aunt Teresa!" Isabel stamped her foot. "No man has made love to me," she repeated, looking at Frank.

"But you are in love with some man?"

Her eyes flashed recklessly. "If I said 'yes' would you leave me alone?"

"I suppose I would," he said huskily. "Yes, I would."

"Very well, then! Think it, if you like!"

Without waiting for his comment, heedless of her aunt's horrified cry of "Isabel!" she swung out of the room, banging the door behind her.

CHAPTER XIII.

WITH Isabel's violent departure a lull fell upon the scene—the dead lull that envelops the sailing-ship when the wind drops at sea. Such personalities as hers are scarcely conducive to peace, but their withdrawal has a property of making remaining things seem singularly dull.

With the closing of the door, Frank's vehemence dropped from him, and he rose from his seat in a limp, inexpressive way. "I suppose I—I had best go?" he said vaguely.

Miss Costello offered no assistance. She was looking nervously towards the door, while her fingers kept locking and unlocking.

"It's no good my staying here, is it? I—I suppose I'll go down to Lady Lane." He pushed back his chair and took a turn or two up and down the room.

Miss Costello, whose one desire centred round the thought of flight, jumped at the last suggestion. "Oh, do! Do! I'd advise you to. There's nothing like going to the fountain-head."

He gave a dreary laugh. "Well, she's the fountain-head—and you heard what she said."

"Oh, I did! I did, indeed. But I wouldn't be

putting any pass on that at all, Frank. I give you my solemn pledge not another man but you ever said a word to her. Have a good talk with your brother, and 'twill be all right yet, please God!" In her anxiety to be quit of the situation, she was ready to hold out any hope, reasonable or the reverse.

Frank took another turn, and then stopped opposite to her.

"Well, anyway you can tell her that, whoever he is, he'll never care for her more than I did." He took up his hat and overcoat, and, without any attempt at farewell, walked out of the room.

Lady Lane was empty, save for one or two loiterers, when the outside car that had driven Frank from New Town drew up in front of his brother's house, and there were only half a dozen pairs of eyes to observe him get down and walk slowly up the steps to the hall door; but Stephen Carey, breakfasting with Daisy, heard the clatter of hoofs and the stopping of the car, and looked up from his morning paper.

"Wasn't that a car?"

Daisy, whose mind was already flying to possible contingencies, dropped the little bit of toast she was buttering, and ran to the window.

"Oh, Stephen, it's an outside car with a bag and a coat on the seat! And there's the hall-door bell! Who on earth can it be at this hour? And I'm in this awful old dress!"

As she stood panic-stricken at the thought of an unexpected guest, the dining - room door opened without ceremony and Julia put her head into the room.

"Mr Carey, 'tis Mr Frank!" she announced in a voice charged with excitement.

"Frank!" Daisy cried, as Stephen wheeled round in his chair in blank astonishment; but her surprise melted to consternation, as she caught sight of the apparition of weariness and despair.

Carey rose abruptly. "It's all right, Julia!" were his first words. "And shut the door after you." Then he turned on his brother. "What the devil is the meaning of this?"

By strong measures he had played father to the six boys left in his charge, for the authority of an elder brother is a thing that needs upholding; and as he looked down now on the weak, jaded figure of Frank, the old methods presented themselves unconsciously.

For the first moment Frank cowered; then his outraged sense of manhood struggled to the surface. "I want fair treatment, Stephen," he said indistinctly. "That's what I want."

"Oh!" Stephen was very laconic, very hard; and, turning to Daisy, he added in the same brusque tone, "If you've finished your breakfast, Daisy, you may as well go."

With the utmost reluctance Daisy moved towards the door. She would have bartered many things for the privilege of overhearing this conversation, but here again habit was strong, and it did not occur to her to disobey.

As she passed Frank, she held out her hand. "How are you, Frank?" she said in her pretty, precise voice. She made this proffer of friendship partly from the sense of conventionality, but also from an overmastering desire to see his face at closer quarters.

He muttered some unintelligible remark, and dropped her hand almost as soon as he had taken it.

"Close the door after you!" Stephen said remindingly; and without further hesitancy Daisy went.

Left alone, the brothers faced each other, each conscious that antagonism lurked in the other's eyes.

"Well," said Carey at last in a measured way, "so you have taken the liberty of throwing up your studies to come back here and demand fair treatment? Now, would you mind telling me what you call fair treatment?"

Frank visibly weakened at this deliberate attack. In a long absence one is apt to underestimate the strength of such men as Carey, and to face it again with disorder of one's forces.

"I think I'm—I'm entitled to the rights of a man, Stephen."

"Indeed! The rights of a man?"

Frank braced his limp muscles. "I mean, Stephen," he blurted out, "that I'm not a schoolboy —that I'm twenty-three — that I have as good a right to live as you—or—or—any other man."

"Did I ever object to your existence?"

"Oh, you know what I mean — that I have as good a right as anybody else to do what I like with my life, without being bullied and threatened and——"

"Sit down!" said Carey peremptorily. "This isn't a time for heroics. Tell me in the fewest possible words what in God's name brought you back!"

From the instinct of long obedience, rather than from any conscious admission of weakness, Frank subsided into the nearest chair.

"Go on now! What brought you?"

"Your letter."

"Oh!" Again Carey was laconic.

"Yes, your letter. I know that I'm a lot younger than you, Stephen, and I know that I owe you a lot of money——"

"Steady! Steady!"

"Oh, well, I know that you've done a heap for me. But, all the same, I couldn't let any man, even if 'twas my own father, dictate to me whether I am to marry—and who I am to select."

Carey was silent.

"And so, when I got your letter and Isabel's letter, I knew that something was wrong, and I came back to see what it was."

"And have you found out?"

"Yes, I have. I went up to New Town the first thing. I saw her and her aunt."

"Well?"

At the thought of his recent adventure, Frank's bravado flickered and went out. "Oh, what I might have expected, I suppose. She doesn't want any more of me."

A fresh expression passed over Carey's face, banishing the aggressive look. "Ah, well," he said more kindly, "you mustn't be too cut up!" He walked round the table, and with a new generosity put his hand on the other's shoulder.

"I suppose I was a bit rough in my letter, but then I always am like that. Cheer up, boy! We'll be good friends yet, for all this business!"

But Frank bent his head and edged away from the friendly hand. "It's no good, Stephen! It's done for me."

The pressure of Carey's hand became heavier, and he twisted the boy round in his seat.

"What do you mean by that?"

Frank kept his eyes lowered. "I mean what I say. I'm done for! I'm not going to stick on, in the face of this!"

Stephen's brow darkened and the line of his mouth became hard. "Look here, Frank," he said, "don't come to me with any of that rot. It won't work with me. While you're in this house you're going to behave as a rational being. I'll send you upstairs presently to have a hot bath and a shave. And to show how little I give for your threats, I'll lend you one of my razors!"

The cool, sarcastic tone stung Frank out of his lethargy, as Carey had meant it should.

"I think you're a brute!" he blurted out. "And she's as bad."

Carey laughed. "Come, come! Be a man! As for the girl, she's thinking of you more than of herself."

Frank gave a bitter echo of the laugh. "Of me, indeed! That's all you know about it."

"I know she's a sight too good for you! She's got more spirit and sense than ever you will have."

"Spirit! Sense! If that was all, do you think I'd care? Do you think I'd give in like this? It's being thrown away like an old glove—chucked for some other fellow — that takes the heart out of you!"

In the pause that followed, Carey turned away and walked slowly to the mantelpiece. "Another fellow?" he said. "What do you mean by that?"

Frank was too absorbed to notice anything of the tone in which the words were said. "I mean what I say—no more and no less," he said. " If you think it's sense that has made her do this, you know very little about women."

"That's quite probable."

"The less the better for you! Spirit and sense, indeed! Why, with her own lips she told me that she doesn't care a brass farthing for me—that she's throwing me over for somebody else."

Carey leant his elbow on the mantelpiece. "And who is the somebody else?"

"You may be sure I didn't ask. What does it matter whether it's Willie Neville or Owen Power, or who the devil it is, so long as it isn't me?"

Carey turned round abruptly. "Do you think that a girl like that would throw herself away on an ass like Neville or an empty-headed coxcomb like Power?"

"Why not? Power is a lady's man. Ask Daisy or Mary if he isn't!"

"But it's ridiculous on the face of it! She hasn't seen any of them half a dozen times!"

Frank gave another of his dreary laughs. "A lot that has to do with it! I only met her three times, when I was crazed about her."

Carey stood pondering these words of wisdom.

"That's the way with women!" Frank broke out again. "You see if she isn't engaged before a month is out! After all, Power is a better match than me, any day!"

"That'll do, Frank! That'll do! We've had enough of this." Stepping to the side of the fireplace, Carey pulled the bell peremptorily.

The door opened with suspicious alacrity, and Julia appeared.

"Take Mr Frank up to my room," he ordered. "Get him some hot water for shaving, and then fill the bath!"

For a moment Frank looked as though about to rebel, but a glance at Julia's inquisitive face deterred him, and he rose mechanically.

"I won't want any breakfast, Stephen," he said, "so you needn't order any."

"All right!" Carey agreed unfeelingly. "We'll call you for lunch."

As the door closed, he turned back again to the fireplace, and his expression was a curious mingling of irritation and some other emotion, less easily defined. With a wide, characteristic gesture, he threw out his arms and, resting both elbows on the mantel-board, stood staring down into the grate. For a while he remained in this attitude of thought; then, with an abrupt movement, he threw up his head, as though impatience of the world had concentrated into impatience of himself.

"Pshaw! Women!" he said with deep disgust.

CHAPTER XIV.

IT was not for a moment to be supposed that such a piece of news as Frank Carey's sudden return, with all its subsequent developments, could be lost to Waterford ears. By eleven o'clock half the Careys' friends were posted in details of the affair, true or false as the case might be; and at half-past eleven Mary Norris appeared at Lady Lane, alert to follow the trail of gossip.

It was Daisy herself who opened the door to her familiar knock; and, taking her arm in mysterious silence, she drew her into the now empty dining-room.

"Well," she said, breathless with her own news, "have you heard anything?"

Mary pulled off her chamois gloves and tossed them on to the table, where the remains of breakfast bore witness to a demoralised household.

"Anything?" she said. "Well, I should think I have!"

"Wait a minute!" Daisy ran back and closed the door carefully. "Now, what is it? What are people saying?"

"Saying? What aren't they saying?"

"Oh, Mary, what?"

"Well, first of all, the Buckleys joined me after

mass, simply brimming over with curiosity, and asked me if it was true that Frank Carey had met Isabel Costello while she was at school and had followed her over here, and that Miss Costello herself had turned him out of the house at nine o'clock this morning? That was bad enough, goodness knows! but then, just as I was coming down Lady Lane, who should rush out at me but that horrid old Miss Green to say that she had heard Frank was barely recovering from malaria and had been ordered back to his native air, and that she had seen him herself arriving this morning, looking like a person risen from the grave! Oh, I've had a time of it, I can tell you! But what's the truth, Daisy? What on earth is it? Is he honestly here?"

Daisy had sunk into a chair under the weight of her sister's information, and now she looked up with bewildered eyes. "Oh, yes, it's true enough! He's upstairs now, walking up and down his room and groaning out loud. I think he's half off his head."

Mary made a gesture of contempt. "Frank always was a fool! But what on earth has brought him back?"

"Honestly, I hardly know! Stephen was so cross after being shut in here with him for half an hour, that he banged out of the house as if everything in the world was upside down."

"And didn't he explain? Didn't he say any-thing?"

"Oh, I saw him for about two minutes, and he just muttered something about Frank being an ass, who couldn't take 'No' for an answer—and that I was to hold my tongue about the whole business."

"Upon my word!" was Mary's expressive comment. Then she turned her head sharply. "Hallo, Daisy! Wasn't that the hall-door bell?"

Daisy looked aghast. "Oh, no, surely! Would I have time to run upstairs?"

"You wouldn't; I hear Julia opening."

"Heavens! And if it's anybody, she'll have them in here in two seconds! And look at the state I'm in! And look at the table!" Her voice quivered with consternation.

Mary held up a warning finger. "Listen! I believe it's Mrs Power! Yes, it is!"

"Oh, how absolutely sickening! What an idiot Julia is!" Then Daisy turned, all smiles, as the dining-room door opened.

"Oh, Mrs Power! How are you!"

Mrs Power came forward with both hands out, and kissed her effusively. "My dear!" she cried, "I can't tell you how relieved I am to see you looking so well; I hear you've gone through a terrible lot! How are you, Mary! I saw you at mass; but you're like quicksilver, I can never overtake you. And now, Daisy, what on earth is it all about?"

Daisy drew forward a chair, at the same time trying distractedly to decide how much she should reveal and how much she should withhold. "Won't you sit down, Mrs Power!"

"Thank you, dear! And now tell me everything from the very beginning."

Here Mary stepped into the breach. "But, Mrs Power," she said, "the worst of it is that we know

so little ourselves. Won't you first tell us what
you have heard?"

" Heard? My goodness, Mary! What haven't
I heard? But just tell me, Daisy, is it really true
that he met her in Paris and fell in love with her
there?"

"He did meet her in Paris with her aunt," Daisy
admitted guardedly.

" And are they engaged? Do tell me that! Are
they engaged?"

"No, Mrs Power. They are not."

Mrs Power leant back in her chair. "Exactly
what I said myself! It's just the gossip of a place
like this. But there you are! You can't stop
people saying nasty things."

"What about?" Daisy was up in arms. "What
about, Mrs Power?"

"Oh, well, 'tisn't worth noticing things like that.
I never listen to them myself."

"Still, I'd rather know them. What are people
saying?"

"Oh well, indeed, Daisy, they're saying things
about you and Stephen. But, as I say——"

"About us?"

"About Daisy?" Mary cried. "What on earth
for?"

Mrs Power arranged the strings of her bonnet.
"Well, I'll give it to you, word for word. What I
heard was that Frank and Isabel Costello were
engaged, and that when Isabel came back to Waterford, Daisy put her foot down and wouldn't hear of
the match because she has no money; and that
Stephen was seen going into Miss Costello's on

Sunday after last mass. Mind you, I'm only re-peating what I heard!"

"Oh!" Daisy stamped her foot with vexation. "Oh, how annoying! How sickening!"

"Of course it is, my dear! But there you are!"

"I wonder if Isabel herself spread the story!"

"Oh, fie, Mary! As if she'd do such a thing!"

Mary shrugged her shoulders.

"Oh, how annoying! How annoying!" Daisy said again.

"Ah, now don't! You'll make me sorry I told you at all. Make the best of it! Make up your mind what you're going to do!"

"I don't know what to do. Stephen will be furious."

"Will I give you a bit of advice?"

"Do! Oh, do! You're awfully good at knowing the right thing." Daisy revived at the prospect of help.

"Well, then, my advice is to be as nice as ever you can to Isabel. Ask her here while you are in town; and as soon as you go out to Kilmeaden have her to stay with you there."

"Oh, Mrs Power, not Kilmeaden!" Mary cried. "She needn't have her at Kilmeaden!"

"And why not, dear?"

"Because Daisy always has who she likes there. It's the country and—and——"

"Oh, I don't know, Mary!" Daisy objected sud-denly. "Perhaps Mrs Power is right. After all, if we have her here, people won't notice it so much; but if we ask her to Kilmeaden they'll say she must certainly be friends with us."

"That's it, Daisy! That's what I say. And now, like a good girl, tell me about Frank. He really is here, isn't he?"

"Oh, yes; he's upstairs now! He wanted a rest, you know, after the journey."

"Poor fellow! To be sure he did! I suppose Stephen is delighted to have him back?"

"Oh—oh, yes! Delighted."

"And, Daisy, dear——" Mrs Power drew her chair close to Daisy's and dropped her voice to the confidential key. "Daisy, dear, tell me now if it's at all true that he's really in love with her?"

Daisy hesitated, mindful of Stephen's warning, mindful too of Mary's deterring eyes; then the unspeakable joy of imparting such a story broke down all barriers.

"Mrs Power," she said, "it's the most deadly secret, and there isn't another person living that I'd tell it to; but if you'll give me your solemn promise not to breathe a word of it——" And so the story was told.

Before a week had passed all Waterford knew for a certainty that Isabel Costello and Frank Carey had seriously contemplated marriage; and that, for some unknown reason, Frank had returned unexpectedly to his native town, and was now in hermit-like seclusion in Lady Lane—with his engagement, and presumably his heart, irrevocably broken. Now, whatever the secret streams that may issue from a wound dealt by Cupid, only one expression of opinion is likely to be obtained from the public— a deep and protracted study of the lady in the case. So while Frank, lovelorn and disconsolate, pined in his solitude, Isabel saw new vistas opening in her social world, and the ten days that followed the eventful morning found her playing tennis at the Powers', croquet at the Burkes', and being initiated into the mysteries of cards at the Nevilles' and the Norris's. Everywhere she went she was stared at, whispered about, and made much of,—for a girl who has broken an engagement in an atmosphere where marriage is not easy of attainment must of necessity have a claim to consideration. There is a good deal of the child in the Celtic nature, in the sense that the eyes and the ears are caught by the passing show; and that, also like the child, the sound of a new drum will send the feet racing down a side street at the heels of a fresh crowd. Some of the mothers may perhaps have had secret misgivings, wondering in their own minds whether it was entirely right that a girl should be socially in evidence while her rejected lover was in the same town; but if they had doubts, their sons had none, and their daughters, from sentiment or expediency, saw fit to have none either—and Isabel was the attraction of the hour.

For Isabel herself this success was not without result. As on the night of her first dance, she expanded in the sun of admiration, as the butterfly spreads its wings to the summer heat. On a larger stage she enacted again the scene that Carey's first coming had interrupted on the night at Fair Hill, when the little group of men had clamoured for her programme. In those pleasant days she tasted adulation for the first time, knowing the joy of giving and withholding, seeing the moves in that subtle game where the head directs while the heart beats steady; and all the time there was the consciousness that, sooner or later, the real man would step out from this background of shadows, drawing her with him into the real world; and as she laughed and talked and jested this consciousness was alive,—a flame burning out of sight, ready to leap up and scorch. Some day, some moment, the call would come, and her nature would flow out, an unsluiced current flooding towards the sea. And in the meantime? In the meantime, she was young and she was alive!

CHAPTER XV.

ALTHOUGH Isabel had been going to and fro for
nearly a fortnight in the Careys' intimate circle, she
had heard no definite news of Frank. Either from
that hyper-sensitiveness that the Irish feel about
approaching a delicate subject, or because there was
no real friendship to warrant the intrusion, people
avoided the matter altogether or skirted carefully
round it when she happened to be present; so,
although she knew vaguely that Frank was still at
Lady Lane, she was entirely ignorant of the mental
conflict that was going forward between the
brothers.

Carey she had not seen since the night of the
dinner-party; from Frank himself no word came;
and Mary and Daisy preserved a resolute silence
on the subject.

It was not until the eleventh day that the position was made clear to her. She had been playing
tennis all the afternoon, and only returned to
New Town to hurry through the tea, that in such
households as Miss Costello's takes the place of
dinner, before changing her dress for an evening
party at Fair Hill. She was flushed with exercise
and in high spirits when she entered the house,

and the gay tune of a song that had caught her fancy rose to her lips as she crossed the little hall and laid her tennis racket on the old-fashioned hat-stand.

"Miss Isabel," ventured the slovenly maid who had admitted her, "there's a letter for you. It come by the last post, an' I put it in the drawer in the stand."

"For me, Lizzie? Who from, I wonder!" Isabel hastily pulled the drawer open and took up the envelope bearing her name. The handwriting was unfamiliar, but the post-mark was Waterford, and her first feeling was of relief that at least it was not from Frank. Then suddenly, by the suggestion of ideas, a flash of intuition enlightened her: she blushed, and with an almost nervous haste put the letter unopened into her pocket.

"Is tea ready, Lizzie?"

Lizzie, who cherished romantic ideas, looked disappointed. "Oh, yes, miss! Tea is on," she said.

"Is Aunt Teresa in the parlour?"

"Yes, miss; she's goin' on wid it."

Isabel received the information with a nod, and passed into the little sitting-room.

At sound of her entry Miss Costello looked up from her meal, which consisted of strong tea, bread and butter, and a boiled egg. "Well, Isabel!" she said, "you seem very pleased with yourself. Did you win the game of tennis?"

At another time Isabel would have replied that she had played seventeen games and won eleven; but now she merely walked round the table and imprinted a kiss on Miss Costello's forehead.

"I did grandly, auntie. 'Twas a lovely day."

"Who was there? Will you have an egg for your tea, or would you like a chop cooked?"

"An egg will do." Isabel seated herself and began to cut a round of bread from the loaf on the table.

"Well, and who was there? I never knew such a girl! You don't tell a person a thing."

"Oh, auntie, indeed I do!"

"Well, then, who was there to-day?" Miss Costello rose and, opening the door, called down the passage "Lizzie, boil another egg!"

"Well?" she repeated, as she seated herself again.

"Oh, let me see! The Nevilles and the Cranes and some of the Power boys—and Mary Norris."

"And who did you play with?"

"With Willie Neville some of the time, and some of the time with Owen Power."

"With Owen Power? And how did Mary Norris like that? Everybody said last year that he was going in for her."

"Well, I don't think he spoke two words to her to-day."

Miss Costello's black eyes took a hurried survey of her niece. "Isabel," she said severely, "I hope you're not a flirt."

"Aunt Teresa!" Isabel's temper flared up, and then, for some mysterious reason, died down again, and was replaced by a sunny laugh. "Why, auntie?" she substituted in a coaxing voice.

"Because you ought to be very careful after what has happened."

"Why?"

"Because people might talk."

At this juncture Lizzie entered with the egg, and Isabel was helped to a cup of the strong tea; but immediately they were alone again she reverted to the subject.

"Auntie," she said, "I told you before that I don't mind one scrap whether people talk or not. I suppose it's my nature, but it doesn't seem to me to matter, as long as you can please yourself and be happy, whether people speak about you or don't. I try and try to work myself up into being terrified of their talk, but it's no good. I can't." She paused in her healthy consumption of bread and butter, and stared into her aunt's face with her bright, eager eyes. "Am I very queer, Aunt Teresa?"

Miss Costello stirred her tea nervously, for she disliked these searching questions. "Well, any priest will tell you that you must consider your neighbours!"

"I know. But supposing your neighbours don't seem half as real to you as you seem to yourself? Supposing you can't keep thinking of whether this is wrong, or that is wrong, no matter how hard you try?"

"Your conscience will tell you that."

Isabel was silent for a moment: then the questioning glance flashed back to her aunt's face. "Auntie, what exactly is conscience?"

Miss Costello dropped her spoon in perfectly unaffected horror. "Good gracious, child! You don't mean to tell me that the nuns didn't teach you that?"

"Of course they taught me in a set sort of a way, but that's not what I mean at all! I mean how do you really and truly know when a thing is right or wrong?"

Miss Costello's lips tightened. "Do you mean to say you don't know when you commit a sin?"

"Oh, I'd know if I told a lie, and I'd know if I stole anything, of course, because 'twould be a fact, and I couldn't help knowing it. But what I mean is that I don't feel things to be wrong here." She touched her breast lightly. "I remember the nuns in Dublin used to talk about people having 'qualms of conscience,' but I never really understood what it meant. Am I very queer?"

Miss Costello finished her tea hurriedly. "Yes, you are," she said agitatedly; "and a young girl like you has no business at all to talk about such things. Leave them to those that know better." She set down her cup with a rattle and, leaving her niece to ponder her words of wisdom, walked out of the room.

Left alone, Isabel took her letter from its hiding-place and looked at it, turning it over and over in her hand; then with a little smile, meant for herself alone, she slipped it back into her pocket and finished her tea with a certain slow enjoyment.

In her own room, with the door locked, she at last felt free to dethrone imagination for reality, and, sitting on the side of her bed, she drew the letter forth once more and slowly opened the envelope. A minute sufficed for the reading of the enclosure, a very short, very commonplace note, which merely ran—

"DEAR MISS COSTELLO,—I have at last brought my brother to see reason, and he will go back to Paris to-night. I did not write before, because I had nothing definite to report.—Believe me, sincerely yours,

"STEPHEN CAREY."

The first feeling that coursed through her mind was keen disappointment: the curtness, the formality of the letter came like sharp blows on the malleable soil of her sensitiveness. He might have said a word of gratitude! He might have sent one kind message! She sprang from the bed in sudden anger, tossed the letter upon the dressing-table, and with quick, resentful movements began to take down her thick black hair and re-dress it for the night's festivity. Her fingers worked rapidly, brushing, coiling, pinning, the long black strands, until at last the work was done; then, with the same resentful haste, she slipped off the blue cotton skirt she had been wearing, and, throwing open the door of her wardrobe, stood considering what she should put on. The choice was not very extensive: she looked at the white cashmir and the blue serge, her uniform dresses that had been lengthened for her by a New Town dressmaker since her return from school, but both were instantly condemned; next came the pink muslin, but that had seen considerable service in the last few weeks and already drooped pathetically; next, she scanned a couple of blouses, and a black alpaca skirt that had belonged to her aunt, but her eye was full of disfavour, and turned instinctively to the last re-

maining garment—a plain, mauve, linen dress, more
suitable for morning than for evening wear, but
which fitted her well, and found added value in her
estimation by reason of being her latest acquisition.

She had worn this dress on the morning of her
interview with Frank, and at another time, perhaps, the disagreeable association would have made
her shrink from it; but to-night her anger and
disappointment gave immunity from such superstition, and without hesitation she took the skirt
from its hook and slipped it over her head.
A few minutes completed her preparations; and
with a last glance into the mirror at her flushed
face and rebellious eyes, she took her way towards
the door; but at the door she stopped, hesitated,
and with an air half-defiant, half-shy, went back to
the dressing-table and picked up Carey's offending
letter. As if ashamed of her weakness, she thrust
it surreptitiously into her pocket; and as it slipped
into the hidden recess, her fingers touched something smooth and cold, and the expression of her
face altered suddenly—memory striving with surprise, as she withdrew her hand and brought to
light the little bottle she had wrested from Frank
a week ago, and had forgotten in the stress of
newer events.

She stood for a moment, unpleasantly moved by
the sight of this small object. With the fascination
of all deadly things, the harmless-looking tabloids
held her gaze: she looked at them with a close,
repugnant curiosity; she shook the bottle until they
rattled against the glass; she even withdrew the
cork and allowed one to roll out upon her palm.

She looked at it, as it lay there,—one key of the many that could open the great gate,—and for a moment the shadow of its potency fell on her chillingly. The personal contemplation of death had always been abhorrent to her; with an almost superstitious dread, her keen vitality had always recoiled from it. Death existed, certainly! Existed for the old, for the exhausted, for the unfit, but not for health and youth—not for such as she!

She stood for a moment longer, magnetised by the small white tabloid in her hand: then, by some curious working of the mind, an overwhelming repugnance surged over her; she dropped it back among its fellows, ran across the room to a cupboard in the wall, and, thrusting the bottle into a drawer, locked it out of sight.

CHAPTER XVI.

MANY emotions chased each other through Isabel's mind as she made her way to Fair Hill; and as she walked into the room set aside for the guests' wraps, the little group of girls already assembled glanced round at her expressive face with the mingled curiosity, admiration, and uncertainty that she always aroused.

Mary Norris, who had taken up her position at the dressing-table, saw her in the mirror, and addressed her without turning round. "Hallo, Isabel! Is that a new dress?"

Isabel laughed. "Nearly new," she said.

"And is the mauve by way of mourning?"

"Mourning? How?"

Mary carefully took a little powder from a box on the table and dabbed it on her cheeks. "The king is dead! Long live the king!" she said in her most aggravating voice.

"Mary is sarcastic, so she's putting on powder," said Amy Hennessy, the pretty girl with the impertinent eyes, who had criticised Isabel on the night of her first dance.

Mary turned round indignantly. "This isn't powder, Amy, it's crushed starch."

No one offered to challenge this jesuitical statement; but Amy pushed past her to the glass.

"Well, let me see my hair, anyway! What's to go on here to-night?"

"Bridge—for those who have brains to play it," said Mary promptly; "and the garden for those who haven't. Would you like a loan of my fur coat, Amy?"

There was a little titter of laughter at this, for it was diplomatic to be amused by Mary's sallies.

"No, thank you, Mary!" Amy retorted. "The conservatory will be quite good enough for me."

There was a fresh laugh; and chatting and chaffing, the band of girls departed, leaving Mary and Isabel alone.

Mary put in a hairpin or two, and settled the black velvet ribbon at her neck.

"Frank Carey is gone back to Paris!" she announced.

"I know," said Isabel.

"Who told you? 'Twas only to-day Stephen got him to see reason; and he shipped him off this evening, before he could change his mind."

"I know. Mr Carey wrote to me." Isabel took up a comb and arranged her hair, which had been blown into untidiness by her walk.

"Oh!" Mary stole a quick glance at her. "That was a condescension of Stephen's! Was the letter more than two lines long?"

"I didn't count."

"You should have. Stephen's private letters always make me feel that he's missing the six-and-eightpence. Are you ready?"

Passing out of the bedroom and down the stairs, the first person they came upon was Owen Power, lounging in a wicker chair in the hall and flirting with Amy Hennessy. Immediately they appeared, he looked up, and, with a superb lack of courtesy, turned his back on his companion, and came slowly towards them. "Well, Mary!" he said. "Well, Miss Costello, you look very fit after your tennis!"

Isabel, still smarting under Mary's sarcasms, seized childishly upon the opportunity to retaliate. "How could I be tired," she said, "when I had such a good partner?"

Mary glanced at her, amazed by the encouragement of her tone, and Power gave a self-conscious laugh.

"Oh, I don't know about that! I don't know about that!"

He laughed again and twisted his short moustache. "What are you going to do to-night? I think myself it's much too hot for cards." He looked directly into her eyes; and then, bidden by some twinge of conscience, turned to Mary, including her in the question.

Mary flushed, but her glance met his with level coldness. "Oh, do you think that?" she said. "I'm longing for a game myself. I'd be very sorry indeed to give up bridge for anything you could find in this house." With a quick, contemptuous nod, she passed him, and crossed the hall to the dining-room.

The two, left to themselves, were silent for a moment, then Power gave another empty laugh. "'Mary, Mary, quite contrary!'" he quoted. "But that needn't spoil things for us."

Isabel hated him for the words; but she hated
Mary Norris more, so she ignored the lesser feeling
and answered with a smile—

"What are we going to do?"

"Go out in the garden, of course, as soon as
you've said how d'you do to the dragon!"

They crossed the hall, as Mary had done, and
passed into the dining-room, where Mrs Burke and
her two daughters were hovering about a table set
out with tea and coffee. Groups of people were
clustering round the good things, eating and talking,
while in the distant corners of the room others were
already sitting down to cards under the direction
of Michael Burke.

As Isabel entered the room at Power's side, her
mind suddenly leaped to interest, for the first person
her eyes lighted upon was Stephen Carey, bending
down to catch the voluble chatter of a little old lady
in a grey silk dress. Carey was here, then! She
smiled at Mrs Burke, without hearing her greetings.
Would he turn his head? Would he see her? The
questions crossed and recrossed her mind in un-
analysed confusion.

She took her tea from Power's hand, laughing at
some jest of his. Life was interesting again—full of
zest, full of possibility.

She lingered over her tea, her eyes glancing
surreptitiously towards the tall figure and the
characteristic head, while her tongue ran on in a
stream of careless talk. At last she was compelled
to set her cup down.

"Won't you have any tea, Mr Power?" she asked,
hoping for an excuse to linger.

Power looked worldly - wise. "Not me!" he whispered. "I've had a whisky upstairs in the old man's room. Are you ready?"

She nodded. After all, Carey was in the house! They must meet, sooner or later! "Yes, I'm quite ready," she said, and with the buoyant sense that everything was still to come, she followed Power, as he edged round the table and out into the hall.

At the open hall-door they paused, and he looked at her. "Well," he said; "and so I'm to have a talk with you at last!"

She laughed. "A talk? What have you got to say?"

"Ah, wait and see! I have plenty to say to you!" He led the way down the steps, and as they crossed the gravelled drive he took out his cigarette case. "Do you mind if I smoke? Or, perhaps, you'll have a cigarette yourself? All the girls here smoke, only they don't pretend it."

Isabel's eyes opened. "Do they, really? We used to smoke at school whenever we got the chance, but I thought they were too good here."

"Lord, no! Won't you have one?"

Her eyes flashed. "I'd love to! Do you think I might?"

"Why not? Come down here, and not a soul will see!" He pointed to a long dark alley leading off the avenue.

For a moment she looked doubtful; then, casting her misgivings aside, she turned as he directed. The path, which was known as "The Lover's Walk," was thickly hemmed in by cedars and laurels, which even in dry weather kept the ground damp and the air moist and close.

"It's a funny place!" she said, as they made their way onward. "I don't think I like it."

"Oh, it's all right! It's a bit of the old garden —the only bit that has managed to hold on through Michael's improvements."

"I don't think I like it. It has a creepy feel."

He laughed and edged a little nearer to her. "Afraid of ghosts, what?"

"Ghosts! As if I believed in ghosts!" Her voice was nervously sharp. "Aren't you going to give me the cigarette?"

"Do you want it so soon?"

"Of course I do. I came for it, didn't I?"

Without further demur he took two cigarettes from his case, and putting one between his lips, struck a match.

"You light yours from mine! Matches splutter so much in here." He handed her the remaining cigarette, which she raised somewhat hesitatingly to her lips.

"I think I'll have the match," she said.

"I tell you 'twill go out. It's as damp as anything under these trees."

"Well, I think I'd rather——"

"What nonsense! Come along!" He made his own cigarette glow, and bent his face towards hers.

Half-uncertainly she stepped towards him.

"That's no good! You must pull on it. Look here, stand nearer!" He put his hand on her shoulder, and as the two cigarettes glowed he looked straight into her eyes.

"Do you know what an awfully pretty girl you are?"

Isabel laughed, shaking his hand from her shoulder. "Am I?"

"Are you, indeed? I should think you are. But I'll tell you what you are, too. You're a flirt."

"Why should you say that?"

"Why? Doesn't all Waterford know how you chucked poor Frank Carey?"

"And because all Waterford says it, it must be true?"

"Well, seeing is believing! Come now! Admit!"

Isabel looked at him, and a certain triumph— half-excited, half-nervous — marked her sense of conquest.

"And suppose I do admit?"

"Well, what do you think?" With a ready movement he caught her hand.

She freed herself sharply, and her laugh rang out high and excited. "Listen!" she said quickly. "Listen! There's somebody coming—somebody coming up the path."

They both looked round, struck into silence by steps on the wet ground.

Power muttered something uncomplimentary to all intruders, and Isabel gave a little gasp.

"Why, it's Mr Carey!" she said.

Carey came towards them down the dark path: he was walking very slowly and smoking a cigar. Reaching them, he half-turned as if to retrace his steps, but Isabel stopped him.

"Mr Carey! Aren't you going to speak to us?"

His eyes travelled from the cigarette between her fingers to the shadowy figure of her companion.

"It's so dark——" he said, "I scarcely knew——"

"Oh, it's me—me and Mr Power."

"Ah! Good-night, Power!"

"Good-night!" Power said ungraciously. "I suppose you're like us—found the house too hot!"

"Yes, I thought I'd desert for a while. I had no smoke after dinner to-night. But I mustn't inflict my company on you!"

He was turning again, but Isabel took an impulsive step forward. "But—but we'd like you to stay."

He paused. "Oh, no! Two is company, you know!"

"Well, if you won't stay, we'll go back with you."

Carey laughed. "Will Mr Power subscribe to that?"

Power ground his heel silently into the path.

"Of course he will!" Isabel answered.

"Rather!" Power said rudely. "I must go back to the house, anyway. They'll be looking for me for bridge."

"I see. And will Miss Costello go back too?"

"No!" Isabel answered for herself. "I'll stay on with you: I want to finish my cigarette." With ostentatious calm, she led the way back to the avenue and, replacing the cigarette between her lips, stepped to Carey's side, while Power ran up the steps and entered the house.

As he disappeared, Carey looked down at her. "I can't make you out!" he said in a slow, deep voice.

"Why?"

He answered by another question. "Do you know that I saw you before you saw me?"

"Just now?"

He nodded.

"Oh!" She flicked the ash from her cigarette.

"Don't you think you might wait till that poor beggar is decently out of the country before you begin turning other heads?"

She stood silent.

"Why do you flirt with men like Power? Why do you give them the chance to talk about you?"

Her lashes lifted, and she shot a swift glance at him. "I don't know."

"You don't know?"

"Something makes me."

He stared at her—angry, perplexed, attracted. "Do you like this chap, Power?"

"No."

"Then, good heavens, why do you let him take you out into the garden in this conspicuous way— give you cigarettes—actually make love to you under the eyes of anybody who might happen to pass by?"

"He wasn't making love." With an attempt at bravado, she raised the cigarette again; but before it could touch her lips, Carey seized it from between her fingers and threw it away among the bushes.

She stared at him, and her pulses gave a sudden unaccountable throb.

"Why did you do that?"

"Because if nobody else will stop you from making a fool of yourself, I will."

The words and the tone were harsh, but they had the inestimable worth of things wrung spontaneously from the speaker. Carey had never been so near to her as in that moment of anger.

"And do you mind whether I make a fool of myself or not?"

For one second he seemed on the brink of speech; then he turned away, avoiding her questioning eyes. "Never mind!" he said. "Come into the house!"

CHAPTER XVII.

It was the day following the evening party at Fair Hill—and Mrs Michael Burke's "At Home" day. She was waiting in solemn state in the big drawing-room, while her daughters, Aileen and Angela, flitted here and there, altering the position of a flower-vase, rearranging a book or a paper, lowering or raising the venetian blinds. Aileen and Angela Burke were what is best described as "nice girls." Round-faced, red-cheeked, ridiculously like their father, they had all the sterling qualities of Michael Burke; and, like him, lived under the iron rod of their mother's rule. As they moved hither and thither now about the showy room, they kept up a little whispered duologue, which they interrupted every minute to take furtive glances at the stiff-backed chair in which Mrs Burke sat reading a novel.

"I wonder if any one will come to-day!" Angela, the younger and brighter-looking of the two, remarked, as she drew a peacock-feather fire-screen into prominence. "Wasn't last night awful?"

"I didn't think 'twas bad."

"Of course you didn't! You were sitting on the stairs with Tom Norris. 'Twas very different for me, having to play bridge all night with old Cusacke. Oh, dear! I'm sick of my grand relations!"

Mrs Burke, whose hearing was as sharp as a needle, looked up from her book. "What are you talking about, children?"

"Nothing, mother!"

"Then come down here near me, Angela! I heard a ring at the door. If this is any one, Aileen, you can pour out the tea."

"All right, mother!"

Mrs Burke opened her book again. "I think Henry Cusacke may turn in later," she said. "If he does, I hope you'll be nice to him. It's lonesome for the poor fellow away from his regiment."

Angela, who had obediently dropped to a stool at Mrs Burke's feet, pouted her red lips. "But, mother, I don't like him."

Mrs Burke patted her cheek. "Nonsense, darling! You know nothing at all about your own mind. Just do as I tell you. Why, here's Mrs Carey! How nice of you to come, Mrs Carey! And Mr Norris! And Miss Norris!" She rose and greeted the guests with just the due amount of artificiality, while Daisy and Mary rustled forward, carefully arranging their dresses as they sank into their chairs.

"I suppose Stephen hasn't been here yet, Mrs Burke?" Daisy said.

"No. Is Mr Carey coming?"

"Yes. He promised that he'd call for us in the motor." She could scarcely conceal the pride that the announcement caused her.

Mrs Burke looked a little patronising. "Oh, the new motor? I hear he drives it himself now. I hope he finds it more satisfactory than poor Mr Leader did."

Daisy smiled graciously at what she considered Mrs Burke's natural jealousy. "Oh, it's the greatest success, Mrs Burke. I'm afraid 'twas poor Mr Leader's own fault that he had so much trouble with it. It takes somebody who understands these things——"

"No doubt, indeed! I hope you weren't tired last night."

"Tired? We were just saying as we came up the avenue what a lovely party it was. Weren't we, Mary?"

"That's what we want, Mrs Burke, you know!" Tom broke in; "that old spirit of sociality that's dying out in Ireland. I agree with my sister that I never enjoyed myself so much in all my life as I did last night."

Aileen Burke blushed hotly behind the big silver urn.

Mrs Burke condescended to smile at his compliment. Tom might not be the pinnacle of maternal ambition, but, failing other schemes, he was not to be despised. "That's very kind of you, Mr Norris," she said affably. "I wish everybody was as easily pleased. Will you make yourself useful now, and help the girls with the tea?"

With great alacrity Tom retired to the tea-table, and presently the sound of muffled laughter gave proof of his awkwardness and Aileen's chaffing criticism.

As the cups were being passed round by Angela, the door opened again, and Mrs Power—large, florid, and smiling—came forward into the circle.

"Well, Ellen, I hear there never was such a party! Josephine can talk of nothing else. How are you, Daisy, dear? How are you, Mary? And Aileen and Angela?" In her motherly way she kissed all the girls, and then shook hands with Norris. "Indeed, Tom, I heard all about you; but we won't tell tales out of school!"

Aileen once more sought shelter behind the urn, and Mrs Burke gave one of her hard laughs. "What did Owen think of our bridge?" she asked, tactfully turning the subject. "I expect we seem very much behindhand after Dublin."

"Indeed I didn't see Owen since last night. He went on to some poker party or other, after bringing Josephine home, and he wasn't up this morning when I was going out to mass."

Mrs Burke said nothing, but her face was eloquent in criticism of Mrs Power's family management.

Mary Norris laughed suddenly. "Oh, indeed, Owen was enjoying himself last night, Mrs Power! Wasn't he, Aileen?" It was Mary's first contribution to the conversation, and it was given in her most telling vein.

Aileen Burke gave an embarrassed little laugh. "I didn't see him at all, Mary."

"Didn't you? Oh, he had a very good time last night."

Mrs Burke looked severe. "I thought Owen was playing bridge all the time."

"Oh, not all the time, indeed, Mrs Burke! He was out in the garden first."

"Who with, Mary?" asked Mrs Power.

Mary tossed her head. "Oh, I'm not going to say who with; but they went down the Lover's Walk, and Lillie O'Farrell saw them both smoking cigarettes."

"Both smoking, did you say, Miss Norris?" Mrs Burke asked, her back stiffening perceptibly. "I can scarcely believe that any girl in my house would do such a thing as smoke."

Mary, who consumed many cigarettes a day in the privacy of her own room, looked becomingly grave. "Not in the house, Mrs Burke. I said in the garden."

Mrs Burke's lips tightened. "I confess I don't see much difference between the two! And I'd like to know who the girl was."

Aileen and Angela, themselves conscious of stolen smokes, drew away behind the sheltering figure of Mrs Power, but Tom Norris came forward into the group.

"Don't, Polly!" he said. "'Twould be mean. After all, what's in a cigarette?"

"Oh, nothing but a little paper and a bit of tobacco—if the girl happens to be pretty!"

"I think there's a great deal, Mr Norris, if you ask me," said Mrs Burke severely. "I know that people are getting more lax every day, but for my part, I'd be very sorry indeed to see a daughter of mine smoking."

"Oh, I don't know!" said Tom stoutly. "I don't see any harm in it."

"Perhaps she picked up the habit abroad!" put in Daisy in her pretty, mincing voice.

Mrs Burke jumped to a quick conclusion. "Abroad?" she said. "Abroad? Why, then it must have been Isabel! Miss Norris, was it Isabel?"

Mary shrugged her shoulders. "'Twasn't I let the cat out of the bag, anyway!"

Daisy laughed a little. "Suppose I oughtn't to have said it! But, really, Isabel seems to be getting herself so much talked about lately—"

"—That it doesn't matter how much more you say?" added Tom. "How like a woman!"

"For goodness' sake, Tom, talk about something you understand!" said Mary irritably.

Tom became mute, and retired again to the tea-table, while Mrs Burke drew her chair nearer to Daisy's. "I believe people *are* talking rather too much about Isabel," she said in a lower tone. "Is it true, now, Mrs Carey, that she really did treat your brother-in-law badly?"

Daisy dropped instantly to the confidential key. "Well, indeed, Mrs Burke, I don't like to say anything, but poor Frank looked more like a ghost than anything else that morning that he came down from New Town. I hardly knew him when he walked into the dining-room."

"Yes, indeed, and everybody in Waterford is saying that 'twas the Careys broke off the match," put in Mary. "It's awfully hard on Daisy."

"And who minds what people say, Mary?" said Mrs Power.

"Not mind, indeed! You have to mind."

"Indeed you have," Daisy added. "A professional man like Stephen can't afford to be talked about: that's why it's doubly hard on me."

"Well, Daisy, I told you how you could stop all talk."

"I know, Mrs Power. By asking her to the house.".

"And then have her going on like she did last night!" Mary supplemented.

"Miss Norris, I insist on knowing where she smoked the cigarette," said Mrs Burke, recalled to the thought of her own grievance.

"In the garden, Mrs Burke. Lillie O'Farrell went out for a couple of minutes with one of the Goulding boys, and while they were walking up and down in front of the house, Isabel came out with Owen. Lillie says she was flirting dreadfully; and she heard him offer her a cigarette."

"But what's in that, Mary!" Mrs Power exclaimed. "Owen is always chaffing and going on. Who knows she ever smoked at all?"

"Oh, yes, she did."

"How do you know? Did Lillie follow them?"

"Not very likely that she would!"

"Then how do you know?"

"I heard. Oh, there was a good deal more, only I don't want to say."

"Oh, Polly, do tell us!" Daisy cried.

But Mary closed her lips. "No; I won't tell any more."

"But, Miss Norris, do you think that's quite fair? Surely, when there is anything to tell, it's our duty to tell it for the good of others."

Mary smiled enigmatically. "Sometimes, perhaps, Mrs Burke," she said, "but not always. Don't you think we ought to be going, Daisy? I'm sure Stephen had a puncture or something, and you know I have that appointment at Mrs Clarke's."

"Oh, wait a little longer!" Mrs Burke urged. "He'll be here presently. You never can be up to time with a motor."

Daisy looked inclined to yield, but Mary intervened again.

"But dressmakers don't take that into account, Mrs Burke," she said; "and I have to try on a new dress at Mrs Clarke's."

Daisy rose reluctantly, and Tom tore himself away from Aileen.

"What sort of a dress is it, Mary?" asked Mrs Power good-naturedly, interested, and forgetful of the preceding passage of arms.

"Oh, it's only a linen for Kilmeaden, Mrs Power. We're going down in a fortnight, you know."

"Oh, yes! And I'm wanting Stephen to let me give a little dance at Lady Lane the night before we go," announced Daisy, as she shook out her skirt and arranged her feather boa. "Everything will be put away for the summer, and it wouldn't be a bit of trouble."

"Oh, Mrs Carey, can't you persuade him?" cried Aileen and Angela simultaneously. "'Twould be simply heavenly!"

"Of course he'll let you, Daisy," said Mrs Power. "Stephen is the soul of good-nature."

"If I were you, Mrs Carey," advised Mrs Burke, "I'd send out the invitations and not tell him a word about it till it was all settled. Men have nothing to do with these things!"

Mary laughed sarcastically. "Say that to Stephen Carey, Mrs Burke! Are you coming, Daisy?"

They shook hands all round, and with a great deal of chattering and laughter, left the room.

"I ought to be going too, Ellen," said Mrs Power, rising.

"Nonsense, Kate! Sit down."

"Ah, no; I must really! I have a lot of visits that are hanging over me for months; and anyway, I don't like to keep the horse standing. Good-bye, Ellen! Good-bye, girls! When are you coming to Skerrybeg? You're great strangers to us."

"Indeed, it's too much amusement they have," said their mother. "Aileen is giving up her painting altogether; and as for Angela, she never touches the piano."

"Perhaps they're beginning to think of other things! I know a little bird whispered to me that it wouldn't be long before we heard something about an engagement. Well, good-bye!" She passed out of the room, smiling and nodding.

"I don't know how Kate Power can bring herself to be so vulgar," said Mrs Burke as the door closed. "And what a fool she has been over those spoiled, worthless sons of hers!"

"Mother, wouldn't it be lovely if the Careys give the dance?" said Angela, her mind bent on her own affairs.

"Indeed, if they do, your father will have to take you! I can't lose another night's rest."

The girls exchanged a glance of secret joy, for it was a red-letter day when Michael Burke played guardian.

"Mother," said Aileen suddenly, "do you think that was true about Isabel?"

Mrs Burke looked severely judicial. "Well, I'd certainly be very sorry to believe everything Mary Norris says," she replied; "but I have thought more than once myself that Isabel is rather free-and-easy in her manner for Waterford."

"She's very pretty," said Angela with unconscious philosophy.

"She's too dark for my taste. Besides, Angela, remember 'handsome is that handsome does.'"

"Listen! Listen, mother!" Aileen cried. "I hear a motor. There's a motor coming up the avenue."

"Oh, it must be Mr Carey! They must have gone the short cut and missed him!" Angela rushed to the window.

"It is! It is, mother! And guess—guess— do guess who's with him? Aileen, come here! Quick!"

Aileen flew across the room to her sister's side, overturning a footstool as she went.

"What, in the name of goodness, is the matter?" exclaimed Mrs Burke crossly. "One would think you never saw a motor in your lives!"

With a crunching of gravel, the car sped round the house, and a little cry of excitement and interest escaped the girls.

"Aileen! Angela! What on earth is it?"

But before either could collect herself sufficiently to give a coherent answer, the door of the drawing-room was thrown open, and Isabel Costello, with her eyes dancing and her hair blown into elf-locks, walked into the room, followed by Stephen Carey.

CHAPTER XVIII.

FOR one moment there was silence in the large drawing-room; then Mrs Burke rallied her social qualities and met the situation.

"Isabel! And Mr Carey! This is a surprise. A very pleasant surprise!" she finished with scrupulous politeness.

Carey stepped forward rather hurriedly. "Isn't my wife here?" he said, as he took her hand.

No; Mrs Carey has just gone; she took the short cut through the fields. Miss Norris had an appointment at the dressmaker's.

"And, of course, nothing is so important as a dressmaker, Mr Carey," said Angela, as the two girls came forward, stealing furtively curious glances at Isabel.

The news of Daisy's departure seemed to disconcert him. He glanced round, almost as though he contemplated flight.

"She might have waited," he said. "I told her I'd be as soon as I could."

"Indeed, he was flying up the hill when he met me," supplemented Isabel. "I felt quite guilty for stopping the car even for a minute—though the lift was too tempting to refuse." Womanlike, it was she who made the explanation of their presence —the explanation that instinct told her would be needed.

"I should think so, indeed!" said Aileen kindly. "I wish I had been walking up the hill!"

Mrs Burke looked a little severe. "Won't you have a cup of tea, Mr Carey, now that you are here?"

Again Carey looked round uncomfortably. "Oh, I don't know that I ought!" Then as his eyes strayed round the room they lit upon Isabel, and unconsciously his expression wavered. "Well, thanks, Mrs Burke!" he said. "Thanks! I will have a cup."

"I'm glad you altered your mind! Aileen, see after Mr Carey. Isabel, come here and sit near me." With the shepherding instinct of the mother, she drew the object of most danger to her own side.

"Well, Isabel, and how do you like motor-cars?" she asked, her eyes, piercing as gimlets, searching the girl's face.

"Oh, I simply adore them, Mrs Burke! This is the first I was ever in, and I thought it was like heaven."

Mrs Burke gave one of her stiff little smiles. "I hope heaven will be more peaceful, Isabel."

Isabel threw back her head.

"Oh, do you, Mrs Burke? I don't. I wouldn't care a bit for anything that was all peace and quiet."

"You mustn't say that, Isabel!"

"Why? Is it any harm?"

"Well, it's a little irreverent, isn't it?"

"Is it? I didn't mean it to be. It only seems to me that heaven must be like all the loveliest things on earth, only a thousand times better."

"The prophet's heaven?" said Carey, smiling, as he handed her her tea.

Mrs Burke coughed nervously. "I don't think girls ought to discuss theology, Mr Carey. But perhaps I'm old-fashioned."

"Is this theology?" said Carey innocently.

She stiffened her shoulders. "Oh, you know what I mean. All that girls need know is that they must say their prayers—and never give bad example."

Isabel drank her tea, striving to keep a still tongue; while Mrs Burke, pleased at what she considered her well-timed reproof, turned to Carey with greater friendliness.

"Well, Mr Carey, so you're off to Kilmeaden soon?"

Isabel looked up. This was the first she had heard of the Careys' departure to the country.

"Yes," said Carey. "My wife is anxious to get down early this year and come back in September. We found Kilmeaden rather damp last October."

"That'll be very nice! And you'll find the motor a great convenience, instead of having to drive up to town."

"Will you shut up the house in Lady Lane, then?" Isabel asked.

"Oh, my wife puts in a charwoman, in case any one wants to come to town for a night. But we live altogether at Kilmeaden—though I come up every morning to the office."

"Ah, there's no place like the country! It's so good for the children," put in Mrs Burke.

Isabel finished her tea hastily, and Carey laughed a little awkwardly. "Oh, yes!" he said; "yes!"

"And what fine little fellows they are! I met them on the road the other day with the nurse. But Mrs Carey tells me you're thinking of giving a little party before you go?"

"Oh, mother, she only said they were talking of it."

"But that's the same thing, isn't it, Mr Carey?" said Angela, looking up at him with her good-natured smile. "'Twouldn't be one bit of trouble, you know, once the house is upset. You'll let Mrs Carey give it, of course. You will, now? Won't you?"

"Oh, do, Mr Carey!" chimed in Aileen. "We were saying only yesterday that there wouldn't be another dance this summer."

Carey looked at Isabel. "Miss Costello, won't you stand up for me? It isn't fair, you know! Two to one!"

"Oh, indeed, Isabel would love it! Wouldn't you, Isabel?"

Isabel's eyes met Carey's. "Mr Carey knows I adore dancing."

"And she's only had one dance since she came home. Oughtn't that soften your heart?"

"Angela, you're very tormenting! Let Mr Carey alone!"

"But, mother, it's his duty! What has he a big house for, if 'tisn't to give parties?"

"Indeed, you're a great tease! I wonder Mr

Carey puts up with you. Isabel, how is your
aunt?"

At this decisive changing of the conversation the
topic of the dance was dropped.

"Oh, she's very well, Mrs Burke, thanks!"
answered Isabel. "Only she has one of her bad
headaches to-day. She said I was to excuse her.
Only for it, she'd have come up with me."

"Oh, poor thing! And what is she doing for
it?"

"Nothing."

"Nothing? What a mistake!" Mrs Burke did
a little amateur doctoring on homœopathic lines, and
took great pride in the results. "The minute you
go home, Isabel, tell her she is to take a tumbler of
soda-water with the juice of a lemon in it; and if
she's not well in half an hour, she's to send up to
me for a globule. Now, don't forget! How many
simple cures there are, Mr Carey, if we only knew
them!"

"Yes, indeed!" Carey murmured.

"You may well say so! I believe myself that it
only requires a little faith and plenty of cold water
to do away with doctors altogether! Isabel, you
won't forget my message."

"Did you ever hear how mother gave father a
Turkish bath in his own room?" whispered Angela
to Carey.

"Never."

She waited until her mother was launched upon
another series of directions to Isabel, then she looked
up at him, her round face brimming with humour.

"It was long ago," she whispered, "one time

father had a cold. He was too bad to go out, so
mother thought she'd give him a sort of Turkish bath
in the house, with blankets and a spirit-lamp. He
fought against it like anything, of course—but, you
know, mother always has her way."

Carey nodded.

"Well, father gave in; but just as everything
was arranged and he was packed up in the blankets,
some people called to see mother. As luck would
have it, who should they be but Wexford people that
she hadn't seen for years, so she told poor father to
keep quite quiet and not to imagine the lamp was
too high, and that she'd just run down and say
'How d'you do?' and be back again before he knew
she was gone!" Here Angela went into an irre-
pressible titter of laughter.

"Well, what do you think happened? She went
down, and in three minutes she was buried in all the
old scandals that had happened in Wexford for the
last twenty-five years, with every bit of thought of
father gone out of her head!"

Carey, seeing the picture of Michael, over the
lighted spirit-lamp, powerless under his weight of
blankets, went off into a peal of laughter.

Mrs. Burke looked round. "Is Angela amusing
you, Mr Carey? She's a terrible chatterbox, I'm
afraid."

"Miss Angela is very entertaining, Mrs Burke,"
he said. "I think she ought to be given her dance.
Miss Angela, what was the end?"

Angela looked at him mischievously. "Oh, father
had escaped back to bed by the time she came up,"
she whispered, "but most of the blankets were still

on fire! But you won't go back of your word about the dance? Promise now, you won't!"

At this juncture Isabel stood up. "I think I must be going," she said. "Good-bye, Mrs Burke!"

To everybody's surprise Carey put down his cup and rose also.

"What, Mr Carey! Are you going too?"

"If Miss Costello will let me, I'll drive her home."

Isabel turned to him, all pleasure, all delight, in a moment. "Oh, no! Why should I?"

"But why not? A foretaste of heaven is good for the soul!"

She laughed yieldingly.

"I am sure it will be very pleasant for her to be driven home," Mrs Burke put in rather frigidly. "Don't forget about the lemon for your aunt's head, Isabel."

"No, Mrs Burke!" Isabel's mind was speeding to other things as she shook hands all round.

"Good-bye!" cried Angela cordially.

"Good-bye!" added Aileen. "We'll come out and see you off."

"No, children, I think you'd better not! There's a treacherous fog these evenings, and you both had sore throats last week."

The girls looked disappointed, but neither offered to oppose the mandate.

"Well, we'll look at you through the window," said Aileen.

"And don't forget the dance, Mr Carey!" Angela cried, as the two guests disappeared into the hall.

The setting in motion of the engines was the work

of a moment, and with a good deal of skill and precision Carey swept his car round the open, gravelled space at the corner of the house.

In a vague flash he saw the faces of the Burke girls pressed against the drawing-room window, but the impression passed with the presence of the house, and he drew a quick, deep breath of relief.

"What a woman!" he said. "What an atmosphere!" It was remarkable that he spoke his thoughts as though he were alone, that by some hidden link of comradeship he did not question whether Isabel would understand.

"Yes, I know!" she said quickly. "Don't you feel that you can't stand it for one second longer —that you must get up and scream in the very middle of what she's saying?"

Unconsciously Carey checked the pace of the car, and they passed almost slowly through the gates.

"Good God!" he said, "I've sometimes felt that no man in his senses would stand this life for a single year! Talk of rats in a trap!"

They swerved out into the high-road; but instead of turning down the steep hill that led directly into Waterford, he drove straight on, making a detour.

Isabel sat with her hands clasped loosely in her lap, every nerve quivering to the moment.

"Have you wanted to get out into the world, then?" she said.

"Yes! Lord, yes! There was a time—— But what's the good——"

Her glance dropped to his hands, strong and steady on the steering wheel. "Won't you tell me?" she whispered. "I'd—love to hear."

There was nothing to alarm in the low, enticing voice, and he yielded, half unconsciously, to its persuasion. "Oh, it's only that I built my castles once!" he said, "and that, with half a chance, I might have made my way. A man isn't a man in a place like this! What sort of a life is it? Stagnation. The same round, the same faces, the same work, autumn, winter, and spring, and in the summer—Kilmeaden!" He gave one of his sarcastic laughs.

"But if you liked you could go away—you have money."

For answer he increased the speed of the car, sending it spinning forward. "Miss Costello," he said, "look at the rut at the side of this road! If I ran the car into that rut, we'd have to get ropes and men and horses to drag her out— 'twouldn't help her one atom that she's forty horse-power in herself."

She grasped the simile, and followed it up.

"Yes, but you'd get the car out, however you managed it!"

"Ah, you're right there! And perhaps I've had thoughts for myself too."

She felt her senses quicken at the sudden fire that touched his voice, glowing up through his words, and her impetuous nature leaped to a response.

"Oh, I wish you weren't going away!"

Carey reddened—reddened as though no span of years or tale of responsibilities had sealed the book of his youth. "Why do you say that?" he asked in a low, controlled voice, from which he resolutely shut out the eagerness, the curiosity that were welling in his mind.

"I don't know. Because — because you're different from the others—and I'll miss you."

The subtle flattery moved him. "You'll miss me? Do you mean that?"

She nodded silently; and as he turned to catch her expression, his glance rested on her eyes, with their thick black lashes—on her warm mouth—on the elf-locks blown across her smooth, soft cheek; and the things of the world, the things he had denied, surged up overwhelmingly. "You oughtn't to miss me," he said unevenly. "'Tis I ought to miss you."

Isabel looked down. "I wish you weren't going!"

"'Twon't be for long; I'll see you again soon."

Her glance flashed back to his, quick and eager. "How?"

The little whispered word sent his blood racing through his veins, and for one fierce moment the temptation to say "I'll be alone at the office every day" rose insistently; but with a sudden shame at his own thought he flung it aside.

"My wife is going to ask you out to Kilmeaden," he said instead.

"Me? To Kilmeaden?" She flushed to her temples with swift, incredulous delight.

"Yes. You'll come, won't you?" Unconsciously he slackened speed again.

Her glance fell.

He misinterpreted her silence. "Oh, but you must come," he said quickly. "I won't allow you to refuse. Look here! I'll make you a promise! You like the car. Well, I'll take you for such drives as you'll never forget! Will that tempt you?"

Isabel still looked down at her clasped hands, her colour coming and going.

"Isabel!"

It was the first time he had used her name, though she had long ago ceased to be "Miss Costello" to all his people, and she started, as though he had touched her, the hot tide of blood rushing back into her face.

The car was barely moving; he bent closer to her. "You're not angry? Say you will come!"

Then at last she met his glance, her own eyes alight with sudden exultation.

"I'm not angry—I will come."

CHAPTER XIX.

"LISTEN, Mary! Will this do?" Daisy looked up from the flimsy little walnut escritoire that was her special pride, and smoothed out a sheet of pink note-paper that she had just covered with round, childish writing.

"Go on! What is it?" Mary was tucking a white muslin collar that was to adorn her linen dress at Kilmeaden, and the attention she gave to Daisy was divided.

"Can't you listen, then!—'Dear Isabel, I am writing to ask you to join us on Thursday evening at about eight. We are having a few people here, as it's our last night before going to Kilmeaden.'"

Daisy put down the note and looked across at her sister. "I must say that, you know. If I said it was a dance, half Waterford would be indignant because they weren't asked."

"Well, go on!"

"'Also, I am very anxious to have you with us for a few days in the country. It will only be a sort of family party; but if you don't mind that, I wish you would arrange to come out for a week. We could fix about it on Thursday. With kind regards

to Miss Costello, I am, yours sincerely, Daisy Carey.'
It sounds fearfully abrupt, doesn't it?"

Mary was threading her needle. "Not at all!"
she said conclusively. "It's too agreeable, if you
ask me!"

"Oh, Polly!"

"Yes, 'tis. And I think you're a great fool,
Daisy, to be led into asking her at all."

Daisy folded the pink note and slowly put it into
an envelope. "It's awfully hard always to do the
right thing," she complained. "I'm sure I don't
want her any more than you do, but I can't have
the Nevilles and the Cranes and all that crowd
saying we ruined her chances; and you know they
have said it!" Strengthened by her argument, she
fastened the envelope and addressed it.

Mary pursed up her lips and began a fresh
tuck.

"Well, I hope it's for the best!" Daisy looked at
the envelope, weakening again.

Mary kept silent.

"Polly, why on earth can't you say something?"

"I never give advice where it isn't wanted. You
can do what you like, of course; I'm sure, I only
hope you won't regret it."

"Don't say things like that! They depress me."

"Don't be depressed without cause — you may
have it some time."

"Mary, what on earth is the matter with you
to-day?"

But Mary was not disposed to be communicative;
and presently, having waited in vain for some sign,
Daisy in common justification of herself was com-

pelled to ring for Julia and send her letter to the post.

"Well, it's gone now, any way!" she said with relief. "For goodness' sake, let us forget it, and talk about the dance!" She got up from her desk and came round to Mary's side.

"Polly, I wonder if 'twould be better, after all, to have a 'sit down' supper?"

"Supper! What on earth for? Isn't it a 'Cinderella' dance?"

"Yes, but you know they won't go at twelve."

"I didn't say they would. But as long as they know it's 'Cinderella,' they know they'll get nothing to eat. Indeed, I'd be long sorry to give them anything but tea and coffee and ices."

"Stephen insists on chicken and ham at least."

"What nonsense! A lot Stephen knows about it!"

"Well, I can't help it. He says men must have something to eat."

"Rubbish! If men have something to drink, it's much more to the purpose."

"Polly, how can you!" Daisy looked shocked.

Mary let her sewing lie idle in her lap. "'Pon my word, Daisy," she said, looking up at her sister, "you're like a girl at school! How on earth a married woman with three children can keep on being shocked at this, and shocked at that, like you do, is more than I can understand! Do you really think life is all visiting and dressing and fussing over babies?"

Daisy looked deeply offended. "I think you say very queer things sometimes, Mary! I don't think a nice woman ought to want to know anything out-

side her home—and I'm sure Stephen wouldn't wish
me to."

Mary's lip curled. "Oh, that's quite likely!
There's nothing so convenient to the ordinary man
as an ignorant wife."

Daisy flushed. "I'm as well educated as you,
Mary—though I may not read Tolstoy and Zola,
and those horrible foreign writers."

Mary laughed. "Oh, I'm not talking of mathe-
matics or Euclid; I know you passed your exams.
at school."

"What do you mean, then?"

"Never mind! Wasn't that a ring at the hall
door?"

In a moment the little skirmish was forgotten.
Mary rolled up her work and thrust it behind a
vase; while Daisy flew to the glass over the mantelpiece to arrange her hair.

"Who can it be?"

"How do I know? Sit down, for goodness' sake!"

As they made a rush for their respective chairs,
the door opened.

"Why, it's only Father James!" Daisy cried in a
tone of relief, and they both rose and went forward
towards the door.

Father Baron came into the room with his usual
deliberate slowness, and put out a hand to each of
them.

"Well! Well! Well! A very dull visitor, I
suppose!"

"Indeed, no!" Daisy cried. "We were just
dreading 'twas some woman. Come in, Father
James! Were you down with Stephen?"

He allowed himself to be drawn into the room. "Indeed, I had lunch with him," he said; "and he told me he'd be on here after me. And how is Miss Mary?" He turned his small, dark, kindly eyes from Daisy's face to her sister's with a glance of absolute goodwill.

Mary looked up at him frankly, for in the light of the old man's simplicity her sarcasm always lost point.

"As well as we can expect to be in this world, Father James."

"Oh, come, come, Mary!" he cried. "That's not the way to talk! It's for the like of me to be saying that, with my sixty-ninth birthday coming on next week, and my poor bones eaten up with the rheumatism! It's a shame for her now, Daisy, isn't it?"

"Oh, Daisy will agree with you! We were fighting when you came in."

He looked from one to the other with a smile. "And what harm if you were!" was his characteristic retort. "Sure, life wouldn't be worth anything at all if it wasn't for a fight now and again. Hard words break no bones!"

They both laughed at his unanswerable philosophy.

"You're awfully funny, Father James! I believe you'd find an excuse for Lucifer!"

"Well, child, and maybe I would," he said. "Daisy, am I going to see the sons at all?"

Daisy flushed with pleasure. "Oh, would you like to? I'll run up for them! I won't be a minute! They'd love to see you." She hurried across to the

door, attractive at once in her spontaneous natural
pride in the thought of her children. "I won't be
long! I won't be a minute!" she cried as she
disappeared.

As the door closed upon her, Father Baron turned
again to Mary. "Well, child," he said affectionately,
"I don't think I saw you since that night of that
dinner-party! Is Master Tom as busy as ever,
regenerating the country?"

"As silly as ever, you mean, Father James!"

"Ah, now! Ah, now!" he said gently. "We
mustn't judge any one too quick, Mary! And tell
me what about that little gipsy that was here?
I asked Stephen to-day if it's true what they're
saying about her and Frank, but he didn't seem
to like the question, so I didn't press it."

"Oh, Isabel Costello! I'm sick of her very name!"

Father James looked grave. "Mary! Mary!
Mary! Is that the child that made her first
confession to me!"

"Oh, well, I can't help it, Father James!"

"And what has the poor gipsy done?"

"I can't explain to you. She is different from
the rest of us."

He smiled indulgently. "And perhaps a little
change is no harm!"

"Or it may be great harm, Father James."

He glanced at her searchingly, but when he spoke
again it was in the same gentle tone. "Ah, well!"
he said; "it's not for us to judge her, Mary. The
poor child will meet her own troubles."

It was Mary's turn to look shrewdly at him.

"What makes you say that, Father James?"

"Well, I only saw her the once, of course—and I'm open to make a mistake ; but it struck me then that maybe life wouldn't be too easy for her. She's one, God help her, that'll be asking too much from it ! "

Mary walked slowly across the room, and took her muslin collar from behind the vase.

"Father James," she said with apparent irrelevance, "how did you think Stephen Carey looking ? "

Whatever may have been Father Baron's thought, his answer was non-committal. "Indeed, we had so much to talk about, Mary," he said, "that I didn't take any great notice. But here's Daisy with the children ! "

As he spoke, the door opened and Daisy entered, smiling and unaffected, with one small boy walking close to her skirts and another, a couple of years younger, held in her arms.

"I'm so sorry, Father James, Baby is asleep! But I brought you Ted and Francis."

"Well! Well! Wasn't that bad manners of Master James, now? To be asleep after his namesake coming all the way from Scarragh to see him! I don't think Ted would do a thing like that." In this roundabout, tactful way he banished any shyness the elder boy might feel, and drew him into speech before he was aware.

"I think Baby is a silly fellow," he said, stepping from his mother's side, and looking up into the priest's face. "He's asleep half the day."

Father James put his hand on the small red head, with a touch as gentle as a woman's, and raised the intelligent, freckled little face.

"Is he, now, Ted?" he said thoughtfully. "Is he, now?" Then he shook off the momentary gravity that the child's presence had aroused, and turned towards the second boy, who was hiding a very fair head against his mother's shoulder.

"Well, young man," he said, making no attempt to touch him, "and what do you think about this brother of yours?"

The child raised his face an inch or two, and took a sidelong look at the priest.

"Come, now! Come, now, love! Speak to Father James! That's a good boy!" Very gently Daisy set him down on the ground, pushing him slowly forward. "Shake hands, now, and give him a kiss!"

Overpowered by the shyness that is the charm of many Irish children, Francis clung to her fingers, pressing close to her skirts for protection.

But the old priest understood the childish heart far too intimately to make any onslaught; so, quietly turning his back, he moved to a distant chair, from which he beckoned confidentially to Ted.

"All right! Very well!" he said. "But I think I know somebody that'll have a ride on Father James's horses. Come, Ted! We're going to take the horses out. Come, now! What are their names?"

"I know! I remember, Father James! 'Trample-the-Daisy' and 'Spatter-the-Dew'!" In high delight, Ted rushed forward and placed himself between the old priest's knees, looking up excitedly into his face.

Father James smiled down at him in as much pride as if he were his own son. "That's it, Ted! That's right! Come, now, they're wild to be off! Pick up the reins like a man." He began to move his feet to imitate the movements of an impatient horse.

Ted, flushed with excitement and earnestness, put his round little hand on the cheap black cord that served the priest as a watch-chain.

"Well, now! Which will you have?"

"'Trample-the-Daisy,' Father James!"

"All right! Up you go!" He hoisted him triumphantly on to one knee, where he sat astride, with tightened legs and hands that gripped the watch-chain for life or death.

But a shriek of protest from the other end of the room stopped the game, as Francis, with outstretched arms and unsteady feet, lurched forward, followed by his mother. Reaching the priest's side, he put one fat hand on the vacant knee, and looked up into his face with bright, shy eyes.

"Me yide, too!" he said.

For an instant Father James looked down into the anxious little face; then with an infinitely gentle movement he lifted the child and held him close. "Why, then, indeed you will!" he said. "You'll ride the best horse in Father James's stable — the best horse vacant," he added, seeing Ted's face fall. "And that's 'Spatter-the-Dew'!"

There was uproar in the drawing-room for the next ten minutes; and while it was yet at its height, the door opened and Carey walked into the room.

Usually Carey's full favour was meted out to his sons. For years past, the sum of pride and of ambition had centred round their sturdy limbs, their bright faces, the promise of intelligence in their halting speech; and usually, coming upon such a scene as this, he would have flung his cares from him and, throwing himself into the tide of young life, have become young himself in his children's happiness. But to-day it was different; to-day he stood just inside the door, looking, but saying nothing.

"Oh, father, father! I'm winning! 'Trample-the-Daisy' is winning! Father, he's won! He's won!" Ted's voice rose shrill with excitement, as Father James allowed his legs to subside into well-earned rest, and, taking his arm from round the younger boy, wiped his streaming forehead.

Then Carey came forward into the room. "Daisy," he said severely, "you oughtn't to allow them to play on Father James like that! It's disgraceful! He's perfectly exhausted."

Father Baron laughed. "I wish I was oftener exhausted, then. That's all I have to say! Now, Francis, are you fond of Father James?"

With a charming shy grace the child looked up. "Is!" he said simply, and put up his mouth to be kissed.

The old priest touched his lips almost reverently, and the two children slid to the ground and ran across to their father.

Stephen put a hand on either head; and to Mary and Father James, both watching closely, it almost seemed that impatience crossed the tenderness of the act.

"Take them upstairs, Daisy!" he said a moment after. "I have a splitting headache. Run off, now, like good boys!" He stooped quickly and kissed them.

Daisy and Mary went out, each leading one of the children, and as the door closed on them Carey threw himself into a chair.

"I'm dog tired!" he said.

Father James—who had instructed him for the sacraments, married him, and baptised his children —knew him too well to proffer any sympathy. He sat quite still, fingering his watch-chain, and waiting for the next outbreak.

It came before very long. "Good God, but I *am* tired!" Stephen sat forward, taking his head between his hands.

"You're overworked. Kilmeaden will put you right."

"Kilmeaden!" He laughed sarcastically; then his tone changed. "You'll come out to us, Father James—next month, anyway?"

Father James looked deprecating. "I don't know that I ought, Stephen! I oughtn't to be going there every year, taking up room. An old priest is a clog on young people."

"What nonsense! I'll be glad enough to have you, for one. The place will be infested with Norrises."

"Stephen! Stephen! You're in a black mood!"

Carey was silent for a while, then he lifted his face. "It's not me, Father James," he said; "it's the world that's out of joint."

CHAPTER XX.

In the bedrooms at Lady Lane the curtains had been removed from the windows, the blinds pulled down, and the mattresses on the beds rolled up and covered with brown paper, while downstairs the drawing - room furniture had been stacked away, chair on chair, and loomed forth, rigid and ghostly, under its holland shroud. With the exception of the dining-room, Daisy's bedroom, and the drawing - room, the house spoke eloquently of immediate desertion; but in these three instances the contrast was marked. In the dining-room the big gasalier was fully lighted—a sure token of festivity, and the long table groaned under a weight of hams, chickens, creams, and jellies; in Daisy's bedroom the dressing-table, brightly lighted with wax candles, was set out with the trays of pins and hairpins, the silver-backed brushes, even the box of crushed starch suitable to a night of entertainment; while in the drawing-room—the centre and pivot of the coming gaiety—a long stretch of waxed floor, a piano drawn into a remote corner, and a row of chairs standing like sentinels against the wall, proclaimed aloud that it was the hour before a dance.

It was eight o'clock, and the soft evening light

was making a valiant attempt to struggle through the chinks of the Venetian blinds and offer a challenge to the flood of gaslight filling the room; by the white marble mantelpiece Daisy, in a pretty gauze dress, was dividing her attention between a bank of geraniums and maidenhair fern clustering on the mantelboard, and her own image reflected in the mirror; while at the other end of the room Mary was sprinkling French chalk from a flour-dredger, while Tom Norris followed after, working it into the floor by long, sliding steps.

At last Mary stopped, shaking some of the chalk from her skirt. "That'll do now! Nobody can walk across the room if it's slippier than this."

Tom took a flying slide down the room. "It's grand!" he announced. "Have a turn, Polly! Daisy, play us a waltz!"

Daisy looked round. "Ah, no, Tom! I'm much too nervous! Supposing anybody came!"

"Well, and if they did, couldn't you stop? We'd hear the ring. Come on, don't be so disagreeable!"

She moved slowly towards the piano. "Isn't it frightful, Miss Maguire not being here yet! I think when you pay a person to play, the least they might do is to be punctual. What waltz do you want?"

"Anything at all, only hurry up!"

Still with reluctance, she began to play a musical comedy tune, and Tom advanced upon Mary. "Come along, Poll! We'll have a fling before anybody comes."

But Mary pushed him off with considerable vigour. "Indeed, you'll put on your gloves if you're going to dance with me!"

"What's the matter with my hands? I washed them before dinner."

"I'll stop, if you don't begin!" Daisy announced. "I'm not going to play all night, while you stand there fighting!"

Tom shrugged his shoulders, and grudgingly drew a pair of white gloves from his coat-tail pocket.

But notwithstanding her little triumph, Mary was never called upon to execute the preliminary dance; for, while Tom was still fumbling with his glove buttons, the hall-door bell pealed loudly and Daisy's waltz came to a confused end.

"Good Heavens! It's somebody!" she cried. "Miss Maguire would never attempt to ring like that. Mary, for goodness' sake, come and stand near me! I wonder where Stephen is?"

"Oh, Stephen has only just commenced to shave!"

"Hurry! Can't you hurry, Mary! I hear them coming upstairs. Tom, remember you must talk, whoever it is; and if it's any one at all *passée*, you must engage dances. Now, don't forget!"

"Don't be afraid! You won't give me a chance to. I'll never forget your picnic last year. I spent the whole of a gorgeous afternoon opening soda-water bottles; and then, when it came to evening, and I might have had some fun, I was packed off to ride home with Mrs Fisher, because she was so short-sighted she might run into something! Oh, no, Daisy, I know my place at your parties!"

"Be quiet, for goodness' sake!" whispered Daisy nervously, as the door was opened and Julia's flushed face was thrust forward.

"Miss Costello, ma'am!" she announced.

Mary, whose back was to the door, made a wry face, but Daisy looked relieved.

"Oh, Isabel!" she said. "How are you?"

Isabel stepped into the room, then paused, disconcerted at finding herself the first guest.

"Oh, I'm too early!" she said. "Our clock must be wrong."

"Not at all, Miss Costello! Not at all!" Tom came forward good - naturedly. "It's only that Waterford people think it fashionable to be late. How are you!" He took her hand, smiling with involuntary admiration.

For Isabel was radiant to-night. For the first time since the Fair Hill dance she was wearing the white muslin dress that had honoured her *début;* and with the consciousness of her finery, some of the first pride had returned. To - night, too, she was carrying an old Spanish fan, and wearing a high tortoiseshell comb, that in a moment of generosity Miss Costello had unearthed from a chest of family relics; and as she stepped into the lighted room, she brought with her an air, a distinction, that might have belonged to another generation,—a charm beside which Daisy and Mary sank into insignificance.

They both looked at her, appraising her shrewdly from her high-heeled slippers to the tip of the beautiful old comb; then Daisy stepped forward. "How are you?" she said again, a little less eagerly.

Isabel took her hand. "I must thank you about Kilmeaden," she said at once. "It's very, very kind of you!"

"Not at all!" said Daisy, a little awkwardly.
"I hope you'll come. Any time next month will
suit us; we'll be perfectly settled in a week or
two."

Isabel's lips parted to reply, but before she could
frame the words, Mary stepped forward, an aggravating little sneer on her lips. "I don't suppose
Isabel will care much for Kilmeaden."

"Oh, why not, Polly?" Tom cried. "Kilmeaden
isn't half bad, as the country goes."

"I wasn't thinking of Kilmeaden itself. I was
only wondering how she'd like the party." She
turned to Isabel. "Can you imagine yourself
having a good time with only Daisy and me and
Tom and Father Baron?"

Isabel coloured under the glance levelled at her,
for Mary's sharp green eyes could convey a multitude of words that never found vent in speech.
"I — I imagine 'twould be very nice," she said
confusedly.

Mary laughed. "Oh, that's all right, then!
And, of course, I didn't count the party quite
rightly. There'll be Stephen as well." Her glance
held the other's in a satirical, unfriendly stare.

Tom and Daisy saw nothing of the little duel of
looks; but Isabel, swift of intuition, acknowledged
the cut and thrust, and in a second pride surged
up, ousting reason, expediency, even personal
desire.

She caught her breath, and the first words that
came to her lips poured out, one upon the other.

"You didn't let me finish while ago," she said.
"I was just going to say to Mrs Carey that

I'm sure 'twould be lovely at Kilmeaden, but that I'm afraid my aunt won't be able to let me go."

Amazement spread over Daisy's face. "But why not?" she said. "I thought it was settled."

"Oh, why, Miss Costello?" Tom cried.

But like the preliminary dance, Isabel's possible explanation was forgotten in the sound of the door bell, and presently Daisy, Mary, and Tom were submerged in a sea of arriving guests.

As they disappeared from her sight, Isabel drew back against the wall. Never until that moment had she realised how poignantly interesting the visit to Kilmeaden had been—how closely she had counted on it—how vividly every hour of it had been pictured by her imagination; and as the vision crumbled, a sick sense of loss and of futility surged up, darkening the world.

While she stood there, hiding herself behind the laughing crowd, the musician passed up the room to the piano, and amid a hum of excitement partners were chosen for the first dance.

With the opening bars of the waltz the throng in front of her melted away, and immediately she was seen and seized upon.

"I thought I'd never find you!" cried the familiar voice of Willie Neville. "Give me a dance, do! The others will be up in a minute, and I won't have a chance."

She smiled vaguely. "If you like," she said, thinking it would be easier to reconcile her disappointment whirling round the room under Willie's laboured guidance than standing awkwardly alone.

So Willie had the privilege of leading her out into the circle of dancers, feeling that the eyes of every man followed him with envy.

They danced the waltz to the end; and, still elated by his triumph, he led her towards the door.

"You'll have a cup of tea, won't you?" he said, wiping his streaming forehead, for the night was hot and the dance had been long.

"Yes, I'll have some tea."

This was the extent of their conversation as they passed downstairs, a dozen noisy couples making a passage in front of them, another dozen following upon their heels; and when they entered the dining-room and Willie, still hot and beaming, forced a way to the table, she took the cup of tea from his hand with scarcely a glance.

"Aren't you enjoying yourself to-night?" he asked, struck suddenly by her silence, and moved to blunt expression.

The question roused her; she looked at him and smiled again, this time more kindly.

"Do you know, I'm not, Willie!" she said candidly; "and I wouldn't have believed it, if anybody had told me I could be at a dance and not adore it!"

"But why?" he asked.

"Because I've been a fool—and because I'm angry with myself."

"It's a great mistake to be angry with yourself," said a voice behind them, "because you'll have nobody to go to for sympathy."

The voice came with absolute unexpectedness, and Isabel's cup made a nervous little clatter in its saucer, as she turned sharply to meet Carey's eyes.

It was only a matter of half a dozen words, but their influence was magical. Interest flashed out like lightning from the black cloud of disappointment; in an instant the chatter of voices about her, the tapping of feet overhead, the hum and stir pervading the house, took on shape and meaning.

Forgetful of her partner's existence, she allowed Carey to take her empty cup, while her heart leaped at his next words.

"The second dance is beginning, will you give it to me?"

Willie Neville drew back, thinking it was unnecessary of Carey, even though he was the host, to appropriate the prettiest girl in the room, and pitying Isabel.

"Can I have another later on?" he ventured, as Carey offered his arm. And Isabel, soaring high on the wings of joy, gave him a smile such as he had never received in all his narrow life.

"Two, if you like!" she said.

Neither she nor Carey spoke as they made their way through the press of people circling round the tea-table, but outside in the hall he paused and looked down at her.

"Do you want to dance?"

"Not unless you like." She was strangely content to do as he willed.

"Then we'll sit it out!" He drew her down the hall towards two vacant chairs. "Sit down here, and tell me what the trouble is!"

There was an unfamiliar note in his voice, a suggestion of protectiveness, a hint of tenderness.

"Oh, don't remind me!" Isabel cried, real pain

in her voice. "I'm so sorry — so disappointed —
I've been such a fool."

"But how?"

She opened and closed her fan with a little
nervous movement. "Please, don't ask me! I'd
rather forget."

"Nonsense! It's worth telling, if it can make
you unhappy." It was remarkable that he, who
had once dealt so summarily with her, should be
so solicitous for her now.

"What does that matter?"

"It does matter."

"To you?"

He was silent for a moment, while the persistent
waltz was hammered out upon the piano overhead
and the feet pounded unceasing. Then at last he
answered without looking up, "Yes."

She had tempted the word, and now that it came
it disconcerted her. She reddened and, to cover
her embarrassment, rushed into speech.

"It was only that when I came here to-night,
Mrs Carey spoke to me about going to Kilmeaden;
and just when I was thanking her and going to
say that I'd love to come, Mary Norris joined in,
and——"

"Yes? Mary generally joins in."

"I can't explain it properly, but she was horrible
—she was detestable! She made me forget everything but that I hated her, and that I couldn't
take anything from — from any of them. And
so——"

"Yes?" His tone was low.

"Oh, before I had time to think, or to realise

what I was doing, I just said that I was sorry I couldn't come to Kilmeaden because Aunt Teresa couldn't spare me. 'Twas a lie, of course!"

When she had finished there was a long pause.

"You might say you're sorry!" she added in a plaintive voice.

Still Carey remained silent.

"You might say you're sorry — even if 'tisn't true!"

Ignoring her half-flippant tone, he turned to her with sudden seriousness. "But you'll have to come," he said. "You gave me your word—you promised me."

It was the first time since the early days that he had used the tone of authority, and to Isabel the familiar mastery brought a sudden thrill.

"But how can I—now?"

"You must."

"But how?" She felt like a swimmer who rejoices in the lift and drop of a strong wave. Carey was so decisive, so set to his purpose — so much a man.

"Shall I show you?" he said.

While she had been telling her story he had caught sight of his wife's figure at the top of the stairs, and the fact had held inspiration. He stood up now, and slowly and uncertainly Isabel followed.

"Come! Come, and I'll show you!"

Without giving her time to remonstrate he led her down the hall, and as they reached the foot of the staircase Daisy came down, chattering and laughing, on her partner's arm.

"Oh, Stephen!" she said, as they passed each

other, "I was wondering where you were. Do see
if anybody is wanting tea!"

But Carey paused. "Just a second, Daisy!" he
said; "MacCarthy will excuse you."

MacCarthy, the partner, immediately relinquished
his rights and passed on to the foot of the stairs,
while Daisy, looking a little surprised, remained
standing where she was, and Isabel, in sudden perturbation, let her fingers slip from Carey's arm.

"It's only that I've been talking to Miss Costello,
Daisy, and that I've got her to admit that her aunt
can very well do without her. So we may expect
her at Kilmeaden, after all."

Daisy looked relieved. "Is that all? I mean, is
it only that?" she added, smiling. "I was terrified
something was going wrong with the dance. I'm
awfully glad, Isabel! We'll fix it all to-night.
Excuse me now. I mustn't keep Mr MacCarthy."
She smiled again in a preoccupied way, and, without a shadow of misgiving, ran down the stairs.

To avoid the stream of couples that was pouring
down upon them, Carey put his hand on Isabel's
arm and drew her back against the bannister. He
was a step above her, and could look down into her
face even more easily than usual.

"Well?" he said, and in his voice there was the
ring of vitality that comes when a man has shaped
some incident of his own desires.

Had they known it then, they were standing upon
the brink: a look or a word might have sealed the
matter. But the look and the word were wanting,
for the comedy of the emotions is not played con-
sciously in such surroundings. When reality is faced

it is as a blinding light suddenly revealed, rather than as a pleasant radiance to which the eyes have grown accustomed through many surreptitious lift-ings of the veil.   Neither knew, neither understood, and, without doubt, fate smiled.

"Well?" Carey said again.

Isabel looked up—laughed—stammered.

Something alluring, something childish in her sudden shyness, changed his mood.   He bent down quickly.   "Come!" he said, "give me a dance!   I feel young to-night!"

CHAPTER XXI.

THREE weeks had passed since the night of the dance at Lady Lane. To Isabel, they had been three weeks of ordinary provincial life; yet in her unconscious psychological development, the span of time might have been three months — even three years, for in that brief chain of days she had learned to breathe a new atmosphere, to survey her life from a changed standpoint. The past days, with their favours, their failures—their friendship with Carey, blowing now hot, now cold—had been as a kaleidoscope in which her excited senses had striven to follow the bewildering patterns, weaving and unweaving themselves under her gaze; but these three weeks with their sudden dulness, their unanticipated stagnation, their consciousness that the interest that had upheld and sustained her had been abruptly withdrawn, were as the merging of the colours into a definite pattern while the mechanism slowly ceased to work.

In those monotonous hours there had been no denying that it was Carey who had given point to the weeks just passed—Carey's antagonism and Carey's interest that had made her little battles and her little conquests seem worth while; and now that

Carey no longer figured as a social quantity, social matters fell strangely flat. Tennis at the Powers' and croquet at the Nevilles' became wearisome when there was no longer the consoling thought that if the afternoon proved tedious there was still an evening at Fair Hill or elsewhere at which Stephen might unexpectedly appear; and realising this, she admitted to herself the change and the reason of the change.

She admitted it, but made no effort to alter the routine of her life, even shrinking with a new shyness from the possibility of a chance meeting with the object of her thoughts. Towards one point all her interests merged—the prospective visit to Kilmeaden. The anticipation of this she hoarded as a miser hoards his gold, bringing it forth from the recesses of her mind in the solitude of her room, dreaming of it, thrilled by the thought of it, living it over in anticipation hour by hour, moment by moment. There she would see Carey day after day, in the close intimacy of daily life, until every characteristic, every trick of voice and manner, would become as familiar as household things; and in this realm of imagination she moved, spinning the scenes from her brain, weaving of them a bridge that spanned the dull monotony that separated her from the day she craved.

Of those about her, no one marked the change, no one suspected. Had Miss Costello been questioned upon the passage of those three weeks, she would first have repudiated the idea of any alteration in her niece; and then, pressed upon the point, she would have grudgingly admitted that perhaps Isabel

had spent more time in her own room, had walked
oftener into the country, and had generally made
life less turbulent since their acquaintances had
begun to go out of town and Waterford gaieties
had diminished.

So the circle of the weeks wore round with a little
gossip, a little shopping, a little tennis, and a formal
visit or two, until the great day dawned.

Isabel was up at five, to scan the first pearly sky
tints that presaged brilliant weather, though if the
heavens had opened upon that particular morning
it would not have counted one black mark against
the day's favour. She came down to breakfast the
incarnation of joy, and never had Miss Costello been
allowed to enjoy a meal under circumstances so
serene. She talked of the weather, of her journey,
of the country; she questioned and re-questioned
her aunt upon the subject of Kilmeaden; she
burned to know what the house was like—whether
the grounds were large — if there were stables?
Everything interested her, she took everything in
good part.

Then came the last touches to the packing, practically completed days before; and to participa-
tion in this sacred act she invited Miss Costello,
laughing and talking incessantly as she folded away
the last handkerchief, the last tulle bow.

Everything was ready a full hour too soon, for
it was at eleven that the Skerrybeg carriage was
to call at New Town on its way to Kilmeaden,
from whence it was to bear Mrs Power back to
Waterford after a week's visit to the Careys.

Isabel had helped Lizzie to carry the trunk downstairs, and was now sitting on it in the hall, as she drew on her gloves.

"Well, and when will you be back?" Miss Costello asked.

"I don't know, Auntie. She said a week."

"Very well so! I'll be looking out for you next Monday."

"Unless I write."

"Oh, of course, unless you write. If they ask you to stay on, don't refuse. 'Twill be the only outing you'll get this summer, and you re looking a little pale."

"Pale, Auntie? Am I?" She put her hand apprehensively to her cheek.

"Well, not to-day. You have colour enough to-day. I'm thinking of lately; you looked a little washy lately."

"Washy? How horrible!" She jumped up and walked out into the garden. The small grass plot was beginning to turn yellow in the summer heat, and in the long bed where the russet wall-flowers had once raised sturdy heads the earth was brown and parched, and the blue of the lobelias and the red of the geraniums were marred by city dust.

"You ought to water the poor flowers, Auntie."

"I ought," said Miss Costello helplessly.

"But will you?"

"I will. I'll get Lizzie to do it when she's washed up after tea this evening."

Isabel shook her head; then she looked up at the hot white sky. "How heavenly the country will be! Is it eleven yet?"

"Just."

"Then the car will be here in a minute. Oh, Auntie, just imagine!"

"You're very excited about it."

Isabel turned away from her aunt's scrutiny, only to see Lizzie peering at her from behind the curtain of the parlour window, and at the same moment the Powers' fat bay horse came ambling up the hill, and the roomy brougham drew up, entirely dwarfing the little gate.

At the visible symbol of social rank, Isabel gave a gasp. "Oh, Auntie, if we only had a man to bring out the trunk. Lizzie looks so fearful!"

"Sure, I'll ask the coachman." Miss Costello stepped forward across the garden.

"Auntie! Don't! Oh, don't!"

"What nonsense, child! Why wouldn't I? Your grandfather kept a footman and a coachman. Good morning!" she added in a louder voice to the lethargic-looking individual on the box-seat of the brougham. "Good morning! There's a little portmanteau inside in the hall, would you mind coming in for it?"

Silently, and with obvious reluctance, the fat coachman fastened up his reins. A long and lazy life in Mrs Power's service had left him unwieldy both of mind and body, and Isabel held her breath as she saw him descend laboriously from his seat.

"We'd better call Lizzie, Auntie," she whispered.

"Not at all, child! Not at all!" Miss Costello was enjoying the unwonted position of director in any affair.

"But how will he ever lift the trunk!"

"Be quiet, can't you!" Miss Costello ran forward fussily and opened the little gate as the coachman stepped to the ground. "Yes! Yes! Up here!" she explained, guiding her unwilling henchman up the strip of garden. "It looks a little big, but it's really no weight at all. I'd think nothing of lifting it myself, and the girl——" She faltered as she caught Isabel's eye. "One— one of the maids brought it downstairs by herself."

Under this fire of words he advanced, breathing heavily, and paused before Isabel's big black school trunk.

"'Tis a fine bit of a portmanteau," he said with sarcasm; and disdaining further comment, stooped and lifted it ponderously to his shoulders.

There was a strained moment of uncertainty as he tottered under the weight and swayed down the path; then Isabel clasped her hands in an agony of apprehension. "Oh, Auntie, why did you? Why did you? He'll get apoplexy or something; and Mrs Power thinks more of him than of any of the family. Look, he'll never get it up on the box-seat! Quick, Auntie! Quick!" Even as she spoke she saw his great bulk yield under its burden, and, rushing forward, she was barely in time to scramble to the box-seat, seize a strap, and drag the trunk into place.

Having saved the situation, she jumped to the ground again, flushed but triumphant. "I've torn my glove—but it's up!" she announced. "Now, I suppose, we're ready!"

With his dignity too much ruffled to permit of speech, Roger, the coachman, climbed slowly to his seat and untied his reins.

"Such nonsense!" Miss Costello muttered. "Sure, I could lift it myself!"

"Well, it's all right now, Auntie, and the great thing is Lizzie wasn't seen. Good-bye!" With sudden enthusiasm, she threw her arms about her aunt's neck.

"Good-bye! Get in now." On pretext of opening the door, Miss Costello peered curiously into the recesses of the brougham. "It's a nice, roomy carriage," she said, enjoying the mere use of the word.

"I wish you were coming, Auntie."

"Well, sure we can't have everything! Have you your purse safe?"

"I have; but, Auntie, are you sure two shillings will be enough to give the parlour-maid?"

"Too much, if anything."

"And, Auntie," Isabel lowered her voice fearfully, "do you think *he'll* expect anything for bringing down the trunk?"

She nodded towards the broad back looming against the front window.

"Indeed, then, let him expect! Good-bye, child!"

"Good-bye, Auntie!"

The door of the brougham was closed, the signal for departure given, and the fat bay horse started off at a cautious trot.

As long as the little house was in sight, Isabel leant out of the window, waving to the gaunt figure of Miss Costello; but, as both house and figure were gradually merged in the suburban picture, she drew back into the cushioned seat and gave herself up to the pleasure of the moment.

At any time this drive would have been a delight,
for all her nature yearned towards the pleasantness
of life; but to-day the delight was subtly enhanced,
being the mere preface to all that was to come.   The
road from Waterford to Kilmeaden has no particular beauty: it is a wide, level road, now open to
the sweep of the winds, again arched over and
shadowed by thick clumps of trees, but the way
made little difference,—it was all an enchanted
pathway leading to the unknown.

Lover of speed though she was, she felt no impatience at the ambling trot of the over-fed horse;
if anything, she would have prolonged the drive,
and regret was mingled with her excitement when
at last the handful of houses dignified by the name
of Kilmeaden came into view, the carriage turned
off into a side road, and she realised that it was
a matter of minutes before her destination was
reached and her curiosity satisfied for good and all.

Turning out of the high-road, they made their way
down a narrow lane, skirted a stream in which a
band of ducks were splashing and quacking, and
lurched across a small stone bridge; then for a
few hundred yards they passed between high hawthorn hedges that enclosed them in a bower of scent
and blossom, until these in turn gave place to a low
fence that girded a stretch of cornfield, and beyond
the waving grain Isabel caught her first glimpse
of the Careys' house.

To know this house, one should know Ireland.
Companion houses to it are to be found by the
dozen in every one of the counties, though the date
of their building and the style of their architecture

are alike impossible to place. The similarity lies in the white-washed exterior, in the solitariness of position, in the air of homely dilapidation so racy of the soil. There is something sad, perhaps, to alien eyes, in these neglected, isolated dwellings; but to one who has ever called such a place home, there is a thrill in the white walls looming out of the neutral-tinted landscape, a memory in the very cracks and blisters on the painted door, in the very rattle of the sashes in the high window frames.

A five-barred iron gate gave access to the avenue, which was more a narrow roadway than a drive and ran in a straight line across the green and marshy fields to the doorway of the house. In winter these fields were wont to degenerate into bogland, but now in the heat of summer they were a shimmering carpet, golden with buttercups, on which a dozen cows browsed peacefully. As a vague background to the picture, Isabel acknowledged this haze of gold; but her glance, her burning interest, centred on the house itself—the white house, with its shabby door standing ajar, its many windows looking out like kindly eyes over the calm green country.

A thrill of pleasure and hope passed through her, and she rose from her seat almost before the carriage stopped.

At the same moment, seemingly from nowhere, Daisy appeared at the open door, looking healthy and sun-burned, and suggestive of country life.

"Ah, there you are, Isabel! I was in the garden with Mrs Power, picking strawberries, when I heard the carriage. How are you? Let me help you out!

Julia!" she turned, calling back into the house,
"get some one to carry up Miss Costello's trunk!"

Then again she turned back to Isabel. "Will
you come into the garden first," she asked, "and see
Mrs Power? We're all by ourselves: Father James
is reading his office somewhere, and Mary went up
to town this morning to do some shopping. Roger,
you can take the horse round to the stable. Mrs
Power won't be going till two."

"Very well, ma'am," said Roger, still upon his
dignity; "an', indade, 'tis a rest the poor baste 'll
want!"

Still chatting and inconsequent, Daisy led her
visitor through the square, airy hall, whose only
furniture was a stand crowded with straw hats of
every age and shape, and a large deal table on which
were ranged a row of cleanly red flower-pots filled
with musk.

From the hall they passed into the drawing-
room, and here again was the sense of air and
space. The room was high; a flood of light poured
into it from two long windows that looked upon
the fields, and a mellow greenness flooded in from
the garden through a glass door at the farther end.
There were some good old pieces of furniture here,
relics of the former owner, and a feeling of homeliness and use pervaded the place : there were flowers
in the vases, an open work-basket stood on the
centre table, a novel of Tolstoy's lay on the top
of the piano.

But these things came subconsciously to Isabel,
for Daisy hurried forward, giving no time for close
observation, and presently the two had passed

through the glass door, and were walking down the old garden path overgrown by moss and weeds. The garden itself accorded with the house, it was an acre of ground run wild with vegetation; gnarled apple-trees ranged side by side with black-branched pear-trees and immense, luxuriant gooseberry bushes, while about their roots a riotous undergrowth of rhubarb, strawberries, lavender, and thyme flourished untended and unchecked. It was a bewildering tangle of greenness, scent, and country freshness, and Isabel paused, enchanted.

"I don't wonder you come here!" she said. "I love this place."

Daisy looked gratified. "Oh, I don't know! 'Tisn't a bad old house, but the garden is a terrible wilderness. I'm always at Stephen to get it put into some sort of order, for I'm really ashamed when people like Mrs Power and Mrs Burke, who have such lovely gardens of their own, come out here. But he's so queer; he likes it as it is."

"Indeed I agree with him. I'd a thousand times rather have it than Skerrybeg or Fair Hill."

"Would you, really? I wouldn't. But here's Mrs Power!"

Mrs Power, in an old black cashmere dress, with an alarmingly unbecoming garden-hat tied under her chin, emerged from a side path: her skirt was tucked up under one arm, and she was carrying a cabbage-leaf full of strawberries.

"And so here's the visitor!" she cried. "How are you, Isabel, dear? Did Roger bring you down safely? And what's the news in Waterford?"

Without waiting for an answer, she kissed

Isabel warmly, and broke into another flow of words.

"Let me look at you, now! Indeed you have quite a colour after your drive down. I suppose they're roasted to death up in town with all this dry weather? Josephine tells me that the lawn at home is more like tow than grass, for the want of a drop of rain."

"Indeed, yes," agreed Isabel. "Every place is parched with the heat and the dust."

"We're near a change, though!" Daisy looked up at the sky, where some copper-coloured clouds were gathering in the west.

"Well, indeed, please God, we are! The country will be destroyed if this goes on much longer. Though, to be sure, the heat is good for the strawberries. Have one, Isabel?"

Isabel was about to comply, but Daisy put her hand over the cabbage-leaf.

"Ah, no, Mrs Power! You'll spoil her appetite for lunch, and we have a nice roast chicken. Would you like to go up to your room, Isabel, before the bell rings?"

"Of course she would!" Mrs Power broke in. "I'll take her up; I have to wash my own hands before lunch."

"All right, Mrs Power! The back-room over the drawing-room. That'll be your window, Isabel!" She indicated one of the windows overlooking the garden.

"How lovely! I'll adore the view!" Isabel smiled in involuntary pleasure, and, with a still further lifting of the heart, followed Mrs Power through the drawing-room and hall, and up the wide, clean staircase, where again she was assailed by the delicious, old-fashioned scent of musk.

Without ceremony, Mrs Power opened the bedroom door and walked in.

"I suppose I may wash my hands here?"

"Of course, Mrs Power! Let me pour out the water for you." With her all-pervading sense of pleasure and anticipation, Isabel hurried forward and filled up the quaint basin with its wonderful design of castles and birds and trees, while Mrs Power laid down the leaf of strawberries and began to draw off her rings.

"Thanks, dear! And I suppose you're delighted to be in the country?"

"Indeed I am. Indeed, yes."

"That's right! And now tell me did you see much of them at Skerrybeg while I was away?"

"I saw Maurice and Eddy and Walter on Saturday, Mrs Power, and I saw Josephine yesterday."

Mrs Power walked to the washstand and buried her hands in the water. "And did you see Owen at all?" she asked in a tone that was carefully diplomatic.

Isabel looked round quickly, but there was nothing to be read from the ample back in its cashmere draperies. "No, Mrs Power," she said honestly, "I didn't."

Mrs Power picked up the soap, and there was the swiftness of relief in the gesture. "Didn't you, now?" she said. "Didn't you, now? Owen is a funny boy, Isabel. I won't be sorry when he takes it into his head to settle down. You know, I used to have great hopes once that he and Mary Norris would take a fancy to one another."

There was a pause. "And why didn't they?" Isabel said at last with elaborate indifference.

Mrs Power shook the water from her hands and took up the towel. "Well, Isabel," she said, still keeping her back turned, "between you and me, I believe they did. But lately a little bird has whispered to me that somebody has come between them. Could you guess at all who the somebody is?"

To her intense annoyance, Isabel felt her face grow red. "I, Mrs Power? How could I?"

Then at last Mrs Power turned round. "Ah, now, Isabel," she said with a change of tone, "don't be pretending! You know very well that you're a good deal a more attractive girl than Mary, and that any man in the world may lose his head over a pretty face!"

Isabel's flush deepened, deepened painfully. With the quickness of her race, she saw Mrs Power's intentions as plainly as we see the wares through the glass of a shop-window. It was a case of Frank Carey over again, smoothed this time by kindness and placid dislike of a scene, but fundamentally the same.

"Oh, Mrs Power," she cried, "if you think that I want to spoil Owen's chances — to come between him and Mary Norris, you make a great, great mistake!"

Mrs Power was alarmed. "My dear, my dear, I never said——"

"I know you didn't. But, all the same, I see—I

understand. Owen has a future before him, and
Mary Norris has position and a fortune."

Horror and pain crossed Mrs Power's face. "My
dear, my dear," she cried in distress, "what are
you saying? You don't surely think that I'd have
Owen—or any son of mine—marry for money or
position or any such thing as that? It's only that
Mary is a nice sensible girl—and the Norrises are
such old friends,—and that Owen bicycled out
three evenings since I've been here, and so I half
thought——"

Isabel laughed—laughed suddenly and almost
rudely—"Oh, don't try to explain, Mrs Power!
Please, please don't! I understand so very well."

For a moment Mrs Power hung upon the brink
of dire offence; then tact, and the consciousness of
a difficult deed accomplished, soothed her hurt pride,
and she came forward with her motherly arms
extended.

"Ah, now, Isabel, you're not to take it in bad
part! Don't see offence where there's no offence
meant. Girls are thoughtless things, and I just
made up my mind this morning to give you a hint
of how the land lies. But it's all over now, and I
must run and take my hat off."

With all the old motherly warmth she kissed
Isabel's averted cheek and hurried from the room;
but, long after the door had closed, Isabel stood
where she had left her in the centre of the room,
oddly conscious that something had chilled the
warmth of the day—that, looking truly into the
heart of things, she stood alone in this circle of the
prosperous and worldly-wise.

CHAPTER XXII.

BITTERNESS reigned in Isabel's mind, rebellion surged in her blood, and her cheeks were hot as she brushed her thick black hair and set her dress in order for the coming meal; and justification lay at the bottom of the rebellion, making its goad the keener. She was one of those whom Nature has moulded for life's easy ways. As the child of a rich man, her qualities would have shone as jewels in a fine setting: her exaggerated pride would have passed for dignity, her reckless independence for strength of character, her passionate impulsiveness for feminine charm, and, lapped in security, hedged round by the impregnable barriers of position, her nature would have expanded, softened, matured, until at last she glided into womanhood; but heredity had shaped the mould, and fate had disposed of the modelled clay. In the fairy tale, Cinderella has but to await the Prince, but upon the stage of middle-class Irish life the godmother's wand has lost its cunning, the rags remain merely rags, and the lean mice gnaw the pumpkin. To girls such as Isabel, the future is cruelly stereotyped: a year or two of social success, while the face and personality are new to the limited circle, then the slow decline of that ardent popularity, the imperceptible drawing out of the years, until eighteen merges into twenty-eight, and the girl wakes up with alarm to find that a newer band of pleasure-seekers is pouring back from the convent schools, ousting her from her supremacy. And then? The question is very poignant. In no country in the world does the feminine mind shrink more sensitively from the stigma of old maid than in Ireland, where the woman-worker—the woman of broad interests—exists only as a rare type. There is, of course, the convent always looming, a large possibility in the Catholic mind, and many are the lives that find abiding peace in its placid grey monotony: but it is not the woman of Isabel's stamp who girds herself in the habit of religion; neither is it the woman of this stamp who can subdue her pride to the petty difficulties, the slow drudgery, that in Ireland spells self-support. Such women either marry or they do not marry; and in that simple statement is comprised the tragedy of existence.

Some glimmering of this immense question was shadowing her youth as she twisted up her splendid hair, and the sombre fear of it was darkening her eyes as she slowly descended the clean, bare staircase in answer to the summoning lunch-bell.

In the hall Daisy was waiting for her.

"Ah, there you are!" she began at once. "Come into the dining-room! There's only Father James and Mrs Power. Ted generally has his dinner at our lunch-time, but he has a cold these last few days and the doctor is keeping him in bed."

The dining-room, like the rest of the house, was

clean and scantily furnished, and to Isabel's eyes it
instantly suggested the refectory of a monastery
in its simple severity. The two other guests were
already seated when she entered, and an appetising
smell was coming from the uncovered dishes of
chicken and ham.

"Ah, there you are, Daisy, dear!" cried Mrs
Power. "Come on at once—I'm simply starving.
I tried to tempt Father James to begin carving,
but he was altogether too punctilious."

Daisy laughed. "What nonsense! He knows
I wouldn't mind. Here's Isabel Costello, Father
James!" She led Isabel round the table and then
took her own place. "And now, who's going to
cut up the things?" she added. "Mrs Power,
will you?"

"Ah, no, Daisy, dear! You carve beautifully,"
objected Mrs Power, who was incorrigibly lazy.

"Sure, I'll do the two, child!" said Father James.
"Bring the dishes down here to me, Julia! And
how are you, Miss Isabel! 'Tis a long time since
we met—and then it was only once,—but I have a
good remembrance of you all the same, and I hope
you haven't forgotten me." He took Isabel's hand
with all the kindly warmth in which his soul
abounded; and as ice inevitably thaws in strong
sunshine, the bitterness in Isabel's heart softened.

She looked up at him and smiled.

"No, I haven't forgotten you."

"That's right, child! That's right! We'll be
great friends yet. Now, Daisy, what'll you have?
A bit of the wing?"

And so on, consulting everybody's taste, unceasingly cheerful and kindly, he carved the chicken, supplementing each portion with a piece of ham that would have fed a ploughman.

"Well," said Daisy, when the meal was in progress, "so you went to read your office before lunch? I saw you starting off when we were in the garden."

Father James laughed and then shook his head guiltily. "Peccavi! Peccavi!" he said. "I did start off with my breviary and the best of intentions; but as luck would have it, I took a look up at the nursery window, and I going down the path——"

Daisy laughed as well. "Oh, Father James, I guess——"

"Indeed, I suppose you do! Faith, they're great young tempters, those sons of yours. Up I went, telling myself 'twould only be for a minute; but between playing horses and playing bear, I only got off in time to wash my hands!"

In this manner—in homely talk and homely laughter—the lunch drew to a close; and presently the chime of the old gilt clock in the drawing-room floated across the hall, announcing two o'clock.

Mrs Power started—if so alert a word could be applied to her round and comfortable person. "Good gracious, Daisy, is that two o'clock? And I haven't a bit of my packing done. Come up with me, like an angel, and help me to fold my things!"

Daisy rose. "And what'll you do, Father James? Make another attempt at your office?"

"Well, no," said Father James, rising slowly. "I'll read it later on, when you're all at tea. Now I think I'll take Miss Isabel for a walk, if she has nothing better to do."

Whether he divined that Isabel might feel neglected when the other two retired it is impossible to say, but his eyes were even more than usually kind as they rested on her face.

She sprang up in ready response. "Oh, thanks, Father Baron! I'd love to go with you."

"That's right! That's right!" he said. "But remember I'm Father James to everybody in this house. Run on now, like a good child, and get your hat, so we won't be wasting any time. The day is calling out for somebody to come and enjoy it."

Again Isabel smiled at him. "But I don't want a hat; I love the sun on my face."

"Ah, that's right! I like to hear you say that! We can't have too much of anything the Almighty gives us. I often go out myself, when 'tis pouring rain, and walk up my bit of a mountain at Scarragh till I'm drenched through and through. Come on now, and I'll show you the path to the wood that they all put so much pass on! Good-bye for the present, Mrs Power! I'll see you before you start; and maybe you'd do a little message for me up in town?"

"Indeed, I will, Father James! A hundred, if you like. Come along, Daisy! You know how impatient Roger is, and I'm sure he has the horse tackled."

The two women departed, and Isabel and Father

James passed out into the hall and through the open door.

The sun was brilliant, though the copper clouds were still banked in the west, and the fields of buttercups shimmered pure gold. Isabel paused involuntarily to drink in the beauty of the scene.

"How splendid it is!" she said. "How free it is!"

A serious look came over the old priest's face. "You may well say that, child!" he said. "'Tis what I say to myself every day out on the side of my mountain, when I watch every little plant filling its own place, and see every change and season working its own end. Indeed, I'd pity no man that had eyes to see — and the country to live in."

He said it so simply, with such infinite earnestness, that again Isabel felt her heart go out to him in sudden sympathy. In the same manner —by this same selflessness—he had won his way with many a sinner in the dim confessional, hearing the old, human tale of temptation and of fall from lips that would have remained closed to pleading or to reason. The man showed himself so naïvely, that his very confidence drew kindred revelation; and in the silence that followed, while they walked together over the flower-covered grass, Isabel felt for the first time what it might be to know the intimate love of father and mother; and something of loss—of dim, vague longing—surged up within her.

As though he divined her thought, his next words were intimate and personal.

"Well, child," he said gently, as they neared the fir wood that bordered the fields, "and what sort of a place do you find the world?"

Isabel started. "The world?" she said quickly. "I—I don't quite know."

He smiled, a wise, indulgent smile. "You haven't made up your mind yet? Well, you're young. You're young."

"How made up my mind?"

"Well, about your future—about what you'll be doing with yourself. You'll have to be making up your mind about it some day, you know. None of us are let off that penalty."

She glanced up quickly, almost fearfully. "My future? How do you mean?"

"Well, I mean that you'll have to be choosing your state in life. You'll have to be getting married or going into a convent one of these fine days—I won't say the word 'old maid.'"

Isabel laughed, but her laugh was tremulous. "I could never be a nun."

"And I'm not so sure that I'd be asking you, child. 'Tis a grand life, no doubt—a grand calling, —but, after all, a wife is a grander calling still. Look at Daisy, now!" He paused to let the words sink in, and Isabel kept silent, her eyes fixed upon the fir-trees.

"Look at Daisy, now!" he said again. "She's not a clever girl; she's not a remarkable girl; she'd make only a very ordinary sort of a nun—but she's a good mother to those three boys of hers; and in time to come there'll be three men at least that'll think her the finest woman in the world. Now,

if that isn't something, I don't know what to
say."

Isabel flushed. "I'd hate to be like Daisy!"

The old priest showed no perturbation at the
violence of the tone. "You needn't trouble yourself about that," he said gently, "because you
couldn't be, even if you tried. We're all as God
made us.'

"For one thing, I'll never marry a Waterford
man!"

"And why is that?"

"Because I know too well what they're like."

"And what's that, child?"

"Oh, dull and narrow-minded and stupid."

They were close to the fir wood now, and Father
James paused and looked at her with new seriousness. "Isabel, child," he said, "you must never say
a thing like that. There are men as good and as
fine and as clever, too, in these towns of ours as ever
you'd find in the big cities. Maybe they don't show
up like the other people, but take my word for
it, they're there. Look at Stephen Carey, for
instance!"

He may have said it innocently, he may have said
it with meaning; but whatever his intention, the
result was instant and definite. The blood mounted
to Isabel's face, words flew to her lips.

"Oh, but Mr Carey! How can you compare Mr
Carey to the others? If he had never settled down
in Ireland—if only he was in England or America,
what a great man he might have been!"

Surprise crossed the old priest's eyes. He had
scarcely expected such an outburst as this; it was

deeper water than he had looked to plumb. But he continued to walk on, encouraging her by his calm.

"And so you think Stephen might be a great man?"

"Indeed, yes. Indeed, I do."

"And I'm not so sure, child, that I don't agree with you. Stephen has the stuff in him."

Isabel threw up her head with one of her swift impulses, and her steps quickened to her quickening enthusiasm.

"Yes; he could rise to anything, if he had the chance."

Father James did not reply at once, but with a very thoughtful gesture he rubbed his shaven chin.

"Yes, yes, yes, child!" he said at last. "Maybe you're right! Most likely you're right! But I have queer notions myself about things like that. I'm an old man now, and within measuring distance of the grave, and do you know what my life has taught me?"

She glanced at him in quick interrogation.

"It has taught me this, child, that it's a false thing ever to be saying that if this man had his chance and if that man had his chance, they'd have done this thing and done that thing, for 'tis a bigger mind than yours or mine that put them where they are—and they're working out bigger things than you or I could ever put our tongue to." They had reached the end of the path, and instead of climbing the stile that led into the wood, Father James seated himself on the lowest step, and with great deliberation stooped down and drew into light a tiny fern growing in the interstices of the stone.

"Look here, Isabel!" he said. 'The Almighty set this fern between these stones, and if He thought 'twould thrive better between the paving-stones of a street, do you think He'd be waiting for you or me to tell Him He ought to have put it there?"

Isabel turned her flushed face to the sun. "Oh, but that's exaggerated. I don't think God ever meant us to be satisfied with things as they are. If we all sat down and did nothing, how would the world move on?".

Again Father James rubbed his chin. Then he smiled, his shrewd, kind, lenient smile.

"Child," he said, "did you ever hear of a man called Æsop?"

"I have heard of Æsop's Fables," she said, a little impatiently.

"Well, then, did you ever hear the story about the fly on the wheel?"

"No, I did not."

"Very well, then, I'll tell it to you." And settling himself in his seat, he began the homely story as he might a fairy tale to a little child.

"Well, now, to begin at the beginning, there was a fly one fine day long ago sat himself down on the axle of a chariot-wheel; and after a while he took it into his head that the chariot wasn't going fast enough, so what does he do but speak to the mule that was drawing it. 'How slow you are, my fine mule!' says he. 'Take care that you won't find me giving you a sting to hurry you on!' But, faith, the mule knew too much for him! ''Tis very little

I care for your sting,' says he; 'I only care about him that sits above you, and that hurries me on with the whip or keeps me back with the reins. So bother me no more, for I go fast or go slow without your ordering.'"

When he had finished, Isabel made another movement of quick impatience. "What a silly story," she said. "I don't see the point at all."

"Don't you?"

"I don't."

"Don't you see that life is the chariot and that we are the flies—all of us, the clever ones like Stephen, and the stupid ones like me—and that the chariot is driven by some great big power that knows what we don't know. I agree with you, child, that Stephen is a fine man, and I'm telling you the plain truth when I say that I'd give my life's blood to save him from harm. But, by the grace of God, he can be as fine a man in Waterford as ever he could be in London or New York—and I'd be sorry to believe otherwise."

A curious, defiant look passed over Isabel's face.

"I don't think that. I'll never think it!"

Very slowly Father James got to his feet. "Very well, child, have it your own way!" he said. "But life is long, and we change our opinions many a time before we travel the whole road. There's the carriage coming round from the yard, and we must say good-bye to Mrs Power; but take my advice and don't forget about the fly on the wheel."

CHAPTER XXIII.

For the rest of that day Father James was a more or less silent observer of the house and its inmates : with his native shrewdness he watched Mrs Power's effusive farewell to Isabel, and read in her smiles and nods and whisperings with Daisy the maternal conviction that at last the most wayward of her flock was to be safely shepherded into the fold of respectability ; then with his well-thumbed breviary under his arm, and his shabby clerical hat shading the sun from his eyes, he betook himself to the garden, and as he walked up and down under the apple-trees, muttering his office with the simple earnestness he brought to every duty, a sub-conscious portion ₒof his mind was strained to catch the sound of voices from the drawing-room, where Daisy sat entertaining her guest.

He was not an inquisitive man, but he admitted to himself in the pauses of his devotions that he would have given a good deal to overhear that conversation, the gist and manner of that entertainment ; and when across the still, hot air of the garden he caught the rattle of an opening door and the light tinkle of teacups, his interest sprang up, and he was ready with eyes and ears alert when

Daisy appeared with suspicious alacrity at the french window.

"Father James!" she called. "Father James, isn't your office finished yet? Tea is in, and you simply must have a cup."

A little smile crossed Father James's eyes, but his lips were serious as he closed his book obediently, blessed himself, and came slowly down the mossy path.

"Faith, 'tis fashionable you'll be making me, with your afternoon tea, Daisy!" he said pleasantly, as he stepped through the long window. "When I get back to Scarragh, I'll be ordering Bridget to call my two-o'clock dinner lunch, if I'm not careful. Isn't that the way, Miss Isabel?"

Isabel was half-sitting, half-lying in a wicker-chair that had been converted into a piece of drawing-room furniture by the aid of muslin cushions. At the priest's words she roused herself; and as she turned towards him, he was struck afresh by her personality—the conflicting tenseness and languor of her pose, the smouldering expectancy in her eyes, the curve and colour of her mouth; and with a touch of instinct he divined where her thoughts had been during the dull hour with Daisy.

"I wish I could order our servant, Lizzie, to call our dinner lunch," she said smilingly. "I love late dinner and afternoon tea and all nice things."

Daisy's refinement was slightly outraged by this bluntness, and she paused in her ministrations at the tea-table.

"I don't know how anybody can bother about

meals," she said. "I think having to eat at all is a great nuisance. I could never care about it myself."

"Oh, I adore eating — eating things that are nice!"

"Do you? Wasn't it Lord Byron who could never bear to see a woman eat?"

Isabel laughed. "'Twas well he never met me! Do you think it really matters, Father James, if nice things make you feel fearfully greedy—feel that you must have them?"

Father James looked out of the window. "I suppose we ought to curb our appetites, child," he said, but his tone was awkward, for preaching out of his church was a thing he abhorred.

"Oh, why?" Isabel cried interestedly. "Why, when life is so horribly short?"

"Don't, Isabel!" Daisy broke in nervously. "I hate to hear people talking like that. I suppose we all must die some time, but what's the good of thinking of it?"

"Oh, I don't know!" Isabel threw herself back in her chair and turned her face to the sun. "I don't care what happens to me when I'm old; I only want to live every second of the time while I am young."

But Father James, who was still standing by the window, put up his hand. "Listen!" he said. "Isn't that Stephen's motor?"

"The motor-car!" In a flash Isabel's body was galvanised into life: she sprang up and ran across the room.

Daisy looked round, a little contemptuous of her

excitement. "Yes, that's the car," she said placidly. "We're quite used to it by now, only I wish Stephen wouldn't sound the horn at the gate; it wakes baby, and then he's so hard to manage." She laid aside the tea-caddy and the silver tea-spoon and slowly followed Isabel across the room.

"Won't you come out and meet them?" she added, looking from one to the other of her guests.

Father James obeyed the invitation, following her into the hall; but for some unexplained reason Isabel hung back at the drawing-room door, and from her solitary position listened with a beating heart to the stopping of the car and the confused greetings of Daisy, Father James, Mary, and Tom Norris.

Meanwhile the old priest, with senses alert, was looking for one set of circumstances—Carey's attitude, Carey's first words. He alone of the little group marked his expression as he stretched his long limbs after the tension of the drive; he alone heard his first words.

"Isn't Miss Costello here?"

It had come then, Father James told himself—the moment he had waited for and dreaded, almost as a mother dreads her son's first lapse from virtue! His heart contracted, then expanded again in sudden, ineffable love and compassion. Stephen, the boy he had instructed for the sacraments, the man he had married, never needed friendship as he needed it now in this hour of coming storm! He went forward as Carey entered the house, and took his hand in a warm pressure.

"Well, boy!" he said affectionately. "Daisy and

Miss Costello and myself are waiting for our tea till
you'd come."

Carey's hand tightened on his.

"So Miss Costello is here?"

"Yes; in the drawing-room over."

Father James stood aside to let him pass, and his
glance was keen as a knife as he slowly followed
and saw the meeting of the two.

The sun was enveloping Isabel in a mantle of
gold as she came forward to offer her tardy greeting; and to Carey's eager gaze, stray shafts of it
seemed to lurk in her hazel eyes, lighting them to
strange new fire. His nature leaped in consciousness of her beauty, as he took her warm hand.

"What ages 'tis since I have seen you! And
how well you look!"

"Ages!" she repeated unthinkingly, and let her
fingers lie in his, while her lips, her eyes, her
whole radiant face, gave unconscious point to the
word.

"I'm glad to see you!" he said. "Very glad!"

Then their hands fell apart as Father James,
hearing Mary's sharp voice in the hall, came gently
up to them.

"Well, Miss Isabel, and what about our tea?"

Isabel laughed—a low laugh of absolute delight.

"Father James! Father James, you must curb
your appetite! Father James has been lecturing
me on my greediness." Her eyes again sought
Carey's, unable to repress the excitement welling
in them.

"What! Lecturing you? Why, that's tres-
passing on my preserves! I don't allow any one

to lecture Miss Costello but myself, Father James.
She's had many a bad half-hour with me!"

Isabel laughed again. Life was a glorious thing!
A tempting, radiant, dancing thing, all glitter of
sun and sheen of flowers! What if Daisy were
dull and Mary bitter, and all the world of women
heartless and scheming! Carey had come—Carey's
eyes had lighted at sight of her—Carey's hand had
held hers in a long, close pressure!

She turned, her whole being joyous and alive, as
Tom Norris came into the drawing-room, while
Daisy and Mary waited to whisper together in the
hall.

Tom's face expressed involuntary admiration.
"Hallo, Miss Isabel! There you are! And, 'pon
my word, it does me good to look at you! How
on earth do you manage to keep that colour, when
all Waterford is as washed out as a corpse from
the heat and dust? 'Tis wonderful! 'Tis indeed!"
He took her hand cordially, then turned to greet
Father James. "And is that you, Father James!
'Tis a cure for sore eyes to see you! I thought
you had deserted us altogether. But, do you know
what! I believe there's work for you brewing outside there." He nodded jocosely over his shoulder
to the hall, from whence little gasps and laughs
and whisperings came in the voices of the sisters.

"What is it you mean, Tom?"

Tom laughed. "Ah, don't be curious! You'll
know all in good time. I have only my suspicions
as yet."

"What's that, Tom?" said Carey.

"Have patience! Have patience, I tell you!

All in good time! All in good time!" And Tom laughed again in the pleased, mysterious way of one who could say much, did he care to speak.

Carey turned away uninterestedly. "Have it your own way!" he said. "Miss Costello, how do you like my garden? Come and have a look at it now, with the sun on the apple-trees." He walked to the french window, and Isabel followed him eagerly.

As they disappeared, Daisy and Mary entered from the hall. They were both flushed, and Mary held herself even more independently than usual. Daisy looked round the room, and seeing that only the priest and her brother were present, she ran forward to Father James.

"Father James," she cried breathlessly. "Father James, do you know what! I have such a secret —such news. Mary and Owen are engaged! Oh, how delighted Mrs Power will be!"

Father James beamed all over his kindly rugged face. Whatever faults Mary Norris might have, she was one of his many children. It was inevitable that he should rejoice in her happiness.

"Do you tell me so, child?" he said. "Do you tell me so? Well, all I can say is Master Owen is getting a good wife! God bless you, Mary, child! God bless you! Does Stephen know, Daisy?"

Daisy looked round, still smiling in her pride and gratification. "Stephen? No!" Then a look of surprise crossed her smile. "But where is Stephen? I thought he was here."

Father James said nothing; but Tom answered readily and unsuspiciously.

"Stephen! Oh, Stephen has gone to show Isabel the sun on his apple-trees."

"The sun on the apple-trees?" repeated Daisy, laughing. "How ridiculous! What it is to have a hobby!"

"What it is to have an imagination!" said Mary with a dry little laugh.

. . . .

Dinner that night was quite a gay affair. The announcement of Mary's engagement gave an excuse for festivity, and Daisy felt pleased and flattered that even Stephen—the self-contained, sarcastic Stephen — should give himself up to the moment. Talk never flagged from the soup to the dessert, when Mary's health was drunk in port specially decanted for the occasion. There was something peculiar, something electric in the atmosphere. Mary was keenly conscious of it; Tom and Daisy felt it vaguely; Stephen and Isabel, sitting side by side, secretly burned to the knowledge of it; while Father James, unusually silent in the midst of the festivity, saw and understood it with a curious sinking of the heart.

At last the meal was over; and, contrary to his usual habit, Stephen followed the party into the hall.

"This is an occasion, Daisy," he said. "I think I ought to go into the drawing-room with you."

Daisy looked gratified. "Do! Oh, do!" she said.

Mary turned and shot a quick glance at them, but she said nothing. To-morrow she would be her old self again, speeding her barbed shafts, deal-

ing her swift thrusts, but to-night—this night of
unalloyed triumph—she had no time to waste upon
Stephen. So without comment she suffered the
party to cross the hall.

In the drawing-room they formed into a group.

"And now, what'll we do?" questioned Daisy,
hospitably concerned for the amusement of her
guests. "What about bridge? You play, Isabel?"

Isabel drew back diffidently. "Oh, please no!
I'm no good at cards."

"Well, you will, Polly! And Tom—that's two!
And Stephen and Father James—that's a four!"

A quick look of annoyance, followed by a quick
look of determination, passed over Carey's face.
' Don't mind me, Daisy! I won't play. You take
my place."

"Oh, but why? You always play."

"I am tired to-night."

Daisy looked incredulous, for Stephen's very attitude belied the idea of weariness.

"You're giving it up because you think I want to
play. Please don't, Stephen."

"No, I'm not. Don't make a fuss about it."
Carey turned away, selfish as every man and woman
are selfish when mind and body are centred upon
one object, to the exclusion of all others.

Daisy laughed her silly, light little laugh. "Oh,
very well! Have it your own way!"

But Father James stepped forward, breaking the
silence he had hitherto preserved. "Stephen," he
said, "listen here! We'll have a game of forty-five,
and not mind the bridge to-night; then we can all
be playing. Do, for the sake of old times!"

Distinctly, unmistakably, Carey hesitated; then some thought of his own or something in the old priest's face made his decision for him.

"All right!   Very well!" he said brusquely.

And until the clock chimed twelve, and exhaustion was written on more than one face, Father James kept the game alive, stifling his own yawns, spurring the lagging players, clinging to his position as a soldier defends his flag.

CHAPTER XXIV.

THAT night the threatened rain came, breaking in a torrent—a deluge—such as Irish skies can so readily produce. All through the night it poured upon the roof, relentless, unsparing; and in the morning Isabel, looking from her window, saw a garden green with moisture, paths that were no longer paths but streams, and a sky that hung grey and low over the earth, seeming to pour forth its very heart in a flood of tears.

At breakfast the one topic of conversation was the weather—its effect upon the crops, its probable continuance, its possible abatement; for now that the longed-for change had come, everybody was clamouring for the dry warmth of the past weeks. At half-past nine Carey's motor-car came round to the door; and in a swish and swirl of mud, Isabel saw him drive away with Tom Norris, while her heart beat to his last smile and to his last words, called back through the storm of rain—" I'll be back as early as I can. Mind you wait tea for me ! "

Then there had begun for her that thing of weariness—a hoplessly wet day in somebody else's country house. After breakfast, Daisy had departed to the kitchen to consult with the cook; Mary, with an air of importance, had announced that she had letters to write; while Father James, taxing his imagination to the uttermost, had volunteered to teach her bézique. Bézique, therefore, they had played until lunch-time, when they had both laid down the cards with secret relief. At lunch the spirits of the whole party obviously flagged, and subjects of interest ran low, the talk for the most part dwelling upon Ted's cold and the fact that the doctor had prescribed another day in bed. After the meal, Daisy's duties being done and Mary's letters written, the three girls were constrained to leave Father James to his office and retire to the drawing-room, to wear away the afternoon as best they could, until five o'clock brought tea and the return of the men.

In the drawing-room all the windows were shut to keep out the rain, and a smell of must seemed to emanate from the furniture, drawn forth by the close dampness of the air. The whole room wore a melancholy suggestion of autumn, impossible to reconcile with yesterday's summer sunshine; and as they entered it, Isabel looked longingly towards the empty grate.

Daisy followed the glance. "We almost might have a fire!"

But Mary looked stern and instant disapproval. "A fire? Nonsense! We'd be suffocated. I wish I had stopped in town last night. The country is sickening on a wet day!"

"Oh, I don't know! If we hadn't a wet day now and then I'd never get my mending done. I may as well go and get my work-basket now!"

Daisy departed, virtuously and unimaginatively

content; and Isabella dropped into the long wicker-chair with an air of lazy indolence. Whether this action had in its essence something irritating to Mary, or whether the wet, disappointing day had worked upon her nerves, it is impossible to say, but she walked to the piano with an obvious air of annoyance and picked up her Tolstoi, lying where she had left it the day before. She opened the book, glanced at the pages, then threw it aside and seated herself on the edge of the piano stool.

For a minute or two she played disconnectedly, then she shot a swift glance at Isabel from under her eyelashes.

"By the way, Isabel, why is it you haven't congratulated me? Everybody else has."

Isabel turned, her colour slightly heightened. "Oh, I don't know! I thought 'twas the man that was always congratulated."

Mary reddened in her own turn, and played a chord or two. "I never knew you were an authority on etiquette!"

"I'm not. I only thought——"

"What?"

"Oh, I don't know!" With a sense of being baited, Isabel turned away and looked through the glass door at the dripping garden.

At the action Mary let her hands drop from the keys, and wheeled round on the piano stool.

"Isabel," she said suddenly, "I'd like very much to know what you really think about Owen and me being engaged."

With the instinct of facing an antagonist, Isabel

withdrew her eyes from the garden and met Mary's interrogative glance.

"I don't think at all," she said. "Why should I think?"

"Because you're not quite an imbecile. You must think something."

"Well, and if I do?"

"Then why won't you tell me what it is?"

Isabel's temper, always quick, rose hotly at the persistence.

"Perhaps if I did tell you, it mightn't please you."

"Then it's something nasty?"

"Perhaps."

This time it was Mary's temper that was stung. She shut the piano sharply, and walked across the room to Isabel's chair.

"Look here, Isabel," she said, "I've had enough of this. Kindly explain exactly what you mean!"

Isabel looked up at her, and all the old dislike was patent in the glance that they exchanged. "Very well!" she said recklessly. "I'll tell you if you like. It's just this. I didn't congratulate you, because I don't think you are to be congratulated. I don't envy any one who is going to marry Owen Power."

Whatever Mary had expected, she had not expected this; and in her amazed anger, she stammered—

"I'd—I'd like to know exactly what that means."

"Nothing. Just what I say."

She laughed loudly and sarcastically.

"Not a very convincing statement, I'm afraid! Have you nothing to add to it?"

"Nothing."

For a moment they continued to look at each other, and in Mary's hard glance and tightened lips there was all the prejudice, the impregnable bigotry that in time to come would hedge round her husband and her children.

"Then I'm afraid it doesn't injure Owen very much," she said; "and if you take my advice, Isabel, you'll be careful for your own sake how you air your sentiments. It wouldn't be wise to make an enemy of him, after that night in the Lover's Walk!" She laughed again, her spiteful, cutting laugh; and before Isabel could retaliate—before she could extricate the barbed shaft lying in the words—turned on her heel and marched out of the room with stiff shoulders and head held virtuously high.

All through the succeeding period of solitude and the subsequent hour of Daisy's chatter, Isabel puzzled over the thrust, trying vainly to find its meaning, striving to understand whether it veiled a threat; then tea and the arrival of Carey and Tom Norris banished it from her mind, and when she retired to her room to dress for dinner her interest, her excitement, and her sense of indefinite anticipation were surging through her again, hot and exhilarating as before.

Carey was alone in the drawing-room when she came downstairs, but at their first words Father James appeared, his breviary under his arm.

"Well! well! well!" he said cheerfully. "And do you know that the rain is nearly stopped?"

"Nearly stopped, is it?" said Carey, not very interestedly.

"Nearly stopped, indeed! Praise be to God! Maybe we'll have a fine day to-morrow."

"Oh, goodness, I hope so!" said Isabel fervently. "To-day was terrible."

Carey looked at her and smiled. "Was it very dull?"

She shook her head, but her eyes sparkled. "I suppose 'twas better than being out in the wet."

"Better! Good Lord, no! The rain was splendid; the rain was magnificent. There's a feeling about scudding along in the car over wet roads that has no equal. Any fool can go out in fine weather. I wish I could show you what I mean!" His eyes turned involuntarily towards the windows, beyond which the grey sky was showing rifts of watery light.

As he looked, Tom Norris strolled in from the hall. "It's going to clear up, after all!" he announced. "Where are the girls? It's ten past seven." He compared his watch with the gilt clock on the mantelpiece.

At that moment Daisy hurried in, full of apologies. "I'm awfully sorry to be late! Let's go to dinner now; Polly will be in in a minute."

"In? Is she out?" asked Tom.

"Yes. She said she should get a breath of air, if she was to catch her death from it. She was awfully cross after lunch, and dashed off without a word to anybody. I don't know what was the matter with her."

Tom laughed and whistled. "I tell you what," he said, "Master Owen will have to mind his P's and Q's with Mary. But come along in—I have a raging appetite."

They all filed into the dining-room, and were barely seated at table when the banging of the hall door announced the return of the truant.

Without ceremony Mary walked in. Her hat and her fair hair were both plentifully sprinkled with rain, and her short skirt was splashed with mud; but her cheeks were red from exercise, and there was decision and energy in the carriage of her head.

Tom glanced up from his plate with a quizzical glance. "Hallo, Polly!" he said. "I never thought 'twould take you like that. 'Pon my word, I didn't!"

Mary took off her hat and threw it on a chair; then she seated herself next to Father James, and began to rub her hands, which were wet and red from exposure to the weather.

"Didn't you?" she said coolly. "I'm glad I'm interesting for once."

Tom pretended not to hear. "Just imagine a sensible girl like you driven to meandering by yourself on a wet evening! God help us! Love must be a terrible disease!"

"'Tis well, then, you were inoculated so young! Stephen, can I have some soup?"

In banter and chaff between brother and sister, the dinner wore on until dessert was laid upon the table; then Tom, losing interest in the game, turned his attention to the rest of the company.

"You're very quiet this evening, Father James," he said. "What's the matter with you?"

Father James, who had been listening to a low murmur of conversation carried on by Carey and Isabel under cover of Tom's noisy jesting, started almost guiltily. "Nothing is the matter," he said. "I suppose I'm a bit dull from being in all day."

"Dull? Lord, no wonder! I felt like a stewed rabbit up in town."

"Why don't you all go out, then?" said Mary. "'Tisn't at all a bad night now."

As she spoke, she pushed away her plate, rose, and sauntered to the window.

"I wouldn't mind another turn myself, if any one else is on for it. Will you come, Daisy?"

Daisy rose. "I can't, Polly. I must go and tuck Ted in. He'll cry if I don't. Perhaps Isabel will go."

Mary received the suggestion in cold silence; Isabel reddened at the obvious slight, and Carey stood up with some precipitation.

"Is there any note-paper in the desk, Daisy?" he asked. "I want to write a letter."

"Yes, there is, Stephen. I was writing there before dinner."

It was Father James who answered; and, as if fearing his statement might be doubted, he went across to the desk and drew forth note-paper and envelopes.

At this point Mary turned away from the window and took up her hat.

"Well, who's coming?"

Father James took an undecided look at Carey; but, as he saw him seat himself at the desk with businesslike decision, his expression relaxed.

"I'm on for a turn, Mary," he said. "If you'll wait while I get my hat."

"All right, Father James! Tom, what about you?"

Tom looked after Isabel, who was walking out of the room in Daisy's wake.

Mary stamped her foot. "Come on, for goodness' sake! Don't be always hanging between two fires. I had a letter to-day from Aileen Burke, and there's a message in it for you."

Mary knew her brother. There was no more hesitation; and when Father James appeared at the doorway with his hat in his hand, the three adventurers sallied forth into the hall.

Carey, sitting at the desk, heard the sound of their feet on the bare boards, heard their talk and laughter, then heard the shutting of the hall door.

Nothing in the world could have seemed to him so significant, so portentous, as that shutting of the door. By its heavy sound, convention,—family influence,—even friendship seemed to be shut away, leaving him alone with the subtle, secret things that lodge in a man's soul. The silence that succeeded was intense; he found himself listening, the pen upraised in his hand, the sheet of paper before him still clean.

But nothing came—not a breath, not a rustle. He dipped his pen into the ink; he wrote the date at the top of his letter; then suddenly, with an overmastering, irresistible impulse, he pushed the writing materials from him, stood up, and crossing the hall, walked into the drawing-room.

In the drawing-room the curtains had been drawn; on the centre table stood a lamp with a yellow shade, and seated within the circle of its light—her elbows on the table, her head supported by her hands—sat Isabel, with Mary's Tolsto open before her.

At Carey's entrance she started and jumped to her feet, causing the book to fall to the ground.

"Goodness! How you frightened me!" she said, a dry, nervous catch clipping her words.

For answer, Carey came forward, picked up the book, and handed it to her.

"Why aren't you with the others?" he asked. "Why are you here by yourself?"

She laughed, still nervous, still over-strung. "Oh, they didn't want me; Mary Norris didn't want me. Couldn't you see?"

The words were poured forth quickly, but it was the quickness of irrelevance. Each knew by intuition that question and answer were mere conventionalities, cloaking the thoughts that were racing through their minds.

For a moment Carey stood silent and undecided; then he walked to the window and drew back the curtain.

"It's quite fine," he said, looking out. "There's even a moon trying to come out. Look!"

Isabel was standing by the table, the book in her hand, the yellow lamplight falling on her dress.

"Look! Come here!"

With her pulses throbbing and with a strange sensation in her throat, she came towards him across the silent room.

"Look!" he said again. "The rain is over."

"Yes." The word was spoken automatically. She was conscious of nothing but his near presence, their intimate companionship in the dim window.

"Look here," Carey said suddenly in a tense, abrupt tone. "Let me take you out! Come with me in the car for half an hour!"

She turned to him, her eyes alight and incredulous.

"In the car?"

"Why not? Where's the objection? If people can go for a walk, why not for a drive?" The faint opposition lent heat to his desire.

"But could we?"

He caught the note of yielding in her voice; he seized upon it greedily.

"Of course. Come on! Any minute they may be back." The fever in his thoughts ran through his voice, and its tone dominated her. Across the room the quiet lamp was making a pool of light; but outside, in the struggling dimness of moon and cloud, there was a sense of elemental things. She looked through the window and her senses seemed to waver, swimming out upon the darkness.

"Very well!" she said below her breath. "Very well!"

CHAPTER XXV.

"WE'LL go by the garden."

Carey's voice was low, betraying the nervous tenseness of the man ridden by his desires and devoured by the fear that they may be thwarted. Walking across the room, he caught the handle of the glass door, and Isabel heard him swear below his breath as the rusty lock creaked and groaned under his pressure.

At last it swung open, and the clear air, drenched into added freshness, blew in across the room, making the lamp flame quiver.

"What about coats?" she whispered. "We can't go like this."

Carey paused in the act of stepping into the garden, and laughed with sudden embarrassment. "Of course!" he said awkwardly. "I was forgetting coats."

With instinctive caution, like people who are subconsciously sensitive of a guilty act, they stepped quickly and silently back across the room and out into the hall.

"There's nothing of mine here," Isabel said in the same lowered voice, as they stopped before the laden hat-stand.

"Never mind! Take anything. What about this?" He unhooked a long tweed ulster and held it up.

"That's Mary's."

"Then put it on—and let Mary be useful for once in her life!"

They both laughed inaudibly, as he held the coat out for her and she slipped her arms into the sleeves.

"Now, a hat! Can you manage this?" He took down a tweed shooting-hat.

She looked at it doubtfully. "'Twill be fearfully big."

"All the better! 'Twill stick on!"

She laughed again softly and excitedly, as she put on the hat and drew it down over her ears.

"What on earth do I look like?"

He paused in the act of putting on his own coat, and looked down at the face raised to his.

"Irresistible!" he said curtly, and turning on his heel he led the way back across the drawing-room and through the open glass door.

As she followed him into the garden, he paused to close it.

"We can come back by the hall door," he explained. "Now, right across the strawberry-beds to the little gate in the wall! Give me your hand. 'Twould be a nasty place to stumble."

Unresistingly she let him lead her through the darkness, the heavy wet rhubarb leaves flapping against her skirts, the ghostly apple-trees drooping dark and rain-laden above her head. It was only when they had passed through the garden door and emerged into the big, paved farmyard that he released her hand.

"Now we're safe!" he said.

Very carefully he struck a match, guarding it from the damp air; and having taken his bearings, walked across to the great gate of the coachhouse and lifted the iron bar from its socket. He swore again, as the bar reluctantly yielded; then he stepped back, and the heavy doors swung outward.

In the shadows of the whitewashed house, the car loomed dark and impressive. He stepped up to it, striking another match.

"Mike hasn't put a sponge to her yet. The idle ruffian! You won't mind?"

"No. Of course not!"

"Right! Then in you get!"

Burning with excitement, living as she had never lived before save in her dreams, Isabel stepped into the car, buttoning up her coat and pulling her hat well down over her hair.

In another moment the lamps were lighted, the engines set in motion, and the car was a restive animal, trembling, quivering to be off. Carey mounted to his place, and with a silence and precision that seemed to Isabel magical, they glided out into the yard and down the long, wet avenue.

She drew a sharp breath, and leant back in her seat, clasping her hands upon her knees, as her eyes took in the fleeting vision of the house with its lighted windows, and her face was assailed by the cool, delicious sweep of damp night air. It was

the same attitude that she had assumed on the day,
weeks ago, that she had first occupied this place at
Carey's side,—the same position, the same circumstance,—yet what leagues had been covered in the
field of emotion since that first drive!

The five-barred gate at the end of the avenue
was open, and without pause he guided the car
out into the boreen with the high white hedges,
where the luxurious scent of the hawthorn was
lying heavy on the air. The remembrance of her
drive in Mrs Power's carriage flashed back upon
Isabel with the warm, enveloping perfume, as they
splashed down the lane and over the small stone
bridge.

Emerging upon the high-road, a choice of ways
became inevitable, and she felt her heart bound
with new excitement as Carey discarded the direction of Waterford, and, turning the car to the right,
headed for the open country.

On any night the adventure would have been
breathless; but to-night the elements conspired
with fate in the making of an effect. As they
passed into the wide roadway, the whole panorama
of the sky opened before them,—the great ragged
space of the heavens rent by the moon's knife; the
clouds, massed in grey banks to the likeness of
towers, ramparts, castles; the moon herself, alter-
nately revealed and hidden, as the rolling veil of
mist was blown over her pale face. It was a
wonderful sky picture, pregnant with mystery, suggestion, peril; but Isabel, looking up from her own
wild thoughts, found no fear, no menace, in its wide,
wind-swept surface.

Like a great beast, the car sped onward over the wet and shining roadway, past thick hedges, trees in full leaf, vast corn-fields that in the ghostly light looked like grey, encroaching seas. No word was spoken as they fled on, gaining speed with the flying moments. It was a mad drive—mad as the thoughts that were racing through their minds. Death would have come to either of them then without a tremor; for in every life there is at least one such hour as this—when physical danger and moral danger are alike meaningless, when the soul lifts to the immensity of conscious power, defying fate.

Onward, onward into the night they ploughed, the mysterious country flying by them, the water hissing from the swirling wheels. Here and there a gate-post flashed by, vividly white; here and there a cottage shot into the darkness, the coppery-pink of its windows forming the high lights in a picture where dense black tree-trunks were the shadows. Each landmark on the road fled past, barely waking recognition in Carey's mind. The Police Barrack with its sharp white outline; the railway cutting, where the car seemed to leap as it shot across the rails; the forked roads, conjuring the gallows of old times or the staked body of the suicide; the scattered lights of Kilmacthomas, where the road for the first time faces the mountains that lie behind Dungarvan!

Like a fiend unloosed, the car thundered on—on towards the mountains and the sea. For the first time since they had left Kilmeaden, Isabel turned and looked at Carey, seated tense and rigid at the wheel.

"How far have we come?"

"Fifteen miles." The words seemed phantom things, caught and tossed to her by the wind.

"How far are we going?"

Either he could not or he would not hear; for he urged the car forward, taking no notice of the question.

Up hill they sped, down hill, then once more up hill to the handful of houses, scarcely worth the name of village, that crowns the summit of the land; then once again the road dropped steeply— down, down, past the sparse trees, past the barren fields that whisper of the coast, until at last, with what seemed like a great convulsion, the car groaned to the sharply applied brake, quivering through all its powerful frame like a living thing, and stopped to its master's bidding.

Isabel caught her breath, sharply, audibly; Carey leant back in his seat, inactive for a moment after the immense strain of the drive. At last he turned and looked at her.

"Was there ever a drive like that?"

His voice was low and unlike itself; and Isabel sat silent.

"That was living, wasn't it?"

She whispered something, but neither of them heard any word.

Then he stood up, a powerful, sombre figure in the deserted silence of the night.

"Let us get out! Do you know that that's Dungarvan just below us—that Helvic Head and Ardmore are round to the right? We're almost in County Cork."

He spoke rapidly, uncertainly, and stepping to the ground, he leant against the car, as if still exhausted from his tremendous achievement.

"Come!" he said at last, turning to her suddenly.

Obediently she rose, and for a moment paused on the step of the car, looking down at him.

That moment was supreme; their eyes, meeting in the gloom, spoke secret things; their souls found each other in the profound solitude. In perfect silence Carey put out his arms and lifted her from her place.

He lifted her down, but his arms did not relax as her feet touched the ground.

Thrilled and quivering, she stood motionless in his embrace, conscious of his eyes fixed upon her, intimately conscious of the hard throbbing of his heart—that sensation which every woman experiences for the first time with wonder and with fear.

"You know, don't you, why I brought you here?"

Her lips parted, but again no word came. She was aware in every fibre of his intensity, of his passion, of the reality that was sweeping through their lives.

"I wanted you away from Kilmeaden—I wanted you all to myself. Do you understand? All to myself. I've been mad for you for weeks — for weeks. Ever since I first saw you I've wanted this. There's no use denying it, there's no use fighting it. Every man has his day. Why shouldn't I have mine?"

She struggled a little in his clasp.

"Look at me!" he said. "Look at me! I've

pictured this a hundred times—a thousand times; and a thousand times I've trampled it down. But it's no good! It's no good! You're always before me—your eyes—your hair—your mouth." He bent suddenly and kissed her—kissed her violently.

"Do you care for me? Tell me! Do you?"

She struggled again; then his passion kindled a fire in her; she threw back her head with a free gesture, and her eyes blazed as they met his.

"Yes, I care. I've always cared."

For acknowledgment he released her suddenly, and taking her face between his hands, turned it up to the wan light.

"Is that the truth? The honest truth?"

Her glance answered his, burningly, seriously. "Yes; the honest truth."

His hands dropped with a gesture of finality. "Then, by God, I'd go down to hell for you!"

CHAPTER XXVI.

NEARLY an hour after the car had sped silently down the Kilmeaden avenue, Daisy—placid, un-thinking, wholly unsuspicious of the mine beneath her feet — came slowly down from the nursery, carrying her work-basket and a handful of socks.

The drawing-room, with its shaded lamp, its bowls of flowers, its quiet atmosphere, wore an air of innocence, as though no breath of passion had swept across it; but if the walls and furniture gave no hint of drama, human emotion was not unrepresented, for Mary stood in the middle of the room, all the rigidity of determination in her small figure, all the suggestion of controlled excitement in the pose of her head.

"So you're back!" Daisy said without looking at her, as she stepped calmly to the table and seated herself in the light of the lamp. "What did you do with Tom and Father James?"

"They're in the dining-room, playing chess."

Mary's tone was sharp, acutely sharp, but Daisy was unobservant.

"Oh!" was all she said; then she added in-differently, "And where's Isabel?"

Mary made a little sound of sarcastic contempt.

"Isabel! Don't ask me!"

Then at last Daisy's attention was caught. "What's the matter, Polly?" she said, looking up.

"I suppose you didn't hear anything, while you were up with Ted?"

"Hear anything? No. What would I hear?"

"I thought you might have heard the car coming out of the yard about an hour ago."

"The car? At this hour of the night? The car?"

"Yes. The car! The car!" said Mary, mimicking her. "Oh, Daisy, you make me sick!"

In blank surprise, Daisy dropped the sock that she was holding.

"What on earth is the matter with you? What on earth do you mean?"

Mary turned upon her. "I mean, Daisy, that you're such a fool that a person can hardly even feel sorry for you!"

The attack was so sweeping and so unexpected that Daisy sat and stared.

Then it was that Mary, stung to definite action, boiling with accumulated knowledge, dealt her swiftest, best-aimed blow.

"Stephen has taken out the car—and taken Isabel in it!"

"Stephen! But, why? Where?"

"Ah, that's left to the imagination! But, then, of course, you have none!"

"Mary, what are you talking about? What do you mean?" For the first time a note of uneasiness sounded in Daisy's voice; her fingers unconsciously fumbled with her work-basket.

For answer, Mary walked over to the table and stood looking down at her. "Daisy," she said with deliberation, "do you mean to tell me that you really are as great a fool as you appear? That all these weeks you have never seen what I saw and what everybody in Waterford saw— that Stephen is head over ears in love with Isabel Costello?"

Like a child who has been dealt a slap across the face, Daisy jumped up, letting her work-basket fall to the ground in a confusion of needles and threads.

"Mary! Mary, you're mad!"

"Mad? Oh, I'm not the one that's mad!"

"But, Stephen! But—but he's married!"

Daisy's mind, trained in a circumscribed space, fed upon chosen food, refused the problem as something irreconcilable.

Mary, overmastered by impatience, threw out her arms in a gesture of exasperation. "Married, indeed! Good heavens, when will you learn sense? I tell you any living soul but yourself would have seen it weeks ago. I saw it at the Fair Hill dance, the very first time he danced with her. 'Tis true, indeed, that there are no people so blind as those who won't see!"

"But, Mary, how could it be? How could it?" There was panic in Daisy's voice now, mingling with the incredulity.

Again Mary threw up her hands. "Oh, you exasperate me! You make me furious, when I see you going on day after day, eating and sleeping and smiling as if nothing was wrong! And all the time those two are laughing up their sleeves, to think what a fool you are!"

A crimson wave flooded Daisy's face. "Polly! Polly! Oh, Polly, don't!" she cried; and her voice ran up the whole scale of emotions until it ended in a cry of pain.

At the sound Mary's manner softened. "I don't mean to be nasty," she said, "but you make me wild. It's too much of a good thing when a married man goes out driving at ten o'clock at night with an unmarried girl!"

With a distracted gesture Daisy pushed the fair hair from her forehead.

"But, Polly," she cried, "it's impossible! It's impossible! It's out of the question!"

"Out of the question, no doubt! But, all the same, Stephen—the immaculate Stephen—is careering about the roads at the present moment with the prettiest girl he's ever met in his life. For she is that, whatever you or I may say!"

This touched Daisy to something nearer and more vital than fear: as far as the great passion could have being in her nature, jealousy flared up.

"Do you mean that he admires her—that he notices her?"

"Indeed I do."

There was no ignoring the conviction in Mary's tone, and before it the poor flimsy rags of Daisy's self-possession were scattered.

"How dare you say that, Mary!" she cried. "How dare you think such a thing! Stephen has always been a good husband—always, always from the very first. What do you know about it? You read those horrible foreign novels, and you think things happen here like they do abroad. But I tell you they don't. It's different—it's different!"

"Men are never different."

Again the conviction in the tone swept Daisy's mind like a cold wind.

"What do you mean?"

"What I say. That you are a fool and that Stephen is—a man."

The pause that followed was long and deadly: when Daisy spoke again it was in a thin, faint voice.

"What makes you say that? Is it only because Stephen has taken her out to-night?"

"No; it isn't."

"Then what?"

"Things that people have told me."

"What people?"

"One person—Owen . . ."

"Owen?"

"Yes, Owen. Owen has summed her up pretty accurately, I can tell you! Oh, he was quite honest about it; he admitted that just at first he was taken with her, like the rest of the men, but he had enough of her that night at Fair Hill. You remember my telling you at the time that there was something behind that story of the cigarette?"

"Yes." Daisy's voice was dry.

"Well, the something behind it was—Stephen!"

There was the weight of a definite fact in this last pronouncement,—to Daisy's narrow conceptions, something final and abyssmal.

"And where are they now?" she cried, her

sudden distraction linking the past with the present. "How long are they gone? Polly, what hour was it? What hour was it when they went?"

"'Twas nine," said Mary, knowing the value of a brief statement.

Daisy's glance sought the clock. "And now it's after ten; it's nearly half-past ten. Mary, what could they be doing for an hour and a half?"

Mary shrugged her shoulders with a world of suggestion; then her eyes met her sister's. "I'll tell you what you can be doing—if you have an ounce of spirit, an ounce of sense."

"What?"

"Be thinking out what you'll say to Stephen when he does come back."

With a frightened gesture Daisy put out her hand.

"Polly! Polly! I couldn't meet them—I couldn't meet her!"

"Don't be afraid! She won't be anxious to meet you. But you must see Stephen. Everything depends on your seeing him to-night; everything depends on what you say to-night. You're his wife. You must assert yourself."

"Polly!"

"I mean what I say. You're his wife; make him know it."

"Polly! Polly, you're not going?" She sprang up, as Mary walked towards the door.

"Yes, I am. It's between you two."

"But, Polly!" Her tone was piteous, her face white. "Polly, I can't—I can't. I'm afraid."

Mary paused with her hand on the door. "But you must! No one can help you to-night. It's between you and him. All you have to do is to remember one thing—that you're his wife."

With quiet decision she walked out of the room, and Daisy sank back into her chair.

The half hour that followed was the worst that had come to her in all her narrow, sheltered life. Pain, jealousy, acute nervous anticipation warred in her brain like a peal of discordant bells. Hot rage scorched her, as the hands of the old gilt clock crept on, marking the minutes; cold dread chilled her bodily, as her imagination strove to conjure her interview with Stephen. A dozen times she started up, imagining the sound of the car; and at the realisation of each mistake, she sank back again, physically sick and faint. When at last the real sound came—no myth of the brain, but the whirr and grind of tyres on the wet gravel—her whole life seemed to ebb away, leaving her utterly cold, utterly impotent.

Holding to the back of a chair, she stood listening with morbid intentness. Mary had closed the drawing-room door, but in the silence of the night each sound of the return came to her distinctly— the throb of the engines, the crunch of the brake, the succeeding silence that told of the entry into the house; she heard the feet on the uncarpeted hall, she heard the hat-stand sway as fresh wraps were added to its load; then she heard Isabel's voice, sounding astonishingly full and vital.

"Good-night!" it said. "I suppose they're gone to bed—if they're not playing cards."

Then Carey's voice, very low in tone. "Good-night! Sleep well!"

Then a silence, a silence in which her strained imagination suddenly took fire, burning up her impotence.

In that second of intense jealousy she could almost have gone forward, have opened the door and confronted them; but conventionality checked her. She waited until Isabel's light step passed down the hall, and Carey walked back to the car; then she ran across the room, pulled back the curtain, and pushed up the sash of the window.

"Stephen!" she called. "Stephen!"

To her own ears her voice was harsh and dry; but to Stephen, stepping into the car, it was merely arresting.

"Who's that?" he called. "Is that you, Daisy?"

"Yes, it is. I'm here, in the drawing-room. I want to speak to you."

Carey had set the engines in motion again; he raised his head, trying to catch the words above their drumming.

"What is it?" he called again. "Do you want me?"

"Yes, I do. I want you now."

This time the voice was sharp and penetrating: without further hesitation he stepped to the ground and passed back across the hall and into the drawing-room.

Daisy, standing in the middle of the room, with agitation and nervous strain written in every line of her figure, fastened her gaze upon him—seeing

with an observation born of the moment that he
was paler than she had ever known him, that his
face looked strained, his eyes very dark.

Had his instincts been less keen than they were
to-night, he must have noticed the intentness of
her regard; but with senses sharpened to a point,
he saw in a flash all that her glance portended, all
that it inevitably presaged.

"Well?" he said very quietly; and Daisy, with
her eyes still upon his face, repeated the word.

"Well?"

Then, manlike, he sought for the worst at once.

"Well?" he said. "What is it? Why are you
looking at me like that?"

"As if you didn't know!" she cried out suddenly.
"What a fool you must think I am—never to know,
never to see what all Waterford sees and knows!"

He drew back a step, steadying his nerves.

"And may I ask what it is that all Waterford
sees and knows?"

"Why, that you're forgetting me—that you're
forgetting that you're a married man—that this
Costello girl——"

"Stop!" said Carey, so violently that her voice
failed and died away. "I know where you got this
idea from. I know the reliable source from which
it comes."

Daisy swayed a little. "Stephen! Stephen, does
she matter as much as that?"

Carey checked his vehemence. "I cannot have
a girl slandered."

"Then she's more to you than me? You put her
before me?"

Again his feelings surged within him, driving the blood to his face.

"Have you ever had to complain of that?" he demanded. "Have I ever failed in the bargain of our marriage? Oh, I've held to it well! You've had nothing to complain of!"

"But now it's different! Stephen, it's true what I said? Isn't it? Isn't it? She matters to you now; you put her before me now?"

Carey stood silent.

"Stephen! Stephen!" Her voice rose, straining his tautened nerves.

"For God's sake, let me alone!" he cried suddenly. "Haven't I done all a man could do? Haven't I made you a position, and earned you money, and given you a house? What more does a woman ask from her husband!"

"Stephen!" she cried again.

In her distress it seemed that she could only articulate his name; and with each repetition came the added pain of a soul struggling into existence. Poor, trivial Daisy, who had sipped so fastidiously at the cup of life, was tasting its dregs in those bitter moments. "Oh, Stephen!" she cried wildly. "Tell me it's not true! Tell me it's all a lie, and I'll believe you!" She ran forward and caught his arm.

But the cry fell on deaf ears; Carey's nerves were strained to snapping-point. At the touch of her hand all the selfish manhood in him revolted against her.

"Let me alone!" he exclaimed. "Haven't I given enough? Haven't you drained me dry— you Norrises?"

It was the first brutal word he had ever spoken to her, and she bent under it. With a piteous little gesture, she threw out her hands and burst into tears.

It was the last straw—this sound of woman's weeping. He turned upon her savagely. "Be quiet!" he said. "Don't bring the house about our ears!"

She sobbed on, immersed in her misery.

"Daisy! Be quiet! I tell you I can't bear this!"

A louder, longer, more despairing sob was all that answered him.

"Very well, then!" With the quick, nervous step of a man resolved, he walked to the door.

As she heard the handle turn she looked round, her fair hair dishevelled, her face flooded with tears.

"Stephen! Stephen, where are you going?"

Carey never paused, never looked back. "I'm going up to town. I'm going to Lady Lane."

The words paralysed her. Never in the five years of their married life had he slept out of his own house—never had he spoken in this voice of cold dislike. A great terror surged over her, and the little card-house of her contentment swayed as in a tornado.

"Stephen!" she cried. "Stephen, don't leave me! Don't go! Stephen!"

But the cry was lost in the swish and splash of the car, as it fled past the house.

CHAPTER XXVII.

A STIFLINGLY hot morning; a house imbued with the sense of desertion and the close, pervading breath of city air, uncleansed by even a day's rain! Such was the atmosphere in which Carey was to enact the most fruitful scenes of the drama he called his life!

At ten o'clock on the morning following his night of stress and passion, he descended from his bedroom at Lady Lane and walked into the breakfast-room. It was characteristic, this breakfast-room— characteristic of Ireland — characteristic of Irish family life. Here all the books of the house were collected in a tall, glass-fronted bookcase; here stood the ink-stained table at which Ted did his lessons each day when his father had gone to work; here were ranged the two immense globes from which Daisy, Mary, and Tom Norris had made acquaintance with the heavens and the earth in their youthful days, and which were now a source of instruction and amazement to Daisy's children; here, also, stood the old-fashioned work-table that had belonged to Daisy's mother, and the big iron safe in which Stephen kept the documents that he brought home with him from the office. It was a common room; but to those who knew it, it held that homeliness that lies in common things. Many a wet day Daisy had found quiet enjoyment in that familiar atmosphere over a book or a cup of tea; and many a winter night Stephen had returned, tired and cold, to find calm solace in a pipe over the fire. But the time for solace, like the season of fires, was past by many months. As he walked into the room on this sultry summer morning, the cold grate stared at him in all its blank ugliness, and a coating of dust lay thick upon the work-table and the globes.

Involuntarily a murmur of disgust escaped him, and walking across the room, he threw open the window; but even here the air was hot and festering, for yesterday's rain had not been sufficient to scour the streets after three dry weeks, and the odours that assailed him were unsavoury. Another expression of impatience dropped from him, and he turned back into the room at the moment that the door behind him opened and Mrs Brien, the charwoman, appeared.

Mrs Brien was a woman of sixty,—inquisitive, talkative, lazy, but, as Mrs Power would have said, "a decent creature." She came into the room now, and stood looking at Carey, whose office she washed but once a-week, and in whom she took a proprietary interest.

She looked at him for a minute or two in silence; then, as he made no attempt to speak, she broached the subject that had brought her from the lower regions.

"An' what about me wettin' you a sup a tay,

sir?" she began. "Shure, you must be perished
alive for the want of a bit to ate!"

Carey looked at her, then looked back again at
the window. "Thank you, Mrs Brien," he said,
"but I don't want anything. I'm not hungry."

Seen in the full light of morning, his face seemed
to Mrs Brien to be strangely unlike itself; it was
set and pale, and his eyes had the hollow look of a
man who has not slept.

"An', shure, isn't that a foolish thing, now!"
she was constrained to say. "The Lord knows
you must be wantin' somethin'—wid nayther bit
nor sup passin' your lips these twelve hours. What
harm if you had a dhrop of whiskey itself last
night, afther the long dhrive you had!"

Here Carey's patience suddenly gave way. "Oh,
for goodness' sake go away and don't bother me!"
he cried. "I thought you were supposed to keep
this place clean?" He passed his hand over the
work-table and showed it to her, black with dirt.

She looked at it without confusion. "Well now,
if that isn't a quare thing!" she said with interest.
"An' meself afther scrubbin' this room as clane
as a barrack-yard yesterday mornin'! But, shure,
'tisn't dirt it is at all, 'tis on'y dust."

Carey shook his head hopelessly. "Oh, go
away!" he said again. "If you have no work
to attend to, I have."

Her face expressed dismay. "Work! An' is
it go down to the office you will, widout a bit
to ate?"

"I'm not going to the office; I've just telephoned to say so. I have work to do here."

"Well, of course you knows your own business; an' 'tisn't for the likes of a poor woman like me to be dhrillin' you about what you ought to be doin'——"

Carey took out his handkerchief, wiped his fingers violently, and crossing to the safe, opened it with an ostentatious clatter of keys.

"Are you going—or will I have to put you out?"

"I'm goin', sir—I'm goin'." She sidled slowly to the door, but on the threshold paused and looked back. "I'll come in agin, to see will you be havin' that sup a tay!"

He groaned, then made a wide gesture of relief as he saw her go, and heard her feet—in a pair of his cast-off boots—flapping away into the distance.

With her departure, a change seemed to pass over him; the mask of caution dropped from his face, displaying a light of sudden, feverish energy. Restraining himself to methodical action with evident difficulty, he threw open the heavy door of the safe and lifted out the bundles of family documents, which it was his habit to keep under his personal supervision. They were not a very imposing array, but such as they were, they represented the march of the Carey family, from the day when Barny Carey, in the first pride of affluence, had seen fit to make a will. Taking them carefully in both his hands, he blew the dust from the pink tape that held them together, and carried them across the room to the ink-stained writing-table. There, he drew up a chair and, seating himself, began a careful perusal of the papers, taking them in order, one by one. The task was absorbing, and he buried himself in it, to the exclusion of all outward sights and sounds. Now and then, as he read, his latent excitement seemed to break bounds, and he would pass his hand nervously across his forehead, pull his chair nearer to the table, or, seizing a pen, would dip it in the ink and make rapid notes from the documents before him.

His task was at its height, his nervous attention fixed, when the hall-door bell pealed with a sudden clanging vigour that echoed through the quiet house. At the sound he gave a start, and made a large blot on the paper before him; then he smiled grimly at his jarred nerves, and settled to his work again, as he heard Mrs Brien flap down the hall. Some milkman or baker, he told himself! Even charwomen had to live! And the more surely to avoid disturbance, he planted his elbows on the table and put his hands over his ears.

In this new attitude he heard nothing of the colloquy at the door nor of the passage of steps that followed it; he heard nothing of the opening of the breakfast-room door under Mrs Brien's tentative hand, or the apologetic scraping of her feet on the threshold. But another and subsequent sound he did hear—the familiar tones of Father James's voice sounding suddenly close behind him; and, hearing it, his hands dropped from his ears, and he wheeled round so sharply that Mrs Brien jumped back in alarm.

"Oh, sir," she cried, "I hope I done no harm. But how could I refuse his rivirence!"

Father James put up his hand. "That's all right, my good woman! Sure, what harm would it be! Go on now back to your work."

Not daring to oppose the priest, Mrs Brien reluctantly withdrew, and Father James was left to contemplate Carey's angry face—his sharp, interrogative glance—the hand that had shot out instinctively to cover the papers spread upon the table. He looked at him for a moment in silence, then his soul's absorbing thought broke from him in one word.

"Stephen! Stephen! Stephen!" he said; and never were love and rebuke and pity so blended in a human voice.

Carey made no response. By set and deliberate purpose he began to collect his papers into a heap.

Father James followed the movement; then he shook his head sadly. "You're gone a long way away from me, Stephen, when you think I'd be spying on you!"

Carey flushed, and with a sudden gesture flung the papers back upon the table. "You can see them if you like!" he cried. "And if you have come here to-day to preach to me, Father James, I'd have you to remember that I'm thirty-eight years old, and that I've heard a sermon nearly every Sunday of my life!"

He pushed back his chair, rose abruptly, and walked across the room to the cheerless grate. It had been bound to come—this moment of conflict, and now that it was here, he would meet it like a man! Standing there, resolute and defiant, he struck the first blow.

Father James met the words, met the antagonistic glance; and in the humble simplicity of his heart prayed that he might do the right.

"Stephen," he said gently, "I have been talking to Daisy; I know it all."

Carey threw up his head in swift indignation. "Then the whole crowd knows! Oh, this is intolerable!"

"Easy, boy! Easy! No one else knows. No one only me knows what passed between you—not even Mary. Her trouble seems to have made a woman of the poor child, all of a sudden."

He searched Carey's face for any softening, but there was none, and he put out his hand towards him in sudden supplication.

"Stephen, Stephen, have you no thought that she's your wife—that she's——"

But Carey flung out his arms in a sharp, uncontrolled gesture.

"Father James," he cried, "I've remembered her for five years! now I'm remembering no one but myself!"

There was revolt and passion in the cry; and Father James, with his knowledge of life, with his instinct of race, admitted with a sinking heart that here was no playing with fire, but a great conflagration induced by a strong hand.

"Stephen!" he exclaimed.

But Carey's tongue was loosed, and his words rushed forth, a torrent that laughed at flood-gates.

"Look here, Father James!" he cried. "You think you know me—you think you've known me all these years since my father died; but you've

never known me. Never! Never! What have I
seemed to you? A plodding, industrious, sensible
man—the sort of man to do well—to marry—to
settle down! Oh, we both know the cant! But
underneath all that—far down—fathoms down—
I have been something quite different all the time.
I tell you I have had big dreams—I am my father's
son!" He paused and drew a quick, sharp breath.

"You've thought me content—you've thought me
satisfied; but I can tell you often and often, sitting
in my office, living out the petty routine, playing
the eternal game, the world has risen up before me
till my head swam. I've wanted it all, all, all, I
tell you—success—riches—women!" He wiped his
damp forehead with the back of his hand and took
another sharp, hard breath.

"Oh, I've kept it under—you needn't remind me
of that. But a volcano is quiet till the fire breaks
out!" He stopped once more to look defiance at
the old priest standing before him with fear in his
heart and faith and prayer in his soul.

"I've kept it under. I've worked and plodded
and slaved till I thought I had reconciled myself;
but I find that I was wrong. I suddenly find that
for me, even for me,—the respectable citizen, the
cut-and-dried lawyer,—there's life to be lived; and,
by God, do you think I'll refuse it?"

"Stephen! Stephen! What are you saying?"

"What you hear. Just exactly what you hear.
I've found a woman who is gold and wine beside
the women I have known, and I'm going to have
her, if hell stood between us!"

Father James looked at him quietly and steadily.

"'Tis easier to bridge hell than to bridge life, Stephen!"

The gentle, sober tone steadied Carey.

"I don't understand you."

"I think you do, Stephen. What I mean is that a man can never undo any single thing that he has done."

Once again Carey wiped his forehead; then he thrust at his antagonist again with renewed fierceness. "I see what you mean! I've expected this —I'm prepared for it. But I'll have it without any of your philosophy; I'll have it in brutal facts. I'm a man who has had to live in spite of the world —a man who has had to work—had to marry— had to conform in every way. I know that I have a wife——"

"And children, Stephen."

Carey's mouth hardened. "Yes—and sons," he corrected. "I have a wife and sons; but a wife who has no more susceptibility than a doll, and sons who cannot fail to make their way, for they will have money and a pack of relations—the two passports to success in this damned country. Am I to stand back because fate has thrust me into this position? Am I to refuse what the gods give?"

"Stephen, you're mad!"

"Am I mad? Is this mad?" He walked back to the table and caught up a sheaf of papers. "When you came, I was going through my papers —no one shall say I left my wife unprovided for."

"Stephen! Stephen, boy! Is it you that are speaking? To pay off your wife with money!"

"My wife! The doll out of the shop window!"

"A doll! A doll, is it? I wish you could have seen her to-day. Faith, Stephen, 'twas a doll with the paint washed off!"

Carey's wrath boiled. "Daisy!" he cried. "Daisy! Is it always to be Daisy! I tell you it's life, not toys, I'm playing with now."

"But that's not life, Stephen! That's not life! It's neither life nor love—but just the temptation of the flesh."

Carey turned on him with fierce contempt. "And what does a priest know of a man's temptations?"

A very humble look came over Father James's face, and for a moment he stood silent; then he raised his head slowly, and something akin to illumination shone in his eyes.

"Don't be too sure about that, Stephen. Priests are men too—and there's more than one sort of temptation. You wouldn't think to look at me now that I had a besetting sin once—and that sin pride—would you?"

Carey was silent—silent and ironical.

"Well, I had, then—I had." Father James's voice dropped. "'Twas long ago, before your time, when I was one of David Marsden's curates down at Ballykarney. He's dead these thirty years—the Lord have mercy on him!—but he was a big man in his own little way, a great aristocrat and a well-read man too; and whatever the reason of it was, he took a fancy to me from the first, and I raw from Maynooth. I never could rightly understand it, but he was always friendly to me in his old-fashioned, grand sort of a way; and often after the early mass, when I'd be after preaching, he'd come up to me in the chapel yard and put his hand on my shoulder.

"'Mr Baron,' he'd say, as we walked together to the gate. He'd never put the 'Father' to our names, always the 'Mister.' 'Mr Baron, you have a brogue that could be cut with a knife; but, 'pon my word, you'd coax the birds off the bushes with that tongue of yours!'

"And so it went on, Stephen, from one thing to another. It seemed like as if his fancy for me was contagious, for people outside Ballykarney began taking notice of me too; I began to be asked up to Waterford to preach charity sermons. At last I was made a curate at one of the city churches. You heard all that, maybe, long ago; but what you never heard was that pride began to grow up in me —pride that I was picked out before older and better men to teach the Word of God—and pride that the space round my confessional used to be black with penitents of a Saturday night. Then it came that people began to flatter me and to call me lucky; they began to say that I had a grand future in front of me, and that the bishop had me in mind for a big parish. But, mind you, Stephen, there's a queer way in all these things! People said I was a great man; but the old bishop—the Lord have mercy on him!—knew better, and the Almighty knew better still. I wasn't a great man, and time was to learn it to me.

"Well, Stephen, the years passed on—Easter and Advent and Christmas—and one by one the parishes fell in, and one by one other men got them; and sick and sore and sorry grew my heart, and less

and less they called me lucky, till at last I would
see them looking at me out of the corner of their
eye, and hear them whispering behind my back,
'Poor James Baron! His chance has passed him
by!'

"Well, Stephen, my heart went near to breaking
all those years, though nobody ever knew it; and
then at last—at long and at last—the parish came.
It came—and I fifty-five years old—and what do
you think it was? What do you think it was,
Stephen? What but Scarragh—Scarragh, a bit
of a mountain-side with the grazing of a handful
of goats! I tell you I had black thoughts the
night I knew it first. I had thoughts of refusing it
altogether and going out to America. In America,
I said to myself, a man can find his level!" He
paused, and threw a quick glance at Carey from
under his lashes. "But the Almighty—thanks be
to Him!—put sense into me, Stephen—and I said
nothing and went where I was told; but the first
Sunday that I said mass in my little barn of a
chapel there was never a sorer man. I tell you
that, priest and all as I was, there was red rebellion in me when I turned round to preach to the
handful of a congregation—savages, I think I called
them in my arrogance and pride!

"But, Stephen, God's ways are queer! I stood
there, not knowing how I was going to put my
tongue to a sermon, when my eyes fell on an old
man kneeling on the bare flags near the altar rails.
I had seen the old fellow the day before, and somebody had said to me, 'That's old Darby Farrell of
the mountain; he's all alone up there now; his six

sons are dead, and his three grandchildren are after
going to America last week.' The words came back
to my mind as I stood there looking at him. His
poor old bones were doubled up with the rheumatism
and the work, his fingers were that twisted that he
could hardly pass the rosary beads through them,
and his face had the look of starvation in it; but
his eyes were fixed on the tabernacle, and his lips
were moving all the time, and I would have taken
my oath then and there that he was thanking God!

"I tell you, if the Almighty had put out His hand
and touched me that minute, I couldn't have felt it
more. All of a sudden my pride melted, and I spoke
to those poor, simple people as I had never spoken
in a grand city church; and when the mass was
over, I went back to my little bit of a house and
I burned every sermon I ever wrote. That's many
a year ago now, Stephen, but there hasn't been a
day since then that I haven't blessed God on my
bended knees; for when I walk out on my bit of
a mountain and see the plants sprouting up out of
the earth, and look up at the sky and see the stars
shining—each one in its own course, each one in its
own place—I see things that, maybe, I'd never have
seen all my life long if I was a great man with a
big congregation and a big church—and perhaps
a big debt harassing my mind!"

Father James stopped. Without artificiality,
without self-consciousness, he had told his story.
With fierce persistency Carey had closed his ears
to the simple sentiment lying within it, but against
his will the truth behind the sentiment had pene-
trated his brain. It was the pronouncement of a

man thirty years older than himself—thirty years
nearer the grave—thirty years further removed from
human prejudice, from human passion. Fear gripped
him—an appalling fear—the fear of renouncing that
which he coveted.

"That's all very well!" he cried suddenly. "That's
all very well for you, but not a word of it applies to
me—not a word of it."

Father James had seen this attitude before; he
had seen it in the condemned criminal, refusing to
make his peace with God; he had seen it in the sick
and sorry of soul, coming with lagging steps and
hot, rebellious hearts to the tribunal of confession,
and never once had his courage failed before it.

"Stephen," he said quietly, "can you dare to tell
me that? Can you look down into your soul, and
dare to tell me that you are so big a man that you
are exempt from the common lot that falls to us all?"

"I'm choosing the common lot—I'm going the
common way!"

"You're going the coward's way!"

In the might of his zeal, the shabby figure of
Father James seemed to tower in the silent room;
there was grandeur in his rugged face, power in his
rough voice. He was fighting for the soul he loved,
and the weapons he used were eternal.

"Stephen," he cried, "your duty is plain before
you! You married Daisy, and the day you married
her you shut every life away from her but the life
with you. You gave your word to the Almighty
God to keep and guard her. Are you a man at all,
that you're forgetting that?"

With sudden violence Carey struck the table.

"Haven't you finished yet? Good God, haven't you finished yet?"

"Not yet, Stephen! Not yet! There's one thing yet I have to say. It's the remembering of a day long ago, when you and I stood like this, and faced out bitter things. 'Twas twelve months after the poor father's death, and it seemed that something near to ruin was staring you in the face. I remember the little room in your lodgings as if it was yesterday, and I remember the pain that was in my heart to see the old look coming on your young face that ought to be turning towards nothing but amusement. I remember it well, Stephen; I remember it well. You stood for a long time with never a word and never a sign; then, all of a sudden, you turned on me, fiercelike and determined.

"'I'll live it down, Father James!' you cried out. 'I'll live it down; but, by God, if ever I have sons of my own, they'll never have a hell of their father's making!'"

It was the old priest's last arrow, and it sped home swift and true. For a long space Carey stood, silent and white; then, like a man dazed, he went forward and put his hands roughly on Father James's shoulders.

"Go away! Go away!" he said hoarsely. "I've had enough!"

Father James made no resistance; he went quietly across the room, but at the door he paused solemnly and looked back.

"Stephen," he said gently, "may the Almighty God bless and help you!" Then he turned and passed into the hall.

Until the last footfall had died into silence, and the thud of the closing door had echoed through the house, Carey never moved: then, haltingly, unsteadily, after the manner of a man who has suffered long illness, he walked back to the table, seated himself at his old place, and, throwing his arms out across the scattered papers, let his head fall forward into his hands.

CHAPTER XXVIII.

THERE are periods in the life of every man when
mind and body seem disassociated, and time and
space become as vague conceptions failing to touch
the personal; when events loom up like a fleet of
ships that, rudderless and with tattered sails,
plough headlong to destruction before the hurri-
cane of fate.

Such a period of cloud and stress enveloped Carey.
No recollection of time, no consciousness of place,
moved him, as he cowered in his attitude of despair.
He felt maimed, mentally and physically; and with
the shame of mutilation, his courage ebbed.

The minutes passed, sultry and leaden; the usual
sounds of an empty house started out of the silence
—the cracking of the furniture, the scraping of a
mouse, the faint flutter of the hideous paper decora-
tion in the grate; then from overhead came the
thud and shuffle of Mrs Brien's feet as she made
up his bedroom, the banging of the basin and jug
on the marble-topped washstand, the scraping of the
casters as she pulled the bed this way and that.
At another time these descriptive noises would
have driven him to action; now they did not even

penetrate the outer wall of his absorption. He sat numbed and impotent, broken by the storm.

Time passed—a quarter of an hour, half an hour, an hour; then at last a new sound broke the quiet —the loud, imperious ringing of the hall-door bell. He heard it as he had heard the rest, without interest, without fear, without curiosity. All the world might come now! Nothing mattered.

Upstairs, Mrs Brien also heard it, and paused in her noisy cleaning of the bedroom.

"Let ye ring agin—whoever ye are!" she said to herself, considering her feet and the long flight of stairs.

As though the unseen visitor were conscious of her remark, the bell clashed forth once more—this time with such vigour that she dropped the dustpan and brush that she was holding.

"How impatient ye are—whoever ye are!" she muttered as she tramped downstairs, straightening her dirty apron as she went.

Passing along the hall, she took an inquisitive glance at the closed door of the breakfast-room; then she hastily pulled down her sleeves and opened the hall door an inch or two.

Through this aperture she took a grudging look at the intruder, and either her heart softened or there was something unusually interesting in the appearance of the visitor, for she opened the door another inch.

"Good morning, miss!" she hazarded in her most amiable tones. "I suppose 'tis Mrs Carey you're after wantin'?"

The visitor flushed a deeper red than that which already mantled her cheeks.

"No," she said quickly. "It's Mr Carey I want to see. He's here, isn't he?"

Mrs Brien took a closer survey of the youthful figure and expressive face, and a dozen questions made medley in her brain.

"Mr Carey?" she repeated. "Sure, 'tis at the office Mr Carey always do be at this time a the day!"

The visitor took a step nearer to the hall door. "I know! I know that! But I was at the office and he's not there. So he must be here. He is, isn't he? Do tell me."

Long afterwards, in the privacy of her family circle, over a teapot of stewing tea, Mrs Brien was wont to declare that the look which accompanied this appeal would have melted the heart of a stone; so her reply when it came was becomingly soft.

"Well," she said, "'twouldn't be wishin' for me to be tellin' you a lie, an' 'tis inside by himself in the breakfast-room he is this very minute. But I don't know at all, God help me, that I ought to be disturbin' him."

"But you will? You will?" In her insistent eagerness the visitor stepped across the threshold. "It's very particular—I promise you he won't be vexed."

Mrs Brien shook her head weakly, and drew back into the hall, giving ingress to the intruder.

"Well, all I can say is, God help me if I'm doin' wrong!" She shook her head once more, led the way down the hall, and very tentatively knocked on the breakfast-room door.

Impatience spread over the visitor's face. "Knock again!" she urged.

"Sure, I'd be in dhread, miss! 'Tisn't an hour since I heard the hall door shuttin' on another visitor—and maybe he's thinkin' 'tis enough of it he had."

"Then, let me!"

"Oh, don't, miss! Don't, for God's sake! 'Tis as much as my place is worth."

"Then go away, and let me do it alone. I'm not afraid of him." The girl put her hands on the charwoman's shoulders and pushed her from the door. "Go back to your work, and he won't even know that you let me in."

The woman yielded; and with a quick gesture, at once triumphant and excited, her conqueror turned the handle of the door and walked into the breakfast-room.

The opening of the door was sharp and sudden; Carey wheeled round in his chair, then sat motionless.

"Isabel!"

Isabel closed the door softly and securely, then turned and looked at him.

It would have been difficult—it would have been wellnigh impossible—to guess at the thoughts, the questions that held sway in her mind at that curious moment,—at the war of sensations that clashed within her. In the expression of her eyes, in the poise of her young body, in her eager, parted lips was the flowering of some subtle promise—the

outpouring of that mystic essence of womanhood
that had enchained Carey by its strange and secret
suggestion in his first vision of her at Fair Hill.

She stood there, waiting, expectant; and as he
made no sign, she tiptoed across the room and
paused beside his chair.

"I came," she said.

It was a breath—a mere whisper—but it ran
like wine through his blood. For one conquering
moment all things became dim; the knowledge
of her presence wrapped him like a perfumed garment; he turned to her, holding out his hands.

With a little cry she caught them.

"Ah! And I thought that you were angry!"

A flood of warmth, of passionate relief, swept
through the words. She confessed herself in that
brief sentence—laid bare her heart without fear or
shame.

"I know something happened last night, but I
don't know what it was." Her tongue, loosed by
her returned confidence, ran on in swift explanation.
"I saw nobody at all at breakfast this morning;
and Julia told me that you went up to town last
night on business, and that Mary and Father James
went up with Tom at nine this morning. At first
I was afraid, and wandered about the garden, wondering what I had better do; and then suddenly
—suddenly." Her fingers tightened about his, her
eyes besought his understanding. "I felt that
whatever had happened—whatever it was—I must
come to you. So I came! Was it any harm?"

Again the confession of allegiance—the sweet,
spontaneous confession in eyes and voice and

words. In sudden torture of mind, Carey freed his hands.

"Was it any harm? Oh, it was! You are angry!"

"No."

"Then what?" Doubt ran through her words like a fine vibration.

"Nothing. Nothing."

"Then why did you turn away?"

"Did I turn away?" He was striving blindly to gain time, attempting vainly to compound with fate.

"Yes, you did. Oh, I don't understand! You must be either sorry I came—or glad. You must be either pleased or angry. Which are you? Which? Which?"

"Glad." The words slipped out.

Again she gave a little cry, seizing upon the admission. "Ah, then nothing else matters!" With a sudden gracious movement she dropped to her knees beside him, and, looking up, strove to read his face.

"If you are glad, nothing else matters! Nothing else in the whole wide world matters! Wasn't that what you said last night?"

There was triumph, love, infinite allurement in the inflexions of her voice. She nestled up to him, drawing about her eyes that web of oblivion that women so deftly weave, shutting from her vision the broader issues of the moment, content in the consciousness of loving and being loved. She caught his hand again and held it against her cheek, and the warmth of the contact passed into him, thrilling him. The wild appeal of the blood woke in him, and with it the opposing cry of his will.

He withdrew his hand suddenly, almost pushing her from him.

"Isabel," he said, "we must forget last night! Do you understand? We must forget last night! It's past and dead and done with. We must forget it!"

Never afterwards could Isabel remember what she did in that moment, when the blood receded to her heart, ebbing from her face, her hands, her feet, and then rushed back—a torrent that sang in her ears. It seemed to her that the world had slipped away—that she was alone with Carey in space, in some vague and nebulous place, where time and circumstance did not exist. When at last her tongue found words, her voice assailed her ears, an uncontrolled, unfamiliar thing.

"What do you mean? We must forget last night?"

Then, for the first time since she had entered the room, he felt the impulse to stand up, not from the sense of courtesy, but from the blind human instinct of facing peril or pain upon one's feet rather than crouching in a seat. He rose, and stood before her, one hand holding the back of his chair, the other resting on the papers that still lay upon the table. There was something inexpressibly hopeless in the pose of his body—something final and tragic that sent the blood back once more to her heart.

"Oh, what is it?" she cried, in sudden articulate fear. "What is it? Don't stand like that. Don't look like that."

"It's nothing — but that we must forget last night. That we must forget it."

She stared at his drawn face. "But why? But why? Oh, but you're teasing me! It's some joke!" She tried to laugh; but it was a laugh that withered away, and in the silence that succeeded—the close, stifling silence that blent itself with the atmosphere of the room—the fear within her turned to panic.

"Oh, say something! Make me understand! I'll feel that I'm going mad if you don't make me understand. Last night you said that nobody existed but me—that I was the one thing in the world that made you want to live—that——"

Carey threw out his hands. "Stop! For the sake of God, stop! I tell you there was no last night. We dreamt it. It never was."

She faltered a little, but her courage was a strong thing. With an impulse, intensely ardent, intensely feminine, she moved towards him again.

"Something has happened that I don't understand. But, look, look, I care for you! I care!" She made a wide, proud gesture, offering herself to him. "I care!"

There was all love—all tenderness—all yielding in the movement and in the words; in both it seemed that nature had struck the chord of a great harmony.

Carey heard it—his soul vibrated to it, but he turned away, blindly, inarticulately.

"What is it? Don't you care any more?"

He was silent.

"Tell me! Tell me! I must know." Fear

rushed in again over her voice, marring the
music. Her words trembled, as she strove to
make him meet her glance.

"I can't explain. We must forget, that's all.
I can't explain."

She drew back very slowly, as though her movements were accommodating themselves to some
strange slow alteration taking place within her
mind.

"Then you're sorry for last night?"

"No! By God, I'm not!"

The cry was torn from him, but he disowned it
even as he gave it utterance. "No! I don't mean
that. I *am* sorry for it."

Her eyes blazed. "But you're not! The first
thing was the true one. You do care. I do matter
to you." She stepped forward, catching his arm.
"Look at me! You must. You must. Nothing
in the world can put last night away. What does
anything else matter? We care for each other. I'm
much more mad now than I was last night; then I
was afraid—I was afraid even to let you kiss me;
but afterwards, when I was alone in my own room
in the dark, I knew that I had imagined all the fear.
If you had come for me then, I'd have gone with
you out of the house, and not cared who saw. If
you were a tramp, walking the roads from one town
to another, I'd rather walk them with you than be
married to a king. I never knew I could feel so
much. It's all here—choking me!" She put her
hand to her throat. "'Tis that that made me come
here to-day—the feeling that I must tell you."

She stopped—breathless, passionate, reckless in

her prodigal giving. The emotions of her ancestors were racing through her—her blood was proving itself in a riot of feeling.

Carey listened—each word, each quickly-taken breath, searing him like a flame. At last his endurance broke.

"Stop!" he said. "Stop! It's all over. It's all over, I tell you. We were mad last night; we're sane to-day."

It was a torrent of water on a kindled fire, and the fire hissed up to meet it, quivering and fierce.

"You mean that? Truly, really, honestly you mean that?"

"I do."

No words in his life had cost him what those two words cost, but he said them steadily.

"You mean it? After all that you said? After all that I said?"

He bent his head.

"Then some one has been here? Some one has changed you?" She flashed round upon him, her body trembling, her eyes alight with question. Her emotions were swaying her from one pole to the other; it was a toss of a coin whether love or hate turned the scale.

He stood rigid—rigid as he had been in Father James's presence.

"I told you I have no defence to make. I know I seem a criminal and a coward; but you are young, you will forget—and it doesn't matter about me. I can only say, thank God I didn't ask you to come with me last night!"

Isabel's face flamed. "You say that? You say

'thank God' you didn't ask me to come with you last night?"

"I do."

"Then I say 'thank God' too!"

The scale had turned. Her face was white with rage—her whole being quivered with it. She seemed the very figure of fury—of outraged pride.

"I told you while ago that I cared for you," she said when she could command her voice. "Now I tell you that I feel nothing—nothing—nothing but that I hate you. I loathe you; I detest you. You are one of the rest—just one of the rest. What a fool I was ever to have thought that you were different! What a fool! What a·fool! I'm all right to dance with and to flirt with, when there's nothing better to do; but next morning, when you've had time to think——"

"Isabel!"

"Next morning you can say 'thank God I'm well out of it!'"

"Isabel!" He stood impotent before the sweeping gale of her rage. All the man in him cried appreciation of her scorn; all the passion in him urged him to one act—to seize her in his arms, to hold her as he had held her last night, covering her lips with kisses, hiding his face in the dark cloud of her hair. But he made no movement; he stood stonily silent, seeing with the eyes of his mind the thronging ghosts that surged between them.

And Isabel saw only the mask—the set face, the impassive figure.

"Oh," she cried again, "I wonder now, when I look at you, how I could ever have been so mad as to care! I wish I had words enough to tell you all I feel. To say that I hate you is nothing—nothing——"

She drew a sharp breath; and their eyes met in a long eloquent glance.

"I feel—I feel that I could kill you!" she said; and turning suddenly, she ran to the .door, ran down the hall and out into the close, deserted street.

CHAPTER XXIX.

Down the street went Isabel — a slim white figure in the still picture of dusty town life, hurrying onward, looking neither to right nor left, seeking her home with the instinct of a hurt animal. The heat was intense, her light cotton dress felt a weight about her limbs, her exhaustion showed itself in a dew of moisture that broke out upon her forehead, but she never paused, never moderated her pace until the New Town hill confronted her with its ironical sense of old association.

Waterford is a lethargic place on a summer morning, and she aroused little comment as she made her hasty progress. One or two passers-by looked after her, to wonder why any one should hurry on so hot a day; otherwise, she passed unnoticed.

There was nobody about, as she opened Miss Costello's little gate; nobody about, as she walked up the little strip of garden, arid in the baking sunshine. It looked like a place of death, and the rage in her heart burned hotter as her glance skimmed over the dry earth and parched flowers.

This was life, a thing of revolt—hot, thirsty, seared!

She raised her hand and pulled the bell until its sound echoed through the house, causing Lizzie, the servant, to rush to the bedroom window, and Miss Costello to drop the bowl in which she was making a pudding for the early dinner.

The bowl was dropped precipitately; and, without waiting to dust the flour from her dress, Miss Costello ran into the little hall and opened the front door.

"What on earth possessed you to ring like that?" she demanded angrily; then amazement overspread her angry face. "Why, the Lord defend us, it's Isabel!" she exclaimed. "What, in the name of Heaven, has brought you, child? And at this hour of the morning? I didn't expect you for a week!"

Isabel made no response, but, pushing past her, stepped into the hall.

Miss Costello stared at her, forgetting in her surprise to close the door.

"What's the matter? Did anything happen to you down at the Careys'?"

The word was a lash to Isabel's soul. "Nothing!" she cried.

"Then, what on earth——?"

"Nothing—nothing—nothing, don't I tell you! I'm back, that's all. Can't you see for yourself!"

"But how did you get here? Where's your trunk?"

"I left it. It's down there."

Miss Costello stood with open mouth. "Is it the way you had a row with them—or what?"

"No. It's not."

There was no room in Isabel's mind for the
thought of conventionality. Once and forever she
had stepped beyond its pale. She was living now
as her feelings prompted—undisciplined, primitive,
careless of all comment.

"But, good gracious," cried Miss Costello, "you
must give some reasons! You wouldn't come back
like this, as if you had dropped out of the sky,
unless you were mad!"

Isabel wheeled round upon her, her face damp
and white. "Then that's the reason," she cried.
"I am mad. I'm stark, staring, raving mad; and
I'd advise you to let me alone!"

Without waiting for an answer, she ran up the
stairs; and Miss Costello heard the door of her
bedroom shut with a crash that vibrated through
the whole flimsy house.

Inside her own room, her first action was to
wrench off her hat. She pulled out the pins
with fierce haste, then stuck them back again
savagely into the straw, and flung the hat from
her across the room. She had known little of
life's sublimities in her short span of years; and
all that was elemental and self-engrossed had been
unloosed by to-day's pain. From her passions and
her prodigality she had given of her best; and
that best had been flung back to her—a rejected
gift. She saw nothing behind that casting back
of her favours. Carey had played with her—Carey
had humiliated her—Carey had branded her as the
poorest of things, the woman who has offered herself and been refused.

As she stood there in the low-ceiled room, so cramped, so tawdry, so intolerable in its herd of memories, she lost touch for ever with those about her: she inevitably proved herself the possessor of alien blood—the southern woman, all instinct and emotion, whose mind in its native environment would have flown straight to the thought of revenge—to some headlong business of swift-turning wrist and deadly knife. The thoughts within her sang to a tune generations old—a tune that the fierce, piratical sailor-folk who were her ancestors had brought with them long ago from Spain, when they swooped down in adventurous spirit upon the misty coast of Ireland.

A woman of these sadder isles would have bent under the misery that assailed her in that hour. Appalled by the blackness of life, she would have cowered upon the ground and wept, until her agony and her bitterness were melted by her tears. But in Isabel the old strenuous spirit was awake, drying up the source of tears, scorching her brain, conserving her impulses for some perfect act of self-expression. She was the primitive being —the being who does not probe and does not analyse—who knows what life offers, and acts instinctively upon the knowledge.

She stood there, giving rein to her passions, her figure erect, her hands holding back the hair from her forehead; and, without conscious desire, her life reacted itself, passing before her like the slides in a magic-lantern. Each poor object in the room quickened some recollection. Here, she had dressed for her first dance, intoxicated with the joy of anticipation; here, she had waited with beating heart on the long-ago Sunday when her aunt and Carey had talked in the parlour downstairs; here, she had met the first disappointment, hidden in Carey's brief letter.

Her mind hung over the remembrance of that night. How young she had been then, in her consideration of trivial things! Mere ink and paper had called forth her emotions; mere contact with Frank's little bottle of poison had been sufficient to make her shudder!

Her mind passed from one train of thought to another. Frank! What a poor, miserable coward Frank had proved himself! From her own red anger she looked back upon her last scene with him. How differently she would have acted on that morning, had she been in his place! Conjuring her own coldness, her own desertion, she wondered now that he had not killed her, rather than leave her for another.

The scene, as it might have been, rose before her sharply; the thought of the consummating deed—the poignant act of killing—closed in upon her so vividly that she drew a nervous, audible breath, and let her hands drop to her sides.

That would have been something worth doing! That would have been a drowning of pain and shame! a justification of himself!

Enmeshed in the dream, she closed and opened her hands, as though she could feel the touch of flesh, the yielding of muscle and sinew. What she would give to be a man! To be a man for one

hour, with Frank's lost opportunity! Again her
fingers locked and unlocked themselves; and her
eyes, driven by her thoughts, turned to the spot
where she had hidden away the little poison
bottle on the night of the Fair Hill card-party.

Instead of that dealing in swift justice, Frank
had played with death — death wrapped in little
white lozenges, like wine in a sweetmeat!

Without definite intention, her feet moved slowly
across the room; without definite intention, they
paused before the cupboard where the bottle was
hidden, and mechanically her hand went out towards
the hiding-place.

How young she had been then, to tremble at the
sight of those white tabloids!

With automatic slowness she opened the drawer,
permitting a scent of dry decay to issue forth upon
the air; and, putting in her hand, groped for and
found the small glass object.

It was certainly small, to carry such potency!
She drew it forth, and her lips twisted scornfully.
No man who was worth the name of man would
have contented himself with these, while he had
his own strong hands! These were the weapons of
a child—of a woman!

The thought flashed through her—flashed through
her, unbidden, trembling like a flame from her brain
to her nerves—so supreme, so overmastering that it
shook her as a gale shakes the sapling.

She held the bottle to the light, and her hand
trembled so violently that the tabloids rattled one
against the other.

After all, death was death! Her muscles suddenly stiffened, her glance narrowed until a mere pin-point of light showed between the eyelids.

After all, death was death! Whether it was an affair of knives, of naked hands, or white lozenges, death was death!

CHAPTER XXX.

THE day of tumult was a Friday, and the Saturday broke at Kilmeaden in a splendour of green and gold—a lavish prodigality of sunlight, that spread itself over tree and stream and meadow in a shimmering banner of gold.

A wonderful morning; a summer morning, when every living creature basked in the consciousness of life; when birds sang riotously, and insects hummed as they hung passive in the haze of heat.

The hour was nine; upstairs in the nursery the three children exulted, as the birds and the insects were exulting in the open, thrilled by the vibrating sense of youth; at the hall door Carey's motor-car stood, a dark motionless object in the scene that palpitated with the suggestion of expansion and growth; in the bare, clean, monastic-looking dining-room, Daisy and Stephen were meeting again in the lull that supersedes the storm.

The scene was plain — plain and undramatic. The table was laid simply for the morning meal; the full light poured in through the uncurtained windows; a country bunch of buttercups adorned the white cloth.

Carey had halted just inside the door; and Daisy

was standing by one of the windows in a blue
cotton dress, her fair hair neatly brushed, the heavy
purple shadows of sleeplessness lying beneath her
eyes. She looked tired and pathetic, but she had
regained her self-control. She was no longer the
despairing creature who had driven him forth
from the house two nights ago; she was a woman
who had bought calm with pain and tears, and
whose glance, as it sped across the room, spoke
many things.

There was no attempt at greeting. In the
middle classes artifice has little place; each knew
that the other knew, and explanations seemed
superfluous.

At last Carey came forward into the light of
the window.

"Daisy," he said, "I have come back."

That was all. No tragedy, no dramatic effect;
and Daisy, the eternal type—the wife, the mother—
accepted the words without question. Looking up,
she saw the suffering in her husband's face—the
revolt, the struggle, the agonising triumph. She
did not understand it, for such women are content
to class the man of their choice as a being inevitably incomprehensible; but the maternal instinct
in her gushed forth in sudden pity for this being
who had returned to her maimed and in pain.

"Oh, Stephen!" she said in a shaken voice.
"Stephen!" and with a new, self-conscious hesitancy, she put out her hand and touched his.

.   .   .   .

So Carey returned to his home, unheralded and
unexcused. The return was in accord with his

life—strong, restrained, without colour; it seemed at once an emblem and a prophecy.

Immediately the breakfast was brought into the dining-room, he passed without interference to a room at the top of the house where it was his habit to read and smoke on wet days during the summer. This room was comfortless; a deal-table and a couple of kitchen chairs were its only furniture, and the whitewashed walls were bare save for a few fishing-rods, a gun, and a pipe-rack. But its very barrenness, its very coldness, suited him on this day of shimmering glory; its plainness fitted with his mood; its isolation almost suggested peace. Locking the door, he threw himself into one of the unyielding chairs, and felt mechanically in his pocket for his pipe and tobacco-pouch — the silent comforters of man's black hours.

Time passed in the locked room; the day waxed, and with it the sun's strength; nothing marked the flight of the minutes except the thickening of the smoke wreaths, as Carey sat slowly smoking, slowly refilling and relighting pipe after pipe. His mood during that deadened space of time was the mood of a man jaded physically and mentally: exhaustion had fallen upon him — a deep lassitude that almost deprived him of the power of thought — and one desire alone found place within his brain, the desire for solitude.

Lunch time came, but the summoning gong passed unnoticed. Two o'clock came, three o'clock; then at four the quiet was broken. A faint and deprecating knock sounded upon the door.

He started like a man caught in some guilty act.

"Who's that? Who's there?"

"It's me, Stephen—Daisy," came the answer.

"Very well! I'll open. Wait a minute!" Quietly, and without hesitation, he rose and walked across the room: it was the same manner in which he had approached Daisy earlier in the morning, and it almost seemed that he had mapped out a course of action in her regard, and was holding to it fixedly.

He opened the door and stood aside for her to pass.

"I'm frightfully sorry to bother you, but the unluckiest thing has happened!" She walked into the room, then turned to look up into his face through the cloud of tobacco-smoke. "Mrs Power and Josephine and two of the boys are below. I never expected such a thing, but they specially hoped to find you here, as it's Saturday, and they haven't seen you since the engagement. I said I'd try if you were in; but if you like I can go back and say you're not——" Her glance lingered over his jaded face.

For a moment the impetuous annoyance of old days surged up within him — the sharp, contemptuous rejoinder rose to his lips; then with the new control, he checked both.

"Would you rather I went down?"

"Oh, no; not if you dislike to. Mary and Father James and I can entertain them. 'Twas only that I was thinking——" She paused and coloured and looked away.

"What? That they'll talk?"

"That, perhaps, they might talk."

Carey nodded grimly. "I'll go down."

"No. No, don't."

"Yes; I'll go. Where are they now?"

"In the drawing-room. You can see them there for a minute, and then I'll take them out. Mary and Josephine and the two boys can play a game of tennis—and Mrs Power and I can look on."

Again the change was visible in Daisy—the new endurance, the new consciousness of responsibility; and through the vapour of his misery, Carey saw and was mutely thankful.

"All right! Go down! I'll follow you." Again he held the door open for her; then he turned back for a moment into the empty room, to brace himself for the ordeal.

All his soul revolted from the task awaiting him —all his sick senses shrank from contact with the common world—but he had made his choice. Henceforth his way would lie along the common path— his life would be the common life! All the fair and splendid circumstance of dreams lay behind him.

He knocked the ashes from his pipe, pushed his chair back into its accustomed place and passed out of the room.

On the stairs, the smell of the washed boards— the scent of the musk in the red pots upon the window-sill — touched him to torturing memory. This morning he had moved past them, numb and unheeding; but now they rose about him poignantly, recalling the brief moments of romance.

Outside the drawing-room he paused to gather

up his strength. He had not seen this room since the night of his adventure, and it lay within his mind as it had looked then—a place of half lights and faded perfumes, pregnant with sentiment. He paused, dazed by the cloud of recollection that surged about him; then he raised his hand, opened the door, and at once Mrs Power's voice—slow, contented, motherly—dispelled illusion.

The visitors were gathered about the centre table where the tea things were laid out, flanked by a large silver punch-bowl and a tray of glasses. The windows were all open; the sun streamed into the room; a little ripple of laughter was trembling on the air, evoked by Mrs Power's last remark.

As Carey entered, she turned to him, a glass in one hand, a silver ladle upraised in the other.

"Ah, here you are, Stephen! Come and be the arbiter! Daisy insists that claret-cup is a temperance drink, and Josephine says it isn't. For goodness' sake, agree with Daisy, for I'm famished with thirst, and the thought of tea on a day like this is enough to give any one apoplexy."

Carey forced a laugh and came forward towards the table. In that first moment he was conscious of nothing but a deep thankfulness for the shelter of Mrs Power's volubility.

"I think Father Mathew himself would exempt you from tea with a temperature like this," he said. "If I were you, I'd take the risk."

Mrs Power beamed, and proceeded to fill her glass generously from the dark, cool liquid in the bowl. "Now, that's what I call logic," she said placidly. "After all, there's no profession like the law—it finds such reasonable excuses for our little peccadillos. What do you say, Father James?"

Father James, who had been standing modestly in a corner, came out into the light at her challenge.

"Well, well, well!" he said. "Sure, after all, what is wine but a gift out of the earth!"

"Very good, indeed, Father James! Though I see Josephine looking a little bit shocked. She's a great total-abstainer, you know, since she attended the last mission!"

Father James smiled across at Josephine Power, a pale-faced, large-boned girl, who was looking with prim disapproval at her easy-going mother.

"Ah, Josephine, that's the way of youth!" he said. "All for total-abstinence or total-acceptance! 'Tis only age brings the happy medium—moderation. Daisy, may I have a sup of that claret-cup myself?"

"Indeed you may! Mrs Power, will you give it to him? We were just going out to the tennis-court, Stephen. The girls are going to play."

She spoke without looking at Carey, and he answered with averted eyes.

"That's right! It's too fine to stay in. Mrs Power, I'll give Father James his drink while you finish yours."

Mrs Power willingly resigned the ladle, and fell to sipping the contents of her glass.

"And what about yourself, Stephen?" she said. "We ought to drink to the engagement, you know. Where's Mary?"

"Mary is gone out with Jim and Eddy, to get

the tennis rackets," said Daisy. "They're waiting on the court for us."

"Ah, well, another time! And now, Stephen, come and talk to me. I haven't thought or spoken of another thing since Owen told me the great news. 'Tis the wish of my heart fulfilled." She moved towards the mantelpiece, still smiling, still sipping her claret-cup.

Carey half filled a tumbler for himself, and followed her across the room.

"I agree with you," he murmured. "It's very satisfactory—very satisfactory for all concerned!"

Strive as he might to fix his attention, the commonness of the scene, its triviality, its futility, warred intolerably with his unhappy thoughts. These people with their petty interests, their familiar, unemotional voices, were things irreconcilable with his mood,—files that grated upon his jarred nerves.

"Ah, 'tis a great thing! 'Tis a great thing!" Mrs Power went on. "After all, 'tis the right end for every young fellow—to marry a nice girl and settle down! Look what it did for you, Stephen! Not, indeed, that you were ever anything but steady! But still, a young man improves so much with a nice wife; it seems to form his character."

Stephen murmured something acquiescent; and Father James opportunely stepped up to the fireplace.

"And how is your own good man, Mrs Power?" he said. "I saw him up in town yesterday."

Mrs Power turned, full of new interest. "He's flourishing, indeed, Father James! Like myself, he's full of delight over this news about Owen.

But all Kilmeaden seems to have been up in town yesterday! Tom and Mary lunched with us; and now Daisy tells me that Isabel was up too."

"She was indeed. 'Twas the way her aunt sent for her," said Father James, telling the white lie nobly. "She had one of her bad headaches, it seems, and got a little bit nervous about herself. Indeed, I pitied the poor child, dragged up to New Town on such a killing day!"

Mrs Power looked interested. "Good gracious! You surprise me!" she said. "I was behind Miss Costello at the ten o'clock mass, and I thought I never saw her looking better."

"Ah, well, old people take notions!"

Mrs Power shook her head sympathetically. "They do. They do, indeed! And all the Costellos are a bit cranky. I suppose Isabel will be back to-day?"

The question was addressed to Stephen; but Stephen had turned his back, and was lost in a study of the old gilt clock on the mantelpiece.

"No doubt! No doubt she will!" said Father James. "But Daisy is waiting for you, Mrs Power."

Mrs Power turned round. "Oh, Daisy, are you going?"

"Yes; Josephine and I are ready. Won't you come?"

"I will, dear; I will. Only give me time to drink this. You go on, and I'll be after you!"

"Very well! But don't forget I'll be by myself when the game begins!"

"No, dear. I won't."

Daisy and Josephine Power passed out through the glass door and down the long green garden, their cotton dresses making patches of colour in the full sunlight. Mrs Power sipped her drink again, then turned to Stephen with a new air of confidence. "Now, Stephen, there's something I want to have a little word with you about. Of course, we're all anxious that this engagement shouldn't be a long one—I don't approve of long engagements; and there's nothing for Owen and Mary to wait for. So Mr Power is determined to make things easy for them; and I think that you, as our solicitor——"

Father James was moving discreetly away, but she checked him with a smile and a wave of the hand.

"Don't go, Father James! Sure, what is there in any of our families that you don't know! 'Twas only that I thought, having Stephen here now, we might as well talk the matter over in a friendly way, instead of going down formally to the office."

Carey looked round sharply, seeming not to have heard Mrs Power's words.

"What was that?" he said. "Wasn't that the hall-door bell?"

"I don't know. I didn't hear anything. As I was saying to Father James, Stephen——"

Carey laid his glass upon the mantelshelf. A nervous look of prescience—a peculiar uneasiness—was visible on his face.

"One moment, Mrs Power," he said. "I think there's somebody outside."

Mrs Power looked slightly offended, and Father James glanced sharply at Carey.

"Will I go and see, Stephen? Maybe 'tis some visitor for Daisy, and I could take them out to the tennis-ground."

"Yes," said Carey quickly. "Yes, do. Ah, there's Julia going down the hall!"

All three stood listening; then suddenly Carey took a step forward, as though he had heard some sound to which the others were deaf.

"Father James!" he said involuntarily; then his voice died away. The door was opened by Julia, and without announcement Isabel walked into the room.

The eyes of the three turned upon her simultaneously, seeing her variously, according to their lights. Mrs Power, from the dazzling pinnacle of her maternal happiness, saw nothing but a figure in a limp white dress, a face overshadowed by untidy hair and a carelessly arranged hat; Father James, in his all-pervading pity, saw a human soul looking out upon the world in revolt and misery; Carey saw nothing but the fire in the dark eyes.

Of the three, Mrs Power was the first to offer greeting.

"Good gracious, it's Isabel!" she cried. "Isabel, dear, how are you! I hope your aunt isn't bad; you look as if you had been up all night."

Father James stepped forward and took Isabel's hand. "Isabel," he said, "we were just this minute talking about you. I was telling Mrs Power how your aunt sent for you yesterday, because she had one of her headaches." He made the explanation insistently, pressing her hand to force it home.

But Isabel only stared at him. It was obvious that her own thoughts, her own emotions, filled her mind to the exclusion of all else. Convention she had thrown aside; expediency she had discarded as a worn-out garment. She drew her hand from Father James's, and stood looking from him to Mrs Power, as if flaunting her unexpected presence, flaunting her dishevelled appearance.

"I don't know what you're talking about," she said.

Mrs Power stared; then she made a motherly gesture of concern. "My dear, what is it? You look tired out. Was the drive too much for you?"

Isabel drew back to avoid the proffered caress. "I didn't drive. I walked."

"You walked? You walked from Waterford? Why, you must have been mad!"

The girl made a curious little sound that might have been a laugh.

Carey turned towards her. "Good God! You walked?"

"Yes, I walked. How else was I to get here? I'm too poor to drive."

He turned from the scorn of her glance.

"Mrs Power," he said indistinctly, "will you come out to the tennis-court. I'll be back again, Father James!"

Mrs Power took another sharp look at Isabel; then she followed Carey across the room. As they passed together through the glass door she laid her hand on his arm.

"Did you ever see anybody look so queer as Isabel, Stephen?" she said. "It's my belief that she got a touch of the sun, coming out. If I were Daisy I'd put her to bed and send for the doctor. She's certainly not herself."

And Carey, from the ferment within his mind, made some inarticulate reply.

CHAPTER XXXI.

ALONE in the drawing-room, Isabel and Father James stood looking at each other. Now, as at the moment of her entry, the old priest saw nothing of her disordered clothes, nothing of her unkempt hair and dusty shoes; all he saw, all he yearned over, was the dumb misery that had stamped itself on her face, blotting out its beauty, its youth, its colour, as a cruel heel might crush the life from a flower.

"Child! child!" he said suddenly. "What's come to you? What's come to you, at all?"

Isabel stared defiance. "What you wanted to come to me—you and the rest!"

The flame within her whipped the words forth, as it had kindled the light in her eyes.

He came a step nearer to her, but she wheeled away from him, unconsciously taking up the position by the mantelpiece that Carey had vacated.

"Oh, yes," she added. "It's all just as it ought to be! Daisy and Mary playing tennis; you preaching; he comfortably eating and drinking!" She paused to catch up the half-filled tumbler. "This is his, isn't it?"

"Isabel, child!"

"This is his, isn't it? Wasn't he calmly drinking this, while I was trudging through the heat and the dust? Wasn't he? Wasn't he?"

"And if he was itself, child, sure mustn't we all eat and drink, whatever happens? Isn't that the tragedy of life?"

"The tragedy!" She laughed and looked again at the glass, as if attracted by the cool red liquid. "I haven't wanted to eat or drink since yesterday."

Concern and compassion overspread Father James's face.

"Glory be to God! You don't mean that?"

"Yes, I do. I have had other things to think about. I suppose women are different from men." She still held the glass, moving it about as the sunlight played upon the wine.

"But that's a terrible thing! You can't go on like that. See here now." Again he ventured to move nearer to her.

With a quick, fierce gesture she laid down Carey's glass and turned upon him. "And why can't I go on like that?" she demanded. "I care nothing more about what any of you say—or any of you think. Why can't I go on as I like?"

Something in her face, something in her voice, alarmed him by its intensity. For a moment he wavered before it; then he collected his quiet strength—his inexhaustible gentleness.

"Look here, Isabel," he said, "I'm going to pour out a glass of that wine, and you're going to swallow it to please me."

Refusal—sharp and violent—sprang to her lips; then some suggestion, some thought, arrested it in the utterance; her expression changed curiously, and she answered unexpectedly.

"Very well! Get it for me."

Immense relief touched Father James, and he hurried across the room to the tea-table.

Isabel stood very still. Only her eyes and her right hand showed any sign of life—her eyes following the old priest's movements with a passion of intentness, her right hand stealing silently, stealthily, towards the pocket of her dress. There was a moment of suspense; then, as he bent over the punch-bowl, carefully measuring out the wine, her fingers found the pocket, shot into the light again, and, with a swift noiseless action, dropped two small white objects into Carey's glass.

It was an absolutely simple act—dexterous, controlled, silent; and as Father James walked slowly back across the room, carrying the wine, there was nothing to tell of a deed accomplished.

"Now, child, to please me! To please an old man!" He held out the glass.

Isabel looked at him; then, with a gesture of finality, put her hands behind her back.

"No, Father James. No." Her tone was no longer stormy, but it was vibrating and tense.

Father James's eyes narrowed in closer scrutiny. "What is it, Isabel?" he said. "What's come to you?"

"Nothing. I'm—nearly happy."

"Happy? How happy?"

"Because I hate him so absolutely much."

Again the chill of fear passed over the old priest.

"Isabel," he said hurriedly, "drink the wine! There's a good child, now! Drink the wine!"

"I'll never drink wine again—never as long as I live, after to-day."

Alarm sprang into his eyes. "Child, what's the matter with you? Why are you so still and quiet-like?"

"I told you."

"But I don't like it! I don't like it!" In his blind sense of misgiving he put out his hand and touched her arm. "Isabel, child, I don't like you like this! I'd rather you raving, as you were while ago; it's more natural. Look now! Rouse yourself!"

Isabel shook off his hand.

"And what does it matter how I am? Who in all the world cares?"

He was silent for a space; then, looking at her, he said steadily, "One person cares."

"Who?"

"Stephen."

"Stephen!" She made a wild, contemptuous sound.

"Don't laugh," he said sternly. "Oh, how cursed we are, that not one of us can see outside his own little life—that God doesn't open our eyes to one another's sorrows. Child! child! can't you see that Stephen is broken over this business? Can't you see anything at all but the blackness in your own heart?"

Isabel's wild eyes turned upon him. "How am I to see it? Where am I to see it?"

"In his face. Look at his face. He's coming

back now; I hear him in the garden. Look at him when he comes in. Look at his face."

Carey's step sounded on the garden path, and Isabel turned as he stepped through the glass door.

He came in quietly, his figure silhouetted against the brilliant afternoon light, and it seemed in a curious way that the long shadow his figure cast emanated from something within him—something dark and tragic—rather than by the mere effect of sunlight. There was tangible suffering, tangible struggle, marked upon him; and its very silence, its very strength, made it the more defined. A long, faint shudder passed through Isabel as she stood watching him with her brooding eyes.

He came into the room; he looked about him, as if dazed by the alteration of lights; then he walked aimlessly forward to the mantelpiece.

Isabel's eyes followed him.

The silence was tense; conscious of her searching gaze, tortured by it and by the ordeal to be re-lived, he looked desperately round for some rational, calming influence. By a common chance, his eye fell upon his untasted wine standing on the mantelshelf.

He felt no thirst; the parched dryness of his throat, the burning heat of his brain, would have demanded more than a cup of iced wine; but it was a natural, rational act to pick up the glass, and he turned like a man unnerved to any rational idea. Slowly, automatically, he put out his hand.

Then suddenly a little cry, very low, very faint broke from Isabel. She put out her hand and arrested his.

"Wait!" she said. "Wait!"

For an instant her fingers lingered upon his; then she drew the tumbler away from him, lifted it slowly, and drank.

The glass rattled against her teeth; the touch of the ice chilled her lips; but, looking down into the wine, her eyes caught the warmth, the redness, the glory of the sun.

THE END.

AFTERWORD

When the *Irish Book Lover* published its obituary of Katherine Cecil Thurston in its October 1911 edition, its reference to the "tragic circumstances" surrounding the death of "one of the most brilliant of the women writers of the day" needed no elaboration. Since early September of that year, both English and Irish newspapers had been following the story of her flamboyant life and shockingly sudden death: daughter of a man who had been both a close friend of Parnell and a popular mayor of Cork city, ex-wife of the prolific English novelist E. Temple Thurston, a celebrated novelist in her own right, Thurston had planned to marry again in the same month in which her body was found in a room in Moore's Hotel, Cork. The inquest into her death fuelled the buzz of speculation, rumour and comment, and although the *Dublin Evening Herald* reports circumspectly avoided mention of the exact nature of its findings, the English *Daily Sketch* was more satisfyingly explicit — Thurston, it revealed, was found to have died of suffocation following an epileptic fit.

It was a verdict which did not entirely satisfy many readers, principally because of the subject and, especially, the ending of her penultimate novel — *The Fly on the Wheel*. As the Irish bibliographer Stephen Brown could not resist remarking in the annotation to this 1908 novel in his catalogue of *Ireland In Fiction* (1911), and as many of Thurston's legion of readers doubtless agreed, "the manner of the Author's own death gives this a poignant interest".

At her death at the age of thirty six, Thurston commanded an enormous audience, a devoted following which had been secured by the spectacular success of her second book, *John Chilcote, MP* (1904), a political thriller set in the Westminster corridors of power. Spiced with themes straight from sensationalist fiction — doubles who switch identities, drug addition, illicit love affairs, the fall of a government, unrest in the Empire — *John Chilcote* was not only deliciously daring but also an immediate success in both popular and critical terms. It went into edition after edition, sold over 200,000 copies in the USA alone, and brought Thurston a world-wide celebrity which not only made her wealthy, but which also gave her an audience for her more experimental novels, such as the "curious" *Max*, which appeared in the year of her death. The plot of *Max*, which concerns a young woman who successfully passes herself off as a man for almost the entire novel, forms not only a clearly-articulated female fantasy of turn-of-the-century strivings toward gender-based equality, but also a passionate *cri de coeur* of personal frustration, even of anguish. "I made myself a man," the heroine explains, "not for a whim, but as a symbol. Sex is only an accident, but the world has made man the independent creature — and I desired independence." These questions of independence and power lie at the centre of all Thurston's writing, but never are they as sensitively probed as in *The Fly on the Wheel*, the novel which was closest to Thurston's heart, and the one in which she is most dextrous in blending those two characteristic — and often warring — elements of her work: a flair for the dramatic and an abiding interest in psychology.

The Fly on the Wheel might, in fact, be described as a psychological novel; it might as easily be categorised as a sociological novel, so intense is Thurston's focus not only on the major protagonists but also on the environment which shapes them. The novel is set in Waterford and its environs, a part of the country in which Thurston herself kept a house, and which she marks out in the novel as the stronghold of the provincial Catholic middle class in the first decade of the new century. The Ireland of *The Fly on the Wheel* is not the wild Celtic Ireland so commonly depicted in the Irish novel of the nineteenth century; on the contrary, Thurston's Waterford, like Joyce's Dublin, is Catholic, English-speaking, petit-bourgeois. It is the territory of a rising yet insecure class that Thurston describes as "strong in its own narrow purpose", "held together by material ambitions and common ideals". In its attempts to consolidate its position, middle-class Waterford is a complex web of interrelatedness, shared history, and mutual aspirations. It forms itself into a comfortable but also claustrophobic world of self-absorbed obligations and self-imposed duties; it tries not to notice such threatening issues as Home Rule and the Gaelic League, preferring instead to look inward and to hug to itself such sureties as custom. As a book about the shared fabric of community, *The Fly on the Wheel* is epitomised by its analysis of Waterford mores. But it is brought to life through Thurston's portrayals of characters who reveal not only the orthodoxies of their society but also the individual lives which are so intimately bound up with them.

Thurston's hero, Stephen Carey, is "a type" of the middle class, a hero only "so far as middle-class Irish life produces heroes", a self-made rarity in a milieu where connections count for everything. It is typical of Thurston's careful detailing that Stephen, representative of the patriarchal forces which shape and control his society, has himself been betrayed; left responsible for his father's undischarged debts as well as the education of his six younger brothers, Stephen's anomalous heroism has been forged in terms which Waterford society appreciates. A successful solicitor when the novel opens, Stephen's position in Waterford is quintessentially middle class not only in professional terms but also in personal ones. Married to the daughter of one of the town's richest men, father of three young sons, owner of both townhouse and a country retreat, secure in the position which he has wrested for himself, Stephen is clearly the dutiful son of the patriarchal order and has been rewarded for his adherence to its values. But he is also aware that he has bent himself to its yoke; that the price of "playing the eternal game" has been the suppression of revolt and passion and the decision to service the "machine called expediency".

It is precisely the opposite decision — the refusal to "feed the monster" — which characterises Isabel Costello. She, too, is a product of the mechanics of middle-class Waterford; she, too, has been betrayed by her father's financial incompetence — a grievous sin indeed in a world which is built on the alliance of position and wealth and soldered by the appropriate marriage. As an orphan with neither money nor position, but with a dangerous beauty, Isabel is clearly, and immediately, perceived as a threat to that world. Even her name, with its suggestion of the voluptuous south, contrasts with the commonplace Marys and Daisys of Waterford; even before she herself appears in the novel she is perceived as a threat to the middle-class order. Her impulsive engagement to Stephen Carey's brother, made within ten days of her departure from her convent boarding-school, is typical of her desire for a life of action and of her disregard for convention. Long before she tempts "mature, controlled, successful" Stephen out of the Victorian family group and the ring of middle-class society which encloses and supports it, Isabel is characterized by the watchful, warning voices of Waterford as "different from the rest of us", one, "God help her, that'll be asking too much from life". In the intense parochialism of the small town's unquestioning Catholicism, Isabel is marked out as a child of nature rather than as a child of God. Her lack of a social conscience is indicated by her indifference as to whether or not local society takes her up; far more serious is her lack of doctrinal morality. Her years with the nuns have made little impression except to fill her with impatience to begin and experience adult life: a girl who genuinely questions the concept of rightness and wrongness, who confesses herself incapable of feeling wrong, is anathema to a world which adheres wholeheartedly to the dictum that "all girls need to know is that they must say their prayers — and never give bad example". From her entrance into Waterford society, dressed in the emblematic white of a sacrificial offering, Isabel is restless and energetic, a "young animal" who takes possession not only of the dance floor but of all of the Waterford menfolk. Every image which Thurston uses to describe her — a flower, a bird, an animal — suggests a being "pulsing in the delight of living and knowing itself to be alive". In a tableau which mimes the drama of sexual choice, Isabel is first seen surrounded by prospective dancing partners; her eyes are "roving from one man's face to another, in transparent joy at the exercise of power". Clearly ripe for life, Isabel's depiction in terms of sexual response suggests her readiness for sexual experience: "As her body was built upon gracious lines, so her mind had already flowered, where others lay folded in the bud."

As George Eliot observes in *Middlemarch*, public opinion is always of the feminine gender. Thurston, too, peoples her novel with Waterford women who act as the protectors of middle-class morality and who uphold and enforce its values. With her cloud of dark hair, her New Womanish public cigarette smoking, her suspect foreign education, Isabel's determined refusal to "squeeze down to fit" Waterford society marks her as a deviant, a temptress who not only flouts the conservative and pious Catholicism of Waterford, but who also threatens to undermine that most essential foundation of society, the family. Matrons such as Mrs Burke and Mrs Power are quick to recognise the implicit danger and to react instinctively by "shepherding" Isabel, by expressing disapproval of her cheerfully-admitted "unladylike" appetites, even, when necessary, by warning her off. Isabel's rejection of the cautious conservatism of the middle class, first expressed through her precipitous engagement — which, ironically, Stephen intervenes to break off "like you'd lop a dead branch from a tree" — subsequently expressed by her seeming inability to recognise the sanctity of marriage-as-institution, points up her relationship to Waterford society.

The exploration of the institution, the "product of the economic and social class realities that make

a mockery of love" is one of Thurston's avowed
interests in the novel; it is also the chief means by
which she lays bare the world of Waterford. In
spite of the Catholicism which permeates the novel,
in spite of the celebrations of communal worship
and the private pieties, marriage is not an expression
of a religious sacrament but an economic and social
arrangement. Like George Moore's *A Drama In
Muslin*, *The Fly on the Wheel* is an Irish novel of the
marriage market. "Without a husband," says the
scheming mother in Moore's novel,

> a woman is nothing; with a husband she may
> rise to any height. Marriage gives a girl liberty,
> gives her admiration, gives her success; a
> woman's whole position depends on it.

It is by this creed that the women of middle-
class Waterford live. But to a woman they deny
even the thought that they might marry for "money
or position or any such thing as that". Isabel, from
her position as outsider, recognises the truth, the
hypocrisy and the carefully-cultivated fiction, and,
in contrast to those who see the truth but prefer to
subscribe to the illusion, she is not afraid to speak
out. Indeed, the reality is so unavoidable that
even her pious and unworldly Aunt Theresa cannot
help bemoaning the lack of money which is the
cause of "a good match like that slipping away
before our very eyes". It is the same reality which
causes Stephen, as a "natural sequence of events",
to follow his professional training with an advantageous marriage. That he thinks of marriage with
the "faint savour of Orientalism so frequently to be

found in his country and his class" enables him to marry a woman whom he considers to have "no more susceptability than a doll".

The contrast between Isabel and Stephen's wife Daisy is more than simply that of relative sensibilities. Thurston employs a number of devices to establish the relative positions of her chief female protagonists. Primary among them is the antimony of the blond wife who typifies the traditional values of the community and the dark temptress/interloper who exists outside the boundaries of the community and threatens to breach them. Daisy, "placid, unthinking" is "the eternal type — the wife, the mother", "one whose days are full of small concerns and who is obviously content to shape the future on the pattern of the past". Her constant mending, a signifier of her domesticity, is the perfect complement to her belief that "a nice woman ought not to want to know anything outside her home". Almost, she seems a domestic stereotype that the reader, like Stephen, can dismiss. But, as Thurston makes increasingly clear, Daisy is a character not only of considerable importance but of considerable interest. Her mending is not imaginative, or creative, but, just as it expresses her acceptance of her role, so it foreshadows her importance as the rebuilder of her marriage. Instead of collapse at Stephen's departure, she moves from innocence to experience and to a growth from doll to woman. In allowing her development, Thurston indicates her closeness to, rather than her distance from, Isabel, and suggests that in fact the docile wife and the social disrupter may share a nexus so close that they are, in reality, the expression of a single self.

Both Daisy and Isabel stand in sharp contrast to Daisy's sister Mary, who serves in the novel as a fierce guardian not only of all that Waterford holds dear, but also of her own prospects. In a society in which marriage is the goal to be attained, the price of failure is high, and inevitable: there is no place in Waterford for the unmarried, the "odd" woman. There is only, as Thurston sketches it, a bleak and "cruelly stereotyped" future, the prospect of which adds impetus to the already-competitive situation of those who find themselves in the marriage mart, for there is nothing less at stake here than a place in society. As the personification of the worst effects of middle-class provincialism and socially-imposed female competition, Mary relies on weapons such as sarcasm and scandal in order to keep her precarious social status while her desperate fear drives her, clear-eyed and chillingly intent, not only to attempt to destroy Isabel, but also to throw herself away on a marriage to a foolish and weak partner whose existence nevertheless ensures that she will not spend the rest of her days caring for her brother and elderly father in bitter old-maidhood.

However repugnant to Isabel, in the eyes of Waterford Mary's campaign is eminently sensible and understandable. Isabel's decision to break off her engagement to Frank Carey, on the other hand, is regarded not only as foolish, but as suspect,

as the act of one who is capricious, immoral, or
lunatic — or, perhaps, all three. Indeed, the words
"mad" and "madness" reverberate through the
novel, and Thurston uses them consistently not
only to describe Waterford's opinion of Isabel as
deviant, but also to record Isabel's own view of her
rejection of Waterford values. In opposing that
logical and expedient code of behaviour, which she
alone finds abhorrent and unnatural, Isabel comes
to accept Waterford's view of her — that there is,
in fact, some inherent badness/madness in her
makeup which not only causes but also explains her
position as alien. Her fruitless questioning on the
subject of her mother is one way in which Thurston
suggests her deep-rooted insecurities; another is
her paranoic response to overheard laughter on
the night of her introduction to Waterford society
and Stephen Carey. Proud, sensitive to the harsh-
ness of Waterford's standards, aware both of the
impossibility of her acceptance and of the contra-
dictions of her desire to be accepted at the same
time that she defies the formula for that acceptance, Isabel experiences a confusion and a lack of
control that is equated with mental illness.

Nowhere, of course, is Isabel's madness so in
evidence as in her increasing involvement with
Stephen Carey. From their initial encounter,
Thurston makes their mutual attraction, and its
consequences, inevitable. Stephen's madness, then,
is not merely a match for Isabel's. Because it is
triggered by their erotic identification with each
other, his madness — and his description of his

mental and emotional state as such — represents
not only aberration but the expression of alliance.
In placing himself in opposition to Waterford sanity
Stephen rejects the Waterford-sanctioned male
role just as Isabel has rejected the feminine. His
madness is not only indicative of his refusal to
subscribe to the mores of the middle class; more
radically, it is a measure of his alignment with the
deviant principle which Isabel embodies. And,
just as she represents for him liberation from the
conventional and the repressive, so he stands for
her as the "real man, unshackled by convention".
It is a misperception which fits neatly into her
Romantic imaging of real and ideal love, a belief
which is sustained by her own character, "passionate, reckless in her prodigal giving" as she is.
What Isabel cannot see is that in loving not only
Stephen but the image and the abstraction of love,
she does not take cognisance of the practical calcu-
lations which she discounts, but which have so
greatly shaped his life.

The tension with which Thurston imbues the
crisis of misunderstanding between Stephen and
Isabel is derived from their relative life experiences
and reflects their differing realities. Isabel's financial predicament is a recurring theme in the novel,
and her countering of economic inadequacy with
incautious emotional expenditure is a matter of
instinctive response with only the weapon of retaliation at hand. As a female outside the patriarchal
structure, Isabel's responses are personal and
individual. Stephen, in contrast, comes from within

that structure: his sense of self is intimately bound up with conformity to both its demands and its recompenses. His alliance with Isabel, Thurston suggests, is in some ways nothing more than a response to a catalyst: his rebellion has been fermenting for years; he has always reserved at least an image of himself as a free being, has always chafed under the restraints which he, as well as circumstance, has placed on himself. And, just as Isabel clings to the belief that Stephen will "draw her with him into the real world" so Stephen persists in his fantasies of breaking away from Waterford. His promise that he "will go down to hell" for Isabel, then, is a sincere pledge which is directly related to his madness, rather than an attempt to deceive her. In his emotional and mental maelstrom, he really believes that he is capable of leaving and beginning a new life with her. Isabel's tragedy is that she sees her ideal Stephen and not the real one, that she has neither the temperament nor the worldly experience which will enable her to reckon with the force which society and family exert.

It is appropriate that their common madness — as well as their common misunderstanding — is expressed in the climactic night drive in which they attempt an escape from Waterford. Stephen's recently acquired motor car is both a literal and symbolic vehicle in carrying them away from the constrictions and compressions of middle-class life. As a symbol of daring, of hope, of exhilaration, it is the fitting — indeed, the only — medium for conducting them into the emblematic territory of freedom. Thurston's animation of the car into a "restive animal", a "great beast", a "fiend unloosed" establishes its symbolic value as a representation of emotions which can no longer be contained, of a state of mind which can no longer accommodate obligatory, or even, voluntary stifling and suggests, too, the dangers which the throwing off of restraints calls up. The flight into the countryside provides the milieu, finally, for their verbalisation of their love for one another as well as for planning to leave Waterford. But, just as the car takes them only to the Cork-Waterford border, so the entire episode suggests that this is an aborted attempt, that the actual elopement will never take place. Just as Daisy's preference for cultivated gardens and Isabel's attraction to wild profusion have served as important signposts to their respective temperaments and values, so the cessation of Stephen's and Isabel's flight at the Waterford border presages the end of their dreams. The reality is that they are incapable of escape; the tendrils of middle-class life, as Stephen realises as early as the succeeding day, have a strength which is easy to underestimate. Their return to Waterford is born of their intention to prepare for their departure; its outcome, instead, is Stephen's resumption of his shackles, his renewed recognition of his place in the patriarchal order.

The agent of Stephen's return to duty is Father James, the exemplary priest, the gentle Christian, the surrogate parent. As the "father" suggests, his is an emotional as well as spiritual parenthood, and, in the face of Stephen's rejection of conven-

tional Christianity, it is Father James who recalls
him to duty. Daisy's confidence in Father James'
ability to effect a change of heart in her husband is
not misplaced, for, in looking to Father James as
the symbol of orthodoxy, his championship of her
rights supports the position which marriage has
conferred on her. And it is highly significant that
when theological and social arguments fail, Father
James's final, and conclusive, argument is based
on his sketch of the burden which Stephen's departure will place on his sons. The priest of the
patriarchal order does not only remind Stephen of
the burden placed on him by his own errant father,
but places before him an argument eloquent in its
simplicity: recalling Stephen to his place in the
patriarchal scheme causes him to recognise that
the betrayal of male fellowship and duty is a
betrayal of infinitely greater magnitude than betrayal of wife, social duty, religious principles or
love. Because the patriarchal code is based on
self-identification, Stephen recognises that breaking
it is not only taboo, but impossible.

Thurston's sympathetic depiction of Stephen's
crisis is counter-weighted by her exploration of
Isabel's. Isabel's interpretation of Stephen's return
to sanity is that it constitutes a rejection and,
indeed, a betrayal of the self that she has proffered.
His suffering represents a fraction of her frenzy,
for his re-absorption into the middle-class world is
a return to his natural habitat. She, on the other
hand, has experienced her final disillusion, her
harshest lesson about the real power of the

charmed circle of prosperous conventionality. Her suicide, however, is not an act of despair, but of affirmation — it is the only direction in which her wish for significant action can take her. Her initial impulse is to kill Stephen; her impulsive decision to kill herself instead arises from complex realisations. Although she is moved as well as gratified by the evidence of tangible suffering which she perceives in Stephen's face, Isabel's suicide is not prompted by a desire to punish him. Nor does it come from chagrin at losing him, nor from mere humiliation. Her choice of death over the living death which she perceives life to be is both a protest and an act of self love. She will not take refuge in a loveless but socially advantageous alliance any more than she will have power to change the middle-class world. Her awareness of herself as a sexual being, as an independent-minded and autonomous being, leads her to see death as a choice of freedom, as a counter to the slow extinction of that selfhood. As she has always been defined through her spontaneous response to the sun, so her relationship with that life-source is expressed in the final line of the novel. As Isabel's eyes catch its "warmth" and "glory" Thurston leaves the reader in no doubt that Isabel is experiencing a spiritual resurrection, that she is, at last, in touch with the exultation of victory against the forces which would oppress her. Her exercise of choice is her expression of her final freedom.

Janet Madden-Simpson, California, 1986

VIRAGO MODERN CLASSICS

The first Virago Modern Classic, *Frost in May* by Antonia White, was published in 1978. It launched a list dedicated to the celebration of women writers and to the rediscovery and reprinting of their works. Its aim was, and is, to demonstrate the existence of a female tradition in fiction which is both enriching and enjoyable. The Leavisite notion of the 'Great Tradition', and the narrow, academic definition of a 'classic', has meant the neglect of a large number of interesting secondary works of fiction. In calling the series 'Modern Classics' we do not necessarily mean 'great' — although this is often the case. Published with new critical and biographical introductions, books are chosen for many reasons: sometimes for their importance in literary history; sometimes because they illuminate particular aspects of womens' lives, both personal and public. They may be classics of comedy or storytelling; their interest can be historical, feminist, political or literary.

Initially the Virago Modern Classics concentrated on English novels and short stories published in the early decades of this century. As the series has grown it has broadened to include works of fiction from different centuries, different countries, cultures and literary traditions. In 1984 the Victorian Classics were launched; there are separate lists of Irish, Scottish, European, American, Australian and other English-speaking countries; there are books written by Black women, by Catholic and Jewish women, and a few relevant novels by men. There is, too, a companion series of Non-Fiction Classics constituting biography, autobiography, travel, journalism, essays, poetry, letters and diaries.

By the end of 1988 over 300 titles will have been published in these two series, many of which have been suggested by our readers.